"I know not knowing doesn't change anything. It doesn't even mean it didn't happen. But..."

She withdrew her hand because she had to pat her chest in order to keep from crying as she continued to force the words out. "If I don't know the particulars, someday when Billy ask̶̶ ̶̶ ̶̶didn't tell him, I can honestly say it's b̶̶ ̶̶ ̶̶ ̶̶'t know." She drew in a breath. "̶̶ ̶̶ paltry to you, but it's not to̶̶ ̶̶ ̶̶ ̶̶ ̶̶ ̶̶ ̶̶ ̶̶ I can give my son, except ̶̶

He grasped her elbo̶̶ ̶̶ ̶̶ ̶̶ ̶̶ ̶̶ ̶̶olid, while being kind. ̶̶ ̶̶ ̶̶ ̶̶ ̶̶ ̶̶ ̶̶ade tears threaten to erupt ̶̶

"I can help you with ̶̶ ̶̶ ̶̶ ̶̶an take you away from here."

Another *if only*. "To where? There's nowhere I can go."

"Yes, there is. There are places you can go. People who will help—"

She pressed a finger to his lips. "I tried that once, Tom." Removing her fingers to press them against her lips, she swallowed before being able to continue. "We made it all the way to Denver. Billy and I. I thought it was a big enough town, that we could get lost in the crowd or move on, when..." There were certain things she refused to remember.

"I won't let anything happen to you or Billy."

Author Note

When my editor asked if I was up to the challenge of submitting a Western ASAP, I was excited at the prospect. After having written several other Oak Grove stories, Tom and Clara's journey had played out in my head and I wanted to get it down on paper. But...two weeks? Well, we don't know what we are capable of until we try, so I agreed, committed myself wholeheartedly and got to work.

My first step was to consult with Kathryn Albright, who was in the midst of writing additional Oak Grove stories, to maintain the consistency of all the characters and events happening throughout each individual story. With the timeline of this story balanced with hers, I set to writing, night and day.

There were bumps in the road, such as my granddaughter's birthday, which included a day of us shopping, baking and decorating her cake, along with other favorites she wanted served the next day, the arrival of company and a major upheaval at the day job, but ultimately, I sent the book to my editor exactly fourteen days after agreeing to write it. Laurie, my editor, was a doll through the process, fully on board beside me and there when I needed her input.

So, here is Tom and Clara's story, the book I wrote in two weeks, and I sincerely hope you become as engrossed in reading it as I was in writing it. These two were meant for each other, but a lot stands in their way of ever obtaining their happy-ever-after.

LAURI ROBINSON

In the Sheriff's Protection

HARLEQUIN® HISTORICAL

Recycling programs
for this product may
not exist in your area.

ISBN-13: 978-1-335-05168-4

In the Sheriff's Protection

Copyright © 2018 by Lauri Robinson

HARLEQUIN®
www.Harlequin.com

Printed in U.S.A.

A lover of fairy tales, **Lauri Robinson** can't imagine a better profession than penning happily-ever-after stories about men—and women—who pull on a pair of boots before riding off into the sunset...or kick them off for other reasons. Lauri and her husband raised three sons in their rural Minnesota home and are now getting their just rewards by spoiling their grandchildren.

Visit laurirobinson.blogspot.com, Facebook.com/lauri.robinson1 or Twitter.com/laurir.

Books by Lauri Robinson

Harlequin Historical
Harlequin Historical *Undone!* ebook

Western Spring Weddings
"When a Cowboy Says I Do"
Her Cheyenne Warrior
Unwrapping the Rancher's Secret
The Cowboy's Orphan Bride
Western Christmas Brides
"A Bride and Baby for Christmas"
Married to Claim the Rancher's Heir

Oak Grove

Mail-Order Brides of Oak Grove
"Surprise Bride for the Cowboy"
Winning the Mail-Order Bride
In the Sheriff's Protection

Daughters of the Roaring Twenties

The Runaway Daughter (Undone!)
The Bootlegger's Daughter
The Rebel Daughter
The Forgotten Daughter

Visit the Author Profile page
at Harlequin.com for more titles.

To my husband, Jess.

Chapter One

"Ma, a rider's comin' up the road!" Billy exclaimed, his legs going the same speed they always were. At a run. "A man on horseback! Maybe it's Pa, Ma! Maybe he's come home!"

Clara Wilson squeezed the edge of the table, willing the fire-hot pain in her leg to ease while trying to find the wherewithal to respond to her son. "Shut. The. Door. Billy," she forced out.

"No, Ma! It's Pa! It has to be."

"Shut the door. Now!" A moan followed her command. One she'd tried to keep down but couldn't stop. The pain was too strong. So was the excitement in Billy's voice, hoping the rider was his father. Hugh had let her down too many times to show up now, exactly when she needed him.

Billy did as instructed, and rushed to the table where she sat with her left leg propped up on another chair. "Is it your leg, Ma? Is it hurting again? Pa will be able to help you. I know he will. That's him coming up the road. I just know it."

And she knew it wasn't. It would be nice if she could believe differently, if things could be different, but they weren't and never would be. Her instincts were too strong, her life too true to form for anything to be different. "Yes, it's my leg. Bolt the door."

"Why? If it's Pa—"

"That's not your father riding in," she said between clenched teeth.

"You don't know that. You ain't even seen the rider."

She wiped at the sweat rolling down her temples and covering her forehead. Why now of all times did someone have to ride in? She could hope it was Donald Ryan, their closest neighbor, but he'd stopped by last week, along with his wife, Karen, on their way back from Hendersonville, a long journey that they wouldn't be making again anytime soon.

Pulling up enough fortitude to talk while fighting the pain was hard, but she had to. "Do as I say and bolt the door." Drawing another shaky breath, she said, "Then bring me the gun out of the drawer."

"But I ain't allowed to touch that gun."

"You can this time." Talking was stealing her strength, making her dizzy, and the flashes of light and dark spots forming before her eyes made it hard to concentrate.

Billy bolted the door and then ran to the cupboard where she kept the good napkins, folded neatly atop the pistol. "Can I get my gun, too?" he asked while closing the drawer.

"Yes." She wanted to say more. Tell him to be careful, but needed to reserve enough strength to address whoever was riding in.

Billy laid the gun on the table. She grasped the handle, pulled it across the table and then dropped it onto her lap, covering it with the corner of her apron. Billy had run into his bedroom and was already returning with the old squirrel gun he'd found last year. It was covered with rust and the trigger was broken off, but he carried it like it could take down an elk if need be.

"Look out the window, but stay back," she instructed.

He did so, peering over the back of the chair. The way his shoulders dropped told her exactly what she'd already known. It wasn't Hugh.

"It's not Pa," Billy said. "This man's got black hair. He's giving his horse a drink out of the trough, and he's taking one, too." A moment later, he said, "He's walking toward the house."

Clara wrapped her hand around the gun handle. "When he knocks, you say your pa's out checking cattle." She pressed her hand to her head, fighting the dizziness and the nausea that had her hands trembling. Her entire body trembling.

The knock sounded. Billy spoke. And the world went black.

Ready for action, for he'd expected some, Tom Baniff had his gun drawn before he heard the familiar sound of a pistol hitting the floor. The young boy, whose thick crop of blond hair looked as if it hadn't been combed in a month, shot a startled look around the edge of the door that was only opened wide enough for the little guy to fit in the opening.

When the boy had opened the door, he'd instantly

claimed his pa was out checking cattle and now, at the sound behind him, boasted he knew how to use the old squirrel gun in his hand.

Pushing the door open wider, Tom said, "Put that gun down before you hurt someone."

"It'll be you I'm hurting," the boy said, holding his stance.

No more than seven, maybe eight, the boy had guts, and that almost made Tom smile. Until he got a good look around the door, at the woman at the table. She wasn't sitting; she was slumped. No, she was falling off the chair.

Tom shot forward, arriving in time to save her head from banging against the floor. She was warm, and breathing, but out cold. "Who else is in the house?" he asked the boy while glancing toward the open doorways of two side rooms.

"No one."

"Your pa's not out checking cattle, either, is he?"

"No, sir," the boy answered, his voice quivering. "Is Ma all right?"

Never one to lie, not even to a child, Tom replied, "I'll figure that out in a minute. Get me a pillow for her head."

The boy was back in a flash. Tom pulled out his hand-kerchief and used it to wipe away some of the sweat covering her face before lowering her head on the pillow. She was burning with fever. "How long has she been sick?"

The boy shrugged. "Couple days. She cut her leg out in the barn going on a week ago."

"Which one?" Tom knew which one as soon as he

pulled aside the layers of her skirt. Her left leg was swollen twice its size, and a jagged and clearly infected gash marred the side of her calf. "Where's her bed?"

"This way," the boy said. "She told me her leg was getting better, just sore."

"I'm sure she did." Tom hoisted her off the floor. Out here alone, she wouldn't want the boy to worry. "Bring the pillow."

She moaned slightly, but didn't regain consciousness as he carried her into the room and laid her on the bed. "Where is your pa?" Tom asked the boy while folding back her skirt to examine the gash thoroughly.

"Don't know," the boy admitted. "Ain't seen him in months." As if realizing he shouldn't have said that, the boy added, "But he'll be back. Soon, too."

"I'm sure he will be," Tom answered drily. That was the reason he was here. "What's your name?"

"Billy. What's yours?"

For half a second he contemplated using an alias, but since this was Wyoming, a place he'd never been before, he doubted anyone had heard of him. However, he did leave the title of Sheriff off because much like the pin he'd taken off his vest and put in his pocket, the title could cause some people to clam up. "Tom Baniff." Resting a hand on Billy's shoulder, he added, "I'm going to need your help. Infection has set in your ma's leg."

"Is it bad?"

There was worry in the boy's blue eyes, but Tom still had to be honest. "It's not good," he said. "But once we're done, it'll be better."

"What are we going to do?"

From the looks of her leg, lockjaw was a real concern, and there was only one thing he knew to do about that. Tom turned Billy toward the doorway. "To start with, we're going to need fresh water."

"Ma already had me haul some in. Just a little bit ago. She set it on the stove to boil."

Tom nodded. She'd probably been preparing to do just what he was going to do. Lance her leg.

Billy stopped in the doorway leading out of the bedroom. "Her name's Clara. Clara Wilson. My pa's name is Hugh. Hugh Wilson. He's tall, but not as tall as you, and he has brown hair."

If Tom had needed confirmation that he was in the right spot, he now had it. Hugh Wilson was the man he was after. The man who'd shot and injured one of the mail-order brides on her way to Oak Grove, Kansas. She'd been on the train Hugh and two other men had robbed. The other two had met their demise by bullets from passengers on the train, but Hugh had gotten away on a black-and-white paint horse. The only clue he'd had to go on had paid off.

"Mister?"

Reining in his attention, Tom patted Billy's shoulder. "Let's see if that water is boiling."

The kettle was on the stove, but the fire needed to be stoked. She must have been about to do that, considering two logs lay near the stove door. Tom grabbed the poker to stir up the coals. "What did your ma cut her leg on?"

"The side barn door is broken. Nellie, she's one of our cows, stumbled and pushed Ma against it, and the hinge cut her leg. Ma said it wasn't bad. It didn't even bleed much. She's been boiling onions to put on it for the past couple of days. I tried to fix the barn door, but couldn't. I did pound the hinge off and…"

As Billy talked, Tom's thoughts bounced from Clara's infected leg to why Hugh Wilson would take to robbery when he had a wife and son and a pretty decent chunk of property. The house was small and needed some work, but it was solid and clean. Clara's leg wasn't. She'd have been better off if that hinge had sliced her leg wide open—the bleeding would have cleaned away the bacteria. As it was, the closed wound had given the bacteria the perfect breeding ground, which could lead to lockjaw. His father, a surgeon who'd served in the army, had told him all about lockjaw, gangrene and a plethora of other infections and ailments that had affected men during the war. Enough so that even at a young age, Tom had realized being a doctor was not his calling.

There'd been a time he'd thought being a lawman hadn't been, either. Until Julia had died and finding her killer and knowing justice would be served—and had been—had somehow eased the pain inside him, and the anger. Now being a lawman was his life. When he'd taken the oath to protect the citizens of Oak Grove, he'd meant it, and wouldn't let them down. It may have been a coincidence that the shot mail-order bride's name was the same as his little sister's, but he considered it more than that. To him, it was proof that he'd chosen the right path. That while the other men in town were head over heels at the idea of getting married, he was right in not having anything to do with the entire Oak Grove Betterment Committee.

"It's boiling."

Tom turned about.

"The water," Billy said. "It's boiling."

"That's good." Tom walked back to the stove. While his mind had been roaming, so had he. The house was in better condition than his first glance had let on, and fully furnished with store-bought items. Not overly expensive pieces, but considering they were a two-day ride from the closest town, several things had him thinking about how long Hugh Wilson had been in the robbery business.

A knife lay on the top of the cabinet near the stove, as did several neatly folded cotton towels and a tin of cayenne pepper. More evidence Clara had been about to lance her leg herself. His stomach clutched slightly, thinking of how difficult and dangerous that would be for someone. The pain could have caused her to pass out, leaving her to possibly bleed out. Which in hand would have left little Billy out here all alone.

Bitterness coated Tom's tongue as his thoughts hopped to Hugh Wilson again. How could a man leave a woman and child out here alone for months on end? The same kind of man who didn't care that his bullet could have killed a woman on her way to getting married.

Tom sucked in the anger that circled his guts and picked up the knife. Lowering the blade into the hot water, he nodded toward the door. "Do you know how to unsaddle a horse?"

"Yes, sir," Billy answered.

"Unsaddle mine, would you? Put him in the barn and give him some feed if you have any to spare."

"Sure. We got some. I'll hurry."

"No," Tom said, walking toward the sink to wash his hands. "Take your time. His name is Bullet."

"You want me to brush him down?"

"That would be good," Tom answered. It wouldn't take long to lance the leg, but he wanted Billy away from the house in case his mother woke up screaming.

"Then I'll help you with Ma," Billy said, already opening the door.

"I'll be ready for your help," Tom answered. "Shut the door."

Billy did so, and Tom scrubbed his hands a bit longer, watching out the window until Billy led Bullet into the barn. Then he dried his hands with one of the clean towels, gathered the other towels and the knife, and walked into the bedroom.

Chapter Two

Struggling through an overwhelmingly thick fog almost wore her out before she'd even opened her eyes, and when she did, the man standing over her, one she'd never seen before, only made Clara close her eyes again. She must be dreaming. Had to be, because even though her leg ached, there wasn't the intense pain of before.

"You feeling better, Ma?"

Billy's voice was so clear in her dream it made her smile.

"You're smiling, so you must be feeling better."

The idea that she might not be dreaming had her pulling her eyelids open. That took effort because they fought her again. When she won the battle and saw Billy, her first instinct was to smile again. He was such a good boy, and she loved him with all her heart. Without him, she wouldn't have a reason to live.

"You are feeling better, Ma. I can tell," he said, grinning. "This here is Tom. Tom Baniff. He cut your leg and put cayenne pepper on it. Then he poured whiskey all over you."

The stranger appeared again, standing next to Billy. This certainly was a silly dream. Only in a dream would a stranger cut her leg and put cayenne pepper and whiskey on her. Cut her leg... A cold shiver rippled over her entire being.

She forced her eyes to remain open, although she blinked several times to chase away the blurriness. Then, as the room became clearer, she glanced around, giving her mind time to catch up and solidify the fact that she wasn't dreaming.

The man was tall and broad, with shiny black hair and eyes as brown as coffee. He was smiling, too. A friendly smile. He must be a doctor. The exact thing she'd needed.

"The infection?" she asked.

"Is clearing up nicely."

His voice was deep but gentle at the same time.

"My leg?"

"Is almost back to being the same size as the other one," he said. "That was quite the infection you had."

Her thoughts became clearer with each minute that ticked by. "The cayenne pepper worked," she said. "My uncle said my grandmother did that to him once. Put cayenne pepper on an infected wound. He said he screamed. That it burned."

"You didn't scream," the man said.

She closed her eyes for a moment, as thankful for the fact that she couldn't remember the pain as she was that she hadn't screamed. That would have frightened

Billy, which was why she'd been putting off lancing
the leg herself. It would have scared the dickens out
of Billy, and there had been the chance she may have
passed out from the pain. As she lifted a hand to feel
her forehead, the pungent scent of whiskey filling her
nose made her cringe.

"I had to get your fever down," the man said. "The
alcohol in the whiskey did the trick."

The sheet was tucked beneath her arms, but she could
tell the only things she wore were her shift and bloomers.
A heat as hot as her fever had been rushed into her cheeks.

"Nothing to worry about, ma'am," he said. "Billy's
helped me take care of you the entire time."

She released a breath, knowing such thoughts of de-
corum were insignificant. "How did you know I was
ill?"

"You fell off the chair when I opened the door," Billy
said. "'Member? I thought it was Pa and you said it
wasn't."

She balled her hands into fists to hide how they instantly started shaking at the memories coming forth.
Thankful it hadn't been Hugh riding in, she glanced
at the window, the east window where the shining sun
showed it was still on the rise, making it no later than
midmorning. Confused, she asked, "Was that yesterday? I—I was out all night."

"No," the man said, "that was four days ago."

She bolted upright, and the blood rushing to her head
had her grasping her forehead.

"Whoa, there," the man said, gently forcing her to
lie back down.

Once her head was on the pillow again, and the room stopped spinning, she said, "Surely not four days. You must be mistaken."

"I'm not mistaken."

Covering her eyes with one hand, hoping that would somehow help her to remember, she shook her head. "I couldn't have slept for four days."

"You were really sick, ma'am," he said. "Really sick. Would you like to see your leg?"

She removed the hand from her eyes. "Yes, please."

He flipped the bottom corner of the sheet aside and mixed emotions filled her. The swelling was considerably less, as was the pain, but the healing that had clearly taken place confirmed what he'd said. She'd been asleep for four days. Billy had been alone with a stranger for four days. Her skin quivered as she glanced toward her son, who was grinning from ear to ear.

"It looks much better than the last time I saw it," she said.

"Like four days of healing?" the man asked.

She pinched her lips together. There was a hint of teasing in his tone, but also affirmation that he hadn't been lying when he said how much time had passed. The yellow color of the bruising confirmed it was old, as did the scabs that now covered her first wound as well as the two slashes that had been made to drain the infection. "Yes," she admitted. "It looks like it's been healing for a few days already."

"Healing nicely," he said. "But now that you're awake, we need to get some food in you."

"We have some eggs boiling," Billy said. "Tom can

cook, Ma. Almost as good as you. And we've kept the cows milked and skimmed the cream off the top, just like you always do."

"I'll make you some tea to go with your eggs," the man said. "Do you think you can sit up? Slowly this time?"

She nodded, and carefully sat up enough for him to put another pillow behind her. Having a man be so caring was uncomfortable, yet she was grateful. Without him, she may not be here. "Thank you."

He gave her a nod, and winked one eye that was charming enough it made her heart thud unexpectedly.

"We'll be back shortly with that tea and an egg," he said, laying a hand on Billy's shoulder. "Won't we, Billy?"

"Yes, sir. We'll be right back, Ma."

The heartwarming sensation that washed over her was one she hadn't experienced in a very long time. So long she couldn't remember the last time. Years. She was still contemplating that when Billy and the man appeared again, along with a tray that the man set down on her lap.

"I made the tea weak," he said. "Your stomach might not tolerate much yet."

She glanced at the tea and the hard-boiled egg that had been peeled and quartered. No one had ever gone to such lengths for her. Ever. A lump formed in her throat that she had to swallow before admitting, "I'm sorry—I don't remember what Billy said your name is."

"It's Tom, ma'am. Tom Baniff."

"Well, Mr. Baniff, I owe you my deepest gratitude."

The hint of redness that appeared in his cheeks was positively endearing. Once again her heart thudded. "It makes me almost believe in miracles," she admitted. "How a doctor was traveling through just when one was needed."

"I'm not a doctor, ma'am."

A hint of a chill had the hair on her arms rising. "You aren't?"

"No, I'm...um—traveling. Just traveling through."

His expression had changed. His eyes had grown so serious the chill rippling her skin increased. As if he knew that, and knew she'd seen it, he turned toward Billy.

Once again setting a hand on Billy's shoulder, he said, "Let's let your mother eat in peace."

A part of her wanted to say that wasn't necessary, but her throat was swelling. When he'd shifted his stance, the black vest covering his chest had caught in the sunlight shining through the window. The vest was made of leather, and though hardly noticeable, she'd seen two tiny holes. Evenly separated and situated in the exact spot a badge would have been worn. A lawman's badge.

A lawman out here meant one thing. He was after Hugh.

She waited for them to leave the room before letting the air out of her lungs, but even then it caught, making it impossible to breathe.

Her eyes were watering and her chest burning by the time she found the ability to draw in another breath. Guilt, shame and other emotions she couldn't name washed over her. Hugh had warned her, more than once, what would happen if she ever went to the law, and she had no doubt he would follow through on those warnings.

Blinking away the moisture in her eyes, she glanced around the room. At the clothes hanging on the hooks, the hand mirror and brush on the dresser, the sewing basket in the corner, the dishes on the tray on her lap. Every item in this house that hadn't been Uncle Walter's had been stolen, or bought with stolen money, and she hated that. Hated knowing that, but as Hugh pointed out, she still wore the dresses, used the dishes, ate the food. Therefore, she was as guilty of committing any crime as he was. Had been since the day she met him.

For eight long years she'd wished she'd never met him, but in all that time, she'd never done anything to change the situation. Other than pray for a miracle.

She bit her lips together as they started to tremble. Through the open doorway, she could hear Billy talking.

"I could show ya when we're done eating," he said.

Clara held her breath, waiting to hear the man's answer. Tom Baniff. She'd never heard the name, but lawmen from as far away as Texas were looking for Hugh. There was no way she could know all of their names.

Tom didn't reply. It was Billy's voice that sounded again.

"My pa says that's the most important thing for a man to know. How to be a fast draw. The fastest. You agree, don't you, Tom?"

The clank of a cup being set down on a saucer sounded before Tom said, "No, Billy, I don't."

He was speaking so softly she had to hold her breath in order to hear what he was saying.

"I believe knowing how to use a gun is important, and that a man needs to know how to use it safely. He also needs to know when to use it. But there are lots of other things he needs to know that are more important."

"Like what?" Billy asked.

"Well, like knowing how to chop wood. You did a fine job with the kindling wood that built the fire in the stove so we were able to cook these eggs to eat. Now, that's important. A man has to eat or he'd starve to death."

"Yeah, I guess you're right about that." After a stilled moment, Billy asked, "What other things are important?"

"Lots of things," Tom answered quietly. "Things you do every day. Right now, the most important thing is taking care of your ma. Making sure she eats and gets the rest she needs so her leg heals. Now, finish eating so we can head outside and she can rest in quiet."

"Think she's done eating?" Billy asked softly, taking a clue from Tom's quiet tone.

"We'll find out once we're done."

Clara quickly ate the egg and took a gulp of tea, and then had to press a hand to her stomach as it revolted, having been empty for so long. She took a couple smaller sips of tea, hoping that would help her stomach accept the food.

It appeared to. When Billy and Tom appeared in the doorway, she no longer feared the egg would find its way back up her throat.

"How are you feeling?" Tom asked. "The egg wasn't too much for your stomach, was it?"

"No, no, thank you," she said. "It was perfect. I'm sorry that—that you've been detained here for so long. Now that I'm awake..." She glanced at Billy and the shine in his eyes as he looked up at Tom. "Billy and I will be fine. I'm sure you'll want to be on your way."

"Tom can't leave yet," Billy said. "Can you? Tom, tell her why."

Her stomach threatened to erupt again and she pressed a hand to the base of her throat while swallowing hard. She didn't have the right to pray that he hadn't told Billy the truth, but sincerely hoped he hadn't.

"We are in the middle of a project, ma'am," Tom said. "One that will take at least another day to complete."

"A project?" Flinching at how fearful she sounded, she pulled up what she hoped looked like a smile, and asked, "Wh-what sort of project?"

Tom's smile was far more genuine as he ruffled Billy's hair with one hand. "When Billy showed me where you cut your leg, we discovered the entire door frame on the barn was rotted."

"Tom used some wood from the corral to fix the door, but first we had to cut down some trees to make poles for the corral," Billy said excitedly. "And guess what, Ma? We got enough poles to use more wood off the corral to fix the porch. Those boards that are missing. But Tom said we couldn't start pounding on the roof until you were awake." As a frown formed, Billy looked up at Tom. "That's important stuff for a man to know, ain't it,

Tom? How to fix a corral and a house. And a barn and how to cut down trees to make poles, and—"

"Yes, it is, Billy," Tom replied, with a wink at her son. "Real important stuff. Now that your ma has eaten, let's go get busy. We have plenty of work to do."

He stepped up to the side of the bed, and as he reached down to take the tray off her lap, Clara willed the tears to remain at bay. Billy had never been treated so kindly, nor had she.

"Thank you, Mr. Baniff." Her throat burned too hotly to say much more.

"You're welcome, ma'am. You have a good boy here. A real good boy."

She nodded but didn't look up. Her eyes were once again staring at the two miniature holes in his vest. If only she could… She closed her eyes to stop the thought.

"Do you need anything else?" he asked.

Pulling her eyes open, she nodded, then shook her head. "No, no, thank you. I'll be fine."

"Just yell if you do. We'll be right outside."

"Yeah, Ma, we'll be right outside," Billy said.

Anger welled inside her as they left the room. That was how it should be. How a man should show a boy what was important in life. How to take care of his property and his family. Hugh had never done that. Would never do that. Whenever he was around, the few days a year he stopped long enough to drop off stolen items and money, he barely had the time of day for Billy.

And he was never alone.

Urgency rose up inside her then. Hugh was rarely

alone. If he rode in, Tom wouldn't stand a chance against Hugh and his cohorts.

She pushed aside the sheet and cautiously swung her legs over the edge of the bed. There wasn't a lot of pain, for which she was thankful, but by the time she'd managed to get dressed, she felt as if she'd just run a mile or more. Exhaustion and weakness were expected after being in bed so long. If it was anyone else, she'd tell them to lie back down. She didn't have that choice. Hugh could show up at any time and she had to make sure Tom wasn't here when that happened.

Chapter Three

"**Y**ou shouldn't have done so much work," Tom told her quietly. He'd struggled saying anything, seeing that Clara was clearly used to working from sun up to sun down. Despite all the work he'd found to keep him and Billy busy the past few days, she'd taken remarkably good care of the property and animals, and her son. Billy was not only well behaved, he was eager to please. From all he'd learned while she'd been asleep, Hugh Wilson deserved no credit when it came to this homestead or Billy.

"I didn't," she said. "I'd canned the venison earlier this year and the vegetables last fall. All I had to do was dump them together and heat it up." She lifted her head from the back of the rocking chair she was sitting in on the front porch, and looked at him. "You, on the other hand, have been extremely busy. I expected the kitchen to be in shambles when I walked out of the bedroom. You must have had a very strict mother."

The serene smile that had appeared on her lips made his heart hammer inside his chest. To the point he had to look away. He'd never taken to a woman before and wouldn't now, but there was something about her that made him want to care. More than he should.

"Or is it a wife I owe the credit to?" she asked.

"No," he said, keeping his gaze locked on the barn. "It would have been my mother. I was the oldest and had to watch over the younger ones plenty, which included cleaning up after them." That had been years ago, long before arriving here, and he'd forgotten what it had been like.

"How many?"

"Four. Three boys and a girl."

"You were lucky."

"Yes, I was," he said truthfully. Though Julia's death had affected all of them, he now appreciated the fact he'd known her. She'd been eleven years younger than him and the apple of everyone's eye. Including his. From the day Julia had been born, he'd felt a deep sense of responsibility toward her that he'd honored. He'd shifted that responsibility to the law after her death, and that was where it would remain until his dying day.

"Where did you live?"

The sun was setting, so he kept his eyes on how the fading rays lit up the rolling hills. "Alabama," he said. "Until we moved to Kansas. My father was a surgeon in the war. The side that lost." That didn't bother him at all; it was just how his father always said it and it was now habit. He stopped there, avoiding telling her about being a deputy in the small town his folks still lived in before moving to Oak Grove and accepting the position as sheriff there.

"My father fought on the other side, but I still don't know if there was a winner or loser. Just lots of lost lives."

He showed his agreement with a nod. Her voice was soft and easy to listen to and that bothered him. Everything about her bothered him in ways he shouldn't be bothered. Mainly because they weren't bad ways. Just unusual. He noticed things about her he shouldn't. Things that shouldn't be any concern of his. Like the sadness that seemed to surround her when she thought no one was looking.

"A surgeon," she said. "That explains your doctoring abilities."

"He's still a doctor. So is my brother Chet."

"My father worked in the salt mines in Iowa before the war, but couldn't afterward." She sighed and her chair creaked as it rocked back and forth. "Perhaps if the North had had a surgeon like your father, mine might have come home with two arms."

Not sure why, except he'd never been one to look at the bad side, he said, "At least he came home."

"You're right," she said. "That's exactly what my mother said. She always said things would work out, too. So when he decided we should move out here, to his brother's place, we packed up and left Iowa."

He pushed a foot against the porch floor, keeping his rocker in motion as he turned her way. "That would be Walter?"

She was staring toward the sunset and didn't look his way, but nodded. "Billy told you this is his place."

"He did. Said Walter died a while ago."

"Three years." She sighed heavily. "I'm not sure Billy really remembers him. He was only four."

"He remembers Walter went out to round up cattle and fell in a ravine. That he's buried out there." The story had come from a seven-year-old, so it could be as off-kilter as a three-wheeled wagon, but Tom sensed even the boy didn't totally believe the Uncle Walter death tale. A man who'd lived here most of his life didn't just fall into a ravine.

He should flat out ask her about that. Normally he would. Normally he'd ask where her husband was, too. Or have already left to keep tracking Hugh Wilson. Instead he'd been here for the better part of a week, mending barns, corrals and roofs, doctoring her and looking after Billy. He couldn't have just ridden on, though, not in good conscience, but now that she was up and showed no signs of the infection returning, he should leave.

Would leave.

"What else did Billy tell you?"

She was do-si-do-ing, wondering if Billy had let it be known that his father was an outlaw. The boy hadn't. Probably because he didn't know. He thought his father was out buying or selling cattle. Billy said he wasn't sure which because his father did both. Tom, on the other hand, figured it was all selling on Hugh's part, and that if Hugh Wilson had a cow to sell, it was because he'd stolen it first.

He hadn't questioned Billy about anything. Children shouldn't be used as informants. He'd never done that before and wouldn't now. Furthermore, he'd bet the reason Billy didn't know was because Clara didn't want him to know. She had to realize she couldn't keep it a secret forever. Sooner or later, Billy would figure it out. Which wasn't, or shouldn't be, his concern.

"Things that are important to little boys," he said. "Where Walter's dog is buried. Where he found that old prairie gun of his. How he saw an Indian up on the ridge one time. Which chickens lay brown eggs, white eggs, and the occasional green one. How you make him take a bath and comb his hair whether he wants to or not." There were a hundred other things Billy had mentioned, but her soft laughter was making him chuckle.

"Oh, dear, I must apologize. He does like to prattle on, and usually has no one but me to talk to."

"No apologies necessary." He enjoyed spending time with the boy and didn't mind her knowing what he thought on that issue. "Billy's a good boy. Smart and caring. You've done a fine job with him and he'll do you proud."

She stopped the chair from rocking and had four fingers of one hand lightly pressed to her lips. Her blond hair was still in the long braid as when he'd arrived, but she'd coiled it and pinned it to one side of her head, which was very becoming. So were her eyes. They were as blue as the sky had been earlier, and right now, shimmered in the evening light.

"Thank you, Mr. Baniff," she said softly. "You may never know how deeply I appreciate what you just said."

It had been years since he'd felt green around the ears, but did so now. For the life of him, he couldn't think of anything to say, nor could he pull his eyes off her. He finally managed, and glanced around the yard before looking her way again. "He is a good boy. And this is a nice place. You've got a lot to be proud of."

She flinched. Slightly, but he saw it, and the way she suddenly grew tense. Her gaze flitted around, landing nowhere, especially not on him, while she gnawed on her bottom lip. He waited, half expecting her to make mention of her husband. He was certain that was what had made her so nervous all of a sudden.

"No, I don't."

She said that so quietly, so softly, he wasn't sure if he heard it or thought it. "Excuse me?"

This time, she acted as if she hadn't heard him and set both hands on her knees. "Speaking of Billy, I best go see that he washed before crawling into bed. He's been known to skip that part."

An unexpected bolt of guilt shot across Tom's stomach. He'd wanted her to say something about her husband. Not necessarily where he was, but maybe that he wasn't a good father or husband. Which was apparent, but inside, Tom wanted her to say it, mainly to confirm his assumptions. That wasn't like him, either. He'd never needed his assumptions confirmed. Nor did he now. He was a lawman tracking down an outlaw. Normally, nothing would get in the way of that. Not a run-down homestead, an injured woman, or a little boy eager to please. And it shouldn't this time. Yet it had. "Let me help you up," he said, rising to his feet.

"No, thank you," she said, slowly rising by using the arms of the chair. "Moving around today has helped my leg tremendously. It's doing well. Better than well. It's fine. Hardly hurts."

She'd said most of that with a grimace that belied her words, yet he kept his distance. The smart thing to do on his part. He then stepped aside as she walked to the door, but hurried around her to open it.

"I—I feel bad that you're sleeping in the barn," she said, holding on to the door frame. "Billy could sleep with me and you could—"

"No, I'll sleep in the barn again. It's fine. More than fine. I've slept in far worse places." He was the one prattling now, and clamped his lips together to stop.

Her eyes were glistening again, and he couldn't stop staring at them. At her. She was a pretty woman. The prettiest one he'd ever seen. Strong and determined, too. Her life out here wasn't easy, yet she hadn't voiced a single complaint.

"All right, then," she said, stepping inside. "I'll see you in the morning."

Tom spun about, but two steps later, stopped before stepping off the porch and turned about. He knocked once on the door and then opened it. She stood near the table, and for a moment, he wondered if he saw something he could only describe as hope in her eyes. That confused him. Hope for what?

Collecting his thoughts, most of them at least, he stepped into the house. "I best carry that lamp for you. Don't want your leg to give out while you're carrying it." Before she could protest, he picked the lamp off the table and started for the room Billy slept in. "I'll put it on the table beside your bed once you're done seeing to Billy."

"Thank you. Th-that's very kind of you."

"Just don't want any setbacks with your leg."

"Nor do I."

There was an odd undercurrent between them, like the tow of water, something he could feel but not see. That was what his problem was. He'd been doing too much feeling since he got here. He needed to get his focus back on the reason he was here. To see justice was served.

Once she'd checked Billy, who was sleeping soundly, she walked back out of the room. He followed, watching her closely. Though she favored the leg, she wasn't grimacing or limping. Her stride was actually purposeful and even.

In her room, he set the lamp on the table and turned about.

She'd stopped near the dresser and was unwinding her hair. His blood turned warm as thoughts entered his head. Thoughts that shouldn't be there.

"Thank you again, Mr. Baniff."

A portion of the good sense he normally had kicked in. "I…uh… The rest of the repairs will be done by tomorrow afternoon. I'll head out then."

She closed her eyes momentarily and then nodded. "I appreciate all you've done."

"Billy did a lot of the work, too, ma'am." He should have just agreed and left, but sensed there was more she wanted to say, so he stood there, waiting.

Turning so her back was to him, she said, "Aren't you going to ask me?"

For some unexplainable reason, he didn't want to be a lawman, didn't want to be the one to cause her more pain. More grief. She had plenty. And it wasn't from her leg. Feigning ignorance, he said, "Ask you what?"

Her back was still to him, and her shoulders rose and fell as she took a deep breath. "Ask me where—where Billy's father is?"

"Billy said he was out buying cattle."

"And you believe him?"

He could point out that he'd seen signs indicating there hadn't been any cattle on her spread for several years and that the fences would need work before any new ones were brought in, but chose not to. "Don't see no reason not to. The boy doesn't seem like one to make up tales."

She turned about, and though her eyes never made contact with his, she nodded. "You're right. He doesn't. Thank you again, Mr. Baniff. Good night."

"Night, ma'am," he said and headed for the door.

On his way to the barn, he stopped at the water trough and gave his face a good splashing of water. With droplets still dripping off his chin, he turned about in a full circle, taking in each and every aspect of the property. What was wrong with Hugh Wilson? He had a wife, a son, both of whom would make any man proud. A solid home, a good barn, and a more than fair chunk of land. Most men could only dream of having all this, yet Wilson would rather rob trains and shoot innocent people. It made no sense. None whatsoever.

Tom made his way into the barn and laid his bedroll out over the mound of straw he'd slept upon the last several nights. He hadn't lied. There had been plenty of nights he'd slept with no shelter since he'd left Kansas.

The train robbery had happened only ten miles outside of Oak Grove. A black-and-white paint horse had been tied to the train tracks. The engineer had blown the whistle, hoping to scare off the horse, but when it wouldn't move, he'd stopped the train, knowing hitting it could derail the locomotive. Witnesses said the train wheels hadn't stopped turning before Hugh and two others had boarded the train. The robbers' first stop had been the mail compartment, but upon not finding any money, they'd made their way into the passenger car, demanding everyone turn over their cash and valuables.

There they'd found what they'd been after. A man from a Kansas City slaughterhouse with a bag of money on his way to buy cattle from Steve Putnam's ranch. That man was prepared, though, and had pulled out a gun rather than give over the money.

Stories varied from there. Some said the outlaws fired first, others said it was the slaughterhouse agent. Either way, the slaughterhouse man and two of the outlaws were dead and a young woman was barely alive by the time the train rolled into Oak Grove.

Everyone's story was remarkably the same when it came to Hugh. He'd had his face covered, but he'd left the train with a bag of money and ridden off on the horse that had been tied to the tracks.

Tom lay down and intertwined his fingers behind his head. The description of the horse had been his only lead when he'd left Oak Grove. Black with white markings, namely one particular mark on its left flank. A long white streak that everyone had described in the same way. Like an arrow.

Not knowing the area well, or maybe he did and was so conceited he wanted to taunt those he stole from, Hugh had ridden right past Steve Putnam's place. Steve and his wife, Mary, had encountered Hugh on the road, not knowing he'd just robbed the train they were on their way to meet.

Hugh had stopped at several other places on his way north, never knowing sightings of his horse were what gave a solid path to follow.

Unfortunately, that path had come to a dead end in northern Nebraska, until Tom had been lucky enough to run into a down-on-his-luck gambler who heard him asking about Hugh's horse. The man knew the horse because he was the one Hugh had won the animal off. Or swindled him out of was how the man put it. The gambler also knew Hugh's name and the general vicinity where Hugh's wife and son lived.

Tom figured he'd come upon the homestead by pure luck. And right now, staring at the ceiling and listening to Bullet snort and stomp at a fly every now and again, he had to wonder if it was good or bad luck that had brought him to Clara's side.

She'd needed help, that was a given, but the fact he'd been the one to provide it was eating at his insides. He wasn't here as some general all-around nice guy who fixed up broken barn doors and repaired leaky roofs. He was a lawman set upon finding her husband and taking him back to Kansas to stand trial for his crimes. When that happened, she'd hate him. Billy would, too, and that was gnawing away at his conscience like a coyote on a fresh kill.

In Tom's eyes, Hugh wasn't much of a husband or father, but there had to be a reason Clara stayed here, waiting for him to return. It was called love. The very thing that could tear a person apart like no other. He'd seen it numerous times. And he'd seen people who by rights were completely unlovable, yet there always seemed to be someone else who'd give their life for that same person, all because they loved them.

His hand slid inside his pocket, where it fiddled with the badge he'd taken off before riding into the homestead. His other hand was on his vest, right where the badge had left two tiny and permanent holes. He'd seen Clara's face today, more than once, gazing fixedly at that spot. She'd never said anything, but the way she wouldn't look him in the eye after staring at his vest had him believing she'd figured it out. Knew why he was here.

Up until tonight, she hadn't mentioned her husband, and he hadn't asked. Billy had said more than enough for him to know he had the right homestead. For some reason, one he couldn't quite explain, he'd refrained from calling her Mrs. Wilson. Actually, he only called her *ma'am*. In the full scheme of things, that didn't mean much, but from the time he'd entered the house and saved her from hitting the floor, he'd felt a draw to her. An uncanny one that just couldn't be explained. He felt sorry for her, that was a given, but this went beyond sorrow.

His reputation of being a straight-shooting lawman who stuck to the law and didn't let anything get in the way of that was the reason why the folks of Oak Grove had singled him out and asked him to move to their small town when their acting sheriff was killed during the Indian Wars. He'd been proud of his reputation, proud to serve the town, and hadn't let a single resident down.

Oak Grove's mayor, Josiah Melbourne, who, for Tom to keep on the straight and narrow, was probably the most trying man in town, had known about how Julia had been killed during a stagecoach robbery years ago and how, as a newly sworn-in deputy, Tom had brought her murderer in and seen justice was served. That was what Melbourne, and the entire town of Oak Grove, wanted again, and that was what he had to do.

Whether Hugh had a family or not shouldn't matter. In most cases it wouldn't, because in most cases he wouldn't have met them.

Maybe that was what he should do something about. Hendersonville was a two-day ride. He could travel there and get the local sheriff to gather up a posse to stake out the place and arrest Hugh.

No, he had no way of knowing if Hugh would show up here or not. He had to get back out there, find Hugh's trail. When he found him and arrested him, Clara wouldn't know it had been him.

But she would eventually find out. And where would that leave her and Billy? She had no income, no way of surviving without the money Hugh dropped off at intervals. That was what it appeared happened. Billy said his father came home every once in a while with lots of presents and money for Clara to give to the neighbors to buy supplies for them whenever they traveled to Hendersonville.

The boy said he'd never been to Hendersonville. Not once. And that Clara hadn't, either.

In all aspects, if anyone was to ask him, he'd say Hugh Wilson, outlawing aside, should rot in jail for the way he treated his wife and son.

Although his thoughts had kept him up most of the night, that didn't prevent Tom from rising early. He'd barely finished his morning routine that included a quick shave before he heard Billy at the well, collecting a pail of water.

"Morning," he shouted from the open barn door.

"Morning, Tom!" Billy called back. "Ma said if I see ya to say breakfast will be ready shortly! It's biscuits and gravy! My favorite!"

"Sounds good! I'll be right there." Tom turned about to finish packing his gear in his saddlebags. During his sleepless night, he'd determined what he had to do. Leave. He'd told Clara that the work would be done this afternoon, and it would be. In fact, if he got right down to it, it would be done before noon, giving him a good start on getting back to tracking Hugh.

Mind set and gear stored, he headed toward the house, only to stop dead in his tracks at the doorway when he saw Clara.

The aching in her leg had awoken her early, only because it had been stiff from being used yesterday after lying around for so long. She'd known what would help, and it had. Long before the sun rose, she'd heated water and filled the washtub she used to bathe herself and

Billy, and to wash clothes. It wasn't large enough for her to completely sit in, but it was deep enough for her to soak her leg. Afterward, she'd given herself a thorough scrubbing, and before the water had completely cooled, washed her hair.

It felt good to be clean and to no longer smell like a saloon from the whiskey dousing Tom had used to bring down her fever. She hadn't taken a bath in a real bathtub since before moving out here, before Billy had been born. It was just one of many things she wanted to do again, but she also knew that most of those things were little more than pipe dreams. This was her life, like it or not.

Tom was the reason she'd even thought about some of those things. Watching him with Billy, talking with him last night, had made her wish harder than ever that there was a small iota of hope that someday things could be different for her and for Billy.

She had put on one of her nicest dresses. A yellow one that she never wore because it would show the dirt too easily, which was silly because there was no one but her and Billy to notice if she got it dirty or not.

Furthermore, she always wore an apron to prevent stains.

Turning, because she'd heard Tom's footsteps on the porch but had yet to hear him enter the house, she frowned at how he stood in the doorway as if scared to enter.

For a split second she was afraid to have him enter. He must have just gotten done shaving. His face was glistening, as was his hair that still showed the comb marks smoothing it back off his forehead. Even if she hadn't already witnessed what a good man he was inside, she'd have to admit he was handsome. Maybe that was what took her breath away, knowing he wasn't just good on the outside, but on the inside where it mattered, yet a person couldn't see. How different her life would be if she was married to a man like that. Good on the inside. Then she'd have something to be proud of.

Tossing her head slightly to catch her wits, she said, "Good morning, Mr. Baniff. Please sit down. Everything will be ready shortly."

He stepped forward, twirling his hat with his hands. "It smells good."

"It's just biscuits and gravy and some fried potatoes. I'm sorry I don't have any bacon or ham, but with my injury I haven't made it over to the Ryan place to pick up a smoked pig lately. I usually do that every few months, and will need to go get one soon. Oh, let me get you a cup of coffee."

"I can get it," he said while hanging his hat on the hook by the door.

"No, I'll get it. You sit down." Her insides were splattering about like water tossed in hot grease. She was talking as much as Billy usually did, too. It was all because she wasn't used to a man like Tom. One who didn't expect to be waited on. One who didn't bark orders or snarl like a rabid dog just waiting for the chance to bite.

She poured him a cup of coffee and set it on the table. "Sit down. I'll have your plate ready in a second."

"What can I do to help? How's the leg this morning?"

"Nothing, and the leg is fine. You really know a lot about doctoring. I hardly know it had been injured."

She quickly filled a plate for him and set it on the table, then filled one for Billy, and walked back to the stove. With the coffeepot in one hand, she returned to the table.

"My cup is still full." Glancing at the table, he frowned at Billy already eating before asking, "Aren't you going to join us?"

When it was just she and Billy, she did sit at the table, but when Hugh was home, he expected her to be at the stove, ready to bring him a second helping.

"Oh, I'll wait until you've had your fill."

"This will be more than enough," he said. "And if I want more, I'm perfectly capable of getting it." He pushed his chair away from the table. "Actually, you've been on that leg long enough already. Sit down while I fix you a plate."

Taken aback, she found it was a moment before her heart slowed down enough for her brain to function. He was already at the stove, piling food onto a plate. Hurrying toward the stove, she said, "I can do that."

"So can I," he said, taking the coffeepot from her hand. "While you sit down."

He set the pot on the stove and with an expectant look, said, "Go on. Sit down."

She did so and smiled, though it felt wobbly, at Billy, who was grinning from ear to ear. When a plate was set before her, as well as a cup of coffee, she thanked him, and withheld the need to insist this wasn't necessary. Although it truly wasn't. She'd never been waited on and wasn't sure how to react to it. Or him. Merely looking his way made her stomach fill with butterflies.

Lots and lots of precious little butterflies. She'd never felt anything even close to that and had to press a hand against her stomach.

"Where do you usually get the smoked pig?"

Her heart sank. "You don't like it." Pushing away from the table, she stood. "I'll make you something else."

"No, sit down. This is good. Very good, actually. I was just wondering where you get the pig from."

"The Ryans are our neighbors," Billy said. "It's a long walk, but they have two kids. They're girls, but still fun to play with."

"How far is it?"

Clara had sat back down, and noted he was eating the meal as if it tasted good. She sincerely hoped it wasn't just for show. "They live about ten miles from here."

"And you walk? Carrying a smoked pig?"

The look of shock on his face almost made her sputter her coffee. Swallowing, and wiping her lips, she shook her head. "Mr. Ryan often gives us a ride home, or if busy, will deliver the pig later."

"Oh, well, that's better." Looking over at Billy's empty plate, Tom then asked, "You need more?"

Billy nodded.

She pushed away from the table again, but Tom shook his head as he stood. "Bring your plate, Billy. I'll fill it while filling my own." He then asked her, "How about you? You need more while I'm up?"

"No, thank you. I'm fine."

"How about coffee?"

"Good there, too."

She couldn't pull her eyes away as the two walked to

the stove, and couldn't stop a smile that formed when Tom asked Billy if he wanted one or two biscuits.

"Two," Billy answered.

"Me, too. They are the best I've ever had."

Her smile gradually slipped away when she realized she only had the supplies to make the biscuits because of money that Hugh had brought last winter, during his last visit. That was going on five months ago, which meant he'd probably be stopping by anytime now. Not ever the best provider by far, since Walter had died, Hugh usually managed to visit three times a year and leave enough money to keep her and Billy fed during his absences.

The irony was that today, that money was feeding a lawman.

Her appetite hadn't been great before, but now it was completely gone. She pretended to eat while the other two finished their breakfast and spoke about what they'd get done today. Not only did Tom fully engage Billy in the conversation, he asked questions and then offered explanations on how they'd repair the porch roof and what they'd each need to do and in what order.

She'd wondered about him long and hard last night. Actually, since awaking and discovering him in her house yesterday. She understood she was lonely and that any visitor would occupy her thoughts, but he was different. He made her question things that she had no business questioning. Like why he wasn't married. A woman would be lucky, extremely lucky, to have him as a husband, and a child wouldn't know a better father. She'd never thought about a man in those terms before, or in the other terms she found herself thinking about.

The kind of thoughts that made those butterflies take to dancing.

"Ma'am?"

Snapping her head up, she pinched her lips at the heat flowing into her cheeks. Praying he didn't guess where her thoughts had been, she said, "Sorry, I was woolgathering."

"What were you doing?" Billy asked.

"Thinking about how good that new porch roof will look," Tom said, with a grin that made her heart skip a beat.

She nodded. "Indeed, it will look wonderful. I'm sure."

"We'll get started on it, if you don't need us to do something first?" Tom asked.

"No, nothing I can think of."

"Well, then, Billy," Tom said while standing up. "Carry your plate to the counter and we'll get started. Don't forget your glass."

Billy followed the instructions and headed out the door while Tom was still setting his things on the counter. He walked to the door and collected his hat, but then turned around. "What are you doing here? So far away from town? Far away from neighbors?"

Her throat clenched up and her cup rattled as she set it on the table. "It's our home."

He glanced out the door Billy had left open before saying, "There are lots of homes out there, ma'am. Lots of homes. Lots of places to live."

She stood and started to clear the table. "I'm sure there are."

"It's an awful lot of work for you and Billy, out here all alone."

Her hands started to tremble. "I don't mind the work, and I prefer it that way. Just Billy and I alone."

"Don't you get lonely? Scared?"

Keeping the truth deeply hidden, she said, "Billy chatters too much for me to get lonely, and what good is being scared?"

His frown deepened, but then, as if not able to come up with another response, he nodded. "Thank you for breakfast. It was one of the best I've ever eaten."

Clara bit her lip as she nodded. She'd wanted to tell him that she was lonely and scared all the time, and that all those other homes out there were for other people. Not her. She was where she belonged.

Very irrational thoughts started racing across her mind then, at the sound of Billy's laughter and Tom's low chuckle. He'd said he'd leave today, after the roof was repaired. She was trying to think of other repairs she could ask him to take care of. Something, anything, to keep him here just a bit longer.

Not for herself of course, but for Billy. Her son needed this. Needed a man to model, to learn from, to grow up to be like. One who was trustworthy and kind and would be there at all hours of the day and night. One a boy could be proud of.

A wife needed that, too. When her husband rode up the road, the wife should be happy to see him. Excited. Thankful he was home.

She'd thought about a man like that before, just hadn't imagined she'd meet one.

Flustered by her own thoughts, Clara set into cleaning up the breakfast dishes. Then, with Tom and Billy busy on the roof, and needing to have her mind occupied, she set into washing clothes, including the sheets off the beds.

That was where she was, hanging clothes on the line behind the house, when she heard hoofbeats. Dropping the sheet she'd been clipping on the line, she ran around the house, fully expecting the worst.

What she saw made her heart drop out of her chest.

It wasn't Hugh riding in, but Tom riding out.

She opened her mouth, but seeing the moisture on Billy's cheeks, she closed her lips and her eyes, trying to ignore the pain in her chest.

Chapter Four

⟡⟡⟡

The porch roof had been done well before noon, as were all the chores and a few other tasks Tom had decided he needed to complete. When he couldn't find anything else to justify staying longer, he'd saddled up his horse. Billy had wanted to ride with him, and had been upset when he'd said there wouldn't be room.

There wouldn't have been. The pig was a good-sized one. Quartered and wrapped in burlap, it hung off his saddle both in front and behind him.

Guilt at not telling Clara where he was going ate at him, but he hadn't been completely sure where he was going. It was to the Ryans to see about a pig for her, and he'd told himself, depending upon what he'd learn, he might not be back. Just leaving wasn't his way, but it might be easier in this instance.

Easier wasn't his way, either.

How? Why had a woman and young boy gotten under his skin so thoroughly, so intensely that he wasn't acting like himself? Thinking like himself.

He hadn't even known them that long. But he did

know them, and knew more about them after visiting with Donald and Karen Ryan.

The couple had been Clara's closest neighbors for five years and had never met Hugh Wilson. Not once. But they'd heard plenty about him from her uncle. Walter hadn't thought much about the man his niece had married. They didn't believe that Walter had fallen in a ravine, and didn't hold back in their opinion that he'd either been pushed, shoved, or shot and then thrown down the ravine. It just so happened that Hugh had been home during Walter's fatal accident. Supposedly helping the old man round up cattle, which had been driven off the ranch and up to Montana, where they were sold within a week of the uncle's death.

Walter, it seemed, had plenty of questions when it came to Hugh, and had confided in Donald about them. The old man felt that Hugh had ambushed and killed Clara's parents while they were on their way west, and then ridden in and rescued her. A scared young girl, distraught after burying both of her parents on the Nebraska prairie. When they'd arrived at his place, Clara was already pregnant, and Donald said Walter rued the day he'd done it, but thinking it was best, he'd forced Hugh to marry Clara.

Hashing over all Donald had said during the ride back to her place stirred a powerful bout of anger inside Tom. One he hadn't felt since chasing down the outlaw who'd killed Julia.

He'd never expected to feel that way again, and knew he shouldn't in this instance, but couldn't stop it. Had no control over it.

Mrs. Ryan had told him something else, that she'd once asked Clara why she stayed out here all by herself and that Clara's only response had been to say, "And go where?"

If he'd ever considered not going back to her place today, Tom had completely changed his mind. Clara was afraid to leave because Hugh would find her wherever she went. She hadn't said that, nor had Mrs. Ryan, but his gut said that was the main reason Clara stayed put. She was afraid for herself and afraid for her son. Afraid for what Hugh would do when he discovered they were gone and found them. His gut told him something else. Hugh had done something to make her that afraid. That goaded him like nothing had before. That a man could treat his wife in such a way. Then again, Hugh Wilson wasn't much of a man. Anyone who robbed, thieved, killed, was a beast, not a man. People like that deserved to be caged up, sent to prison, where they couldn't hurt anyone else, ever again.

Especially not a woman as gentle and kind as Clara.

The more he thought about that, the more he wanted to know.

Both Clara and Billy were in the front yard when he rode up. He'd watched Billy run from the barn to the house and then saw Clara rush out the door while he was still riding down the hill into the valley where the house sat. He tried to ignore what the sight of that did to him, how it lit up his insides, but in the end, gave in and let the smile that tugged on his lips form as he rode in the yard.

"We thought you'd left," she said.

There was a hint of accusation in her voice, and though it shouldn't, for he'd said he'd planned on leaving, it bothered him. He didn't want to cause her any unjust pain. She was good at pretending. He'd seen how she'd favored the leg, but acted as if it was already healed. She was good at keeping things hidden. A lot of things. So was he.

"I did." He patted one of the burlap quarters hanging off the saddle. "I went to get that smoked pig you talked about this morning."

"I hadn't meant for you to go get one," she said.

The utter surprise on her face made his smile grow. "I know. But it'll be a while before that leg's good enough for you to walk that far." He stopped Bullet and swung out of the saddle to walk the horse the rest of the way to the house.

She shook her head while fighting to hide a smile that kept creeping forward on her lips. "Well, you left before lunch and it's nearly supper time. You must be starved."

"I had two helpings of your amazing biscuits and gravy to tide me over."

"Two helpings weren't enough for all day."

"Want me to help you carry that pig down into the cellar?" Billy asked.

"Can't do it without you," Tom replied.

"Can I unsaddle Bullet for you afterward, and feed him, too?" Billy asked.

"He'd like that," Tom said, watching how Clara's face shone at her son's offers.

Catching him watching her, she patted her hair, as

if checking that the coil was still pinned to the side of her head. Then, as if embarrassed by her actions, she spun around. "I'll have supper ready by the time you two are done, so wash up afterward and come inside."

"Don't have to tell us twice," Tom said, rubbing Billy's patch of wayward hair and watching her step onto the porch. "Does she?"

"No, sir," Billy replied while making a fist and pumping one arm.

A short time later, when walking into the house, Tom was still grinning at the boy's antics, and hers, or maybe it was just that he was happy. It had been a long time since someone had been there to greet him upon arrival. Someone happy to see him, anyway. Most folks weren't smiling when a sheriff rode into their yard.

It was more than that, though. Sitting down at the table, sharing a meal with Clara and Billy, carrying on conversations with them, all of those were things he was looking forward to. He'd shared many meals with families back in Oak Grove, and enjoyed them, but this was different. This was something he wanted. There was something else he wanted, too.

"I hope you like fried chicken, Mr. Baniff. I had a hen that was pecking at the others."

"I do like fried chicken, but I'm wondering if you'd mind calling me Tom." He shouldn't be so forward, but if he was going to convince her to leave, he needed her to consider him a friend. Someone she could trust.

"Boy, it smells good in here, doesn't it, Tom?" Billy said.

The boy's timing or comment couldn't have been

more perfect. Tom didn't say a word, merely lifted a brow that he hoped she read as saying that if Billy could use his first name there was no reason she couldn't.

Her cheeks turned pink as she bowed her head slightly before turning to the stove. "Sit down, both of you."

Other than the platter she was piling pieces of fried chicken on, the table was set, so he waited until she'd forked the last piece out of the pan before he lifted the platter, signaling he'd carry it to the table.

She didn't protest as she wiped her hands on her apron while walking to the table. He appreciated that. A woman should expect a man to assist her in all aspects of life, and a man should want to.

As they ate, Billy talked about all the kindling he'd chopped that afternoon, and about helping Clara pluck the chicken clean, stating it had been a long time since they'd had fried chicken. It had been a long time since Tom had eaten fried chicken, too, and doubted he'd ever had any this tasty.

"That was the best chicken I've ever eaten, Clara, thank you," he said when he couldn't take another bite. Food, no matter what it was, tasted better when shared with others, but that chicken had been exceptional.

"Me, too, Ma," Billy said.

"I'm glad you like it," she answered. "Both of you."

"We liked it so much, we're going to do the dishes for you," Tom said.

"We are?" Billy asked.

"Yes."

"No."

He and Clara had spoken at the same time. Him nodding while she shook her head.

"You've been on that leg long enough today," Tom said. "It can't heal completely without rest, so you just sit there and tell us if we're doing something wrong."

"How can you do dishes wrong?" Billy asked.

"I couldn't just sit here, Mr.—Tom. I'd feel guilty."

"Then go lie down, or go sit on the porch," he said before turning to Billy. "Considering we did the dishes the entire time she was ill, I don't think we'll get anything wrong, do you?"

"Nope," Billy said, now more than happy to help. So happy, he stood up and carried his plate to the counter. "I forgot about us doing them while she was sick. That wasn't so bad, so I reckon it won't be tonight, either."

"I reckon you're right," Tom said, stacking the empty potato bowl atop the empty platter. Looking at Clara, he stood. "Go sit on the porch if watching us will make you nervous." He was concerned about her overdoing it after being so ill, mainly because if he could convince her to leave, actually doing so wasn't going to be easy. She didn't own a horse and walking all the way to Hendersonville was out of the question. He'd have to ride there, rent a rig and return for her and Billy. Or involve the Ryans. The trouble with that would be how Hugh would react to her and Billy's absence, which could put the Ryans in danger.

"I'm not nervous."

He was, but not about doing dishes. "Good. Then you'll have no worries while you sit out there and watch the sun go down."

* * *

Another first, sitting on the front porch while someone else cleaned her kitchen. She'd had many firsts since Tom had arrived, and it saddened her to know that she would never experience a man with his qualities again. They had to be few and far between. If-onlys started to form in her head and she purposefully ignored them. There was no sense wishing things were different when they couldn't be. She'd tried to change things once, and despite the consequences she'd faced, would have tried again if it had only been her. Billy was the only thing about her life she didn't want to change, would never change, and he was worth whatever she had to do to keep him safe.

She couldn't help but wonder if Tom could be her savior. Take her and Billy someplace that Hugh would never find her. It was a nice pipe dream, but she couldn't wager his life just to make hers better. Nor did she believe such a place existed. Why should it? She'd chosen her life and now had to live it.

Still sitting on the porch trying to bury her grief, she glanced toward the door when it opened.

"All done, Ma," Billy said, barreling out the door as usual. "Tom says I should bury these here bones so the scavengers don't come sniffing around, so that's what I'm gonna do. Bury them good and deep."

"That sounds like a good idea," she said. "And thank you for doing the dishes. I appreciate that."

"You're welcome," he said, already running down the steps. "Doing dishes ain't so bad when you got someone doing them with you."

"That's how most things are," Tom said, walking out the door. "Life in general is more fun when you have someone sharing it with you."

Although her mind screamed to know, Clara waited until he sat down in the chair beside her and set her chair back in motion before asking, "Do you have someone who shares your life?" He'd said there was no wife, but that didn't mean there wasn't someone ready to become his wife.

"I have lots of someones," he said.

Not entirely certain what he meant, she waited for him to say more while trying to hide the disappointment stirring her stomach. Which wasn't right because she had no reason to be jealous of the people in his life. Except she was. Especially whoever was waiting to become Mrs. Tom Baniff.

Setting his chair in motion with the toe of one boot while staring out at the slowly setting sun, he said, "The town I live in down in Kansas is full of people I share my life with every day."

More curious than ever, she asked, "Who are these people?"

"Well, let's see. There's Chester Chadwick. He's a really good sort, would give a stranger the shirt off his back without a single thought as to why not to. He and his wife, Joyce, have a boy, Charlie, about Billy's age, who sneaks off to go fishing every chance he gets. Chester is forever having to collect Charlie from the river and take him back to school. There are weeks where I wonder if Chester spends more time in the school building than Charlie does. And there's Brett

Blackwell, who is about as tall and wide as your barn door, and his heart is almost as big. He has two boys about Billy's age, too, and Brett's wife just had a baby girl this past winter. Then there's Teddy White. He owns the newspaper and—"

"Let me guess," she interrupted. "He has a boy Billy's age."

His grin was as enchanting as it was charming. "Nope. Teddy's wife just had a baby girl on Christmas Day, but Rollie Austin has two boys around that age. Kade and Wiley. You never know where you're going to find those two. Not even Rollie does."

Her gaze had gone to Billy, who was on the far side of the barn digging a hole to bury the chicken bones that had been licked clean. More often than not, she wished Billy had others to play with. "Seems everyone in your town has children."

"Not everyone," he said. "Steve and Mary Putnam don't. Not yet, anyway, but they do have two pet raccoons, and Mary has a twin sister, Maggie. I can't tell them apart. Maggie's husband is Jackson Miller. He builds the finest furniture in all of the state."

He laughed then, and the sound was so delightful it made her giggle. "What's so funny about that?"

"Jackson also builds coffins, and Angus O'Leary has had him build three for him so far, but none have suited him."

She covered her mouth to hide a louder giggle. "You mean he's ordering his own coffin while he's still alive?"

"Yes, ma'am. Angus is a silver-haired little Irishman who came into some money a few years ago. No one knows exactly how—some sort of inheritance—and because he's getting up in years, Angus has planned his funeral in advance, including having his casket built. I can't recall what was wrong with each one of them, but last I heard, Jackson was ordering wood for another one. Angus also wants to go out in style, so he wears a three-piece suit and tall top hat every day. Gets a shave every day, too. The barber, Otis Taylor, opens his shop even on Sundays, just for Angus. Of course, Otis had to get a special permit from the mayor to be open on Sundays."

Enjoying all he was saying, she said, "Your town sounds like a fun place to live. What's its name?"

"It is a fun town. A good town, too. Oak Grove. Oak Grove, Kansas. It's somewhat in the middle of nowhere, but most towns in Kansas are in the middle of nowhere."

Looking around, at land she'd stared at for years and years, Clara said, "Lots of places are in the middle of nowhere."

"They are," he answered with a nod. "But sharing them with others makes them somewhere to call home."

She called this place home because it was the only place she could live, not because she wanted to or because she shared it with others, yet she nodded. "I suspect you're right about that." Still curious, she asked, "Are there any women in Oak Grove? Those who aren't married?"

"Funny you should ask that."

Her heart skipped a beat. "Why?"

"Because there weren't too many women in Oak Grove, so the town decided to do something about it.

The Oak Grove Betterment Committee has paid for several mail-order brides to come to town from back east."

"And have they? Brides come to town?"

"Yes, they have. Steve and Jackson, Brett and Teddy, Rollie and several others have all married women who came in on the train."

"Really?"

He grinned again and gave a single head nod. "Yep, really."

"Are there others?"

"Yes. Doc Graham married—"

"I mean other brides waiting to marry someone."

His gaze was on Billy as the boy carried the shovel back to the barn. "Josiah Melbourne, he's the mayor, paid for a full dozen."

Although she truly wanted to ask if one of those dozen mail-order brides was for him, she couldn't get up the nerve. However, she did say, "If Oak Grove is so wonderful, what are you doing traveling through Wyoming?"

He had his elbow on the arm of the chair and his fist beneath his chin. "Looking for someone."

His chair stopped and she held her breath, preparing for him to say Hugh's name. She had no clue what her response would be. There was no loyalty inside her to Hugh, but there was to Billy. And there was shame. Shame that Hugh was her husband.

"Will you look at that?"

Her heart stopped. Afraid to look toward the roadway that was little more than a pathway through grass that was slightly shorter than the rest due to seldom use, she kept her gaze on him, swallowed hard and prayed there wasn't a rider on the roadway. "What? What is it?"

"The biggest toad I've ever seen," he said, leaping to his feet. "Billy! Come quick!"

What transpired next soon had tears rolling down Clara's cheeks, and she had to cross her legs to keep from peeing. There wasn't one but two toads, and watching Billy and Tom run, jump and trip over one another in their attempts to catch the toads had her laughing harder than she'd ever laughed. She giggled and squealed at their antics and gave directions, when she was able to speak, at which way the toad had gone. When they both finally stood, each with a toad in their hands, she clapped at their accomplishments.

After a short bout of comparing the toads, Tom knelt down and let his go, and a moment later, Billy did the same. They then stopped at the water trough and washed their hands. While Billy ran to get the scrap bucket he'd dropped by the barn door, Tom walked to the porch.

With a huff, he sat back down in the rocking chair. "That was fun."

His grin was still as large and glowing bright as the sun making its way behind the hills.

"It looked fun."

"You should have joined us," he said.

Though the pain was more tolerable every hour, her leg was still too sore for such shenanigans. Not wanting him to question her recovery, she said, "I'm too old to chase toads."

"Too old?" He shook his head. "Chasing toads is like going fishing. And no one's ever too old to go fishing."

"Are we going fishing?" Billy asked, running up the steps. "When? Now?"

"No," Clara replied. They hadn't gone fishing since Uncle Walter had died and Hugh had sold the horse and wagon. The river was too far away to walk. "You two worked so hard to catch those toads, why did you let them go?"

The look Billy and Tom shared was identical. It was as if they couldn't believe she'd just asked that.

"Keeping them isn't any fun," Tom said. "It's the catching them that's fun."

"Yeah," Billy said while nodding in agreement. "And I'm gonna go see if I can find some more."

She was about to tell him to put the pail in the house first when Tom held out a hand.

"I'll take that inside for you," he said.

"Thanks!" Billy handed over the pail and was gone in a flash.

Tom set the pail down beside his chair and pushed a foot against the floor to set the rockers in motion. She rocked in her chair, too, as her mind wouldn't let go of what he'd said.

"Is that how it is with most things? Fun to catch but not fun to keep?"

He shrugged. "I suspect that depends on what you catch."

"I suspect," she said, not certain why a statement so simple troubled her mind.

"Take fish, for instance. Keeping them isn't as fun as catching them, but some are mighty tasty."

She nodded. "That's true."

"Whereas toads, well, no one wants to eat toads." He turned her way and gave an exaggerated look of shock. "You don't, do you?"

She tried, but couldn't suppress a giggle. "No."

"Well, that's good," he said, turning back to watch Billy run around while keeping his chair rocking slow and steady.

She wondered if he liked chasing outlaws, for that was what he did. It was dangerous and hard, but he must like doing it or he wouldn't do it. He hadn't told her that, just as he hadn't told her he was a lawman, but she knew. Was certain of it. He was the good in the good against bad. The lessons he'd already taught Billy proved it. The most intriguing part was that Billy hadn't even known he was being taught a lesson, yet the things Tom had shown him would stay with him forever.

They sat in silence, listening to nothing but the wind rustling the leaves of the cottonwood tree at the side of the house, a few evening birds and the echoing thuds of Billy's footsteps as he ran about, searching the ground for toads.

Maybe Tom was listening to a few more things than that. She certainly was. Her inner thoughts were screaming inside her head. Proclaiming things that could never be and denying things that were certain.

Those certainties won out. The barn door was fixed, as were the corral and the porch roof; there was enough wood piled up to make it until this time next year; and he'd brought home a smoked pig. Withholding a heavy sigh that threatened to collapse her chest, Clara rose to her feet and took a step in order to press a hand against one of the rough-hewn beams holding the porch roof overhead. "You're leaving tomorrow, aren't you?"

She felt more than heard him rise and step up behind her, and when she turned around, she was unable to look away. His eyes were so dark brown, and so, so full of sincerity. If only...

"That depends on you, Clara."

Her heart stalled in her chest and she leaned heavier against the post. "On me?"

"You know why I'm here."

She did, so it shouldn't be so hard to admit. But it was. Swallowing the lump in her throat, she said, "I don't know anything. Don't know where he is or what he did." When his lips parted, she shook her head. "And I don't want to know."

He folded his arms across his chest. "Not knowing—"

Reaching out, she laid a hand on his forearm. "I know not knowing doesn't change anything. It doesn't even mean it didn't happen. But..." She withdrew her hand because she had to pat her chest in order to keep from crying as she forced the words out. "If I don't know the particulars, someday, when Billy asks why I didn't tell him, I can honestly say it's because I didn't know." She drew in a breath. "That may sound paltry to you, but it's not to me. There is very little I can give my son, except love and protection."

He grasped her elbow. His hold firm, solid, while being kind. Just like him. Which made tears threaten to erupt.

"I can help you with that, Clara. I can take you away from here."

Another if-only. "To where? There's nowhere I can go."

"Yes, there is. There are places you can go. People who will help—"

She pressed a finger to his lips. "I tried that once, Tom, shortly before Walter died." Removing her fingers to press them against her lips, she swallowed before she was able to continue. "We made it all the way to Denver. Billy and I. I thought it was a big enough town, that we could get lost in the crowd, or move on when..." There were certain things she refused to remember.

"I won't let anything happen to you or Billy."

He was sincere and it was easy to believe he thought that, but she knew different. Didn't want to, but did. "And I don't want anything to happen to you. But it will." Touching one of the tiny pinholes on his vest, she said, "Just like lawmen, outlaws band together. Even those who don't know each other. They have rules they live by, and though they don't put out wanted posters, they let each other know who they're looking for and why, and how much they'll pay to get them back."

Twisting, she watched as Billy dived to the ground and a toad hopped away, barely missing being captured. "Here we only have one outlaw to worry about. Out there, in the rest of the world, there are hundreds."

With a gentle touch, Tom laid a hand on her cheek, forcing her to turn back to him. "I'll find him. Arrest him."

Her heart was wrenching so hard her entire chest burned. "Oh, Tom, if anyone can, I believe it could be you. Which is one more reason why Billy and I can't go anywhere with you. I don't even want Hugh to know you were here."

"That doesn't make sense."

"It does to those who know how outlaws think. When someone rats on an outlaw, all the other outlaws hear about it, whether they ran together or not, and if there's any chance that person knows anything about them, they'll be on the lookout for that person."

That was a simplistic way of explaining an integral lifestyle that she'd come to understand thoroughly over the years. One there was no escape from.

Tom's gaze was thoughtful as he asked, "Do you have any idea where he's at?"

She shook her head.

"Would you tell me if you did?"

Once again, though it pained her, she shook her head.

Chapter Five

Frustration like he'd never known burned inside him, but Tom couldn't determine if it was because of her commitment to Hugh Wilson, or his desire to pull her into his arms and hold her there until she realized how big he was. How strong and steadfast. How the reputation that preceded him, the one he lived up to every day, said he always got his man. He would this time, too, and he would protect her.

He tried to keep his emotions in check, but the fear and sorrow that had surfaced in her eyes as she talked was eating away at him.

"Hugh didn't just decide to become an outlaw one day." Her voice was soft and low and cracked as she spoke. "He was born and bred that way, and his circle of connections spreads far and wide."

Tom wanted to tell her that his years of being a lawman had already taught him all that she'd said, and more, but instincts said it wouldn't do any good. Hugh had a hold over her, and it infuriated him to recognize that hold was Billy. She hadn't said it, but Hugh was holding her son over her head to the point she'd give up any opportunity for a normal life for her son. Instincts also told him she'd fight to the death for her son, too. Most mothers would, but she was beyond most mothers. Beyond most women.

As thoughts twisted inside his head, he started, "What if I—?"

"I'm sorry, Tom. I really am." She stepped away. "But there's nothing you can do. Nothing anyone can do."

"I don't believe that."

She closed her eyes for a moment. When she opened them, her lashes were damp. "Will you believe me when I say I will never leave here? Not willingly? Because I won't. Not for anyone or anything."

He had little choice but to believe her. And he didn't like that. Not at all.

She turned about and shouted, "It's getting dark, Billy. Time to come in and get ready for bed." As she turned back around, she said, "I'll have breakfast ready early, and a bag of food for your travels."

Without waiting for his reply, she walked into the house.

Tom didn't follow, telling himself he had to be satisfied with the fact he'd tried.

Billy leaped up onto the porch. "You coming in, Tom?"

"No, I'm heading to the barn."

Billy nodded, but then bolted forward and, to Tom's surprise, wrapped both arms around his waist, hugging him with all the strength a seven-year-old had.

"Thanks for catching toads with me, Tom. That was the most fun I've had in my whole life."

His heart took a solid tumble as he patted the boy's back. "Me, too, Billy. Me, too."

As quick as the hug had started, it ended, and Billy shot toward the open doorway. "See you tomorrow, Tom."

"See you," he replied, catching sight of the tears on Clara's cheeks as she pushed the door closed behind her son's entrance.

Though it was no different than any other night that he'd slept out there, the barn was quieter and lonelier, and his thoughts darker. Ultimately, he couldn't force her to leave, and the longer he stayed here, the colder Hugh's trail became. If he didn't want to return to Oak Grove empty-handed, he needed to hit the road.

Empty-handed. Hell, he felt empty all the way to his toes. Clara had made it clear there was nothing he could do, nothing anyone could do, to make her leave here.

Tom considered packing up and heading out, stopping miles away, wherever exhaustion would finally kick in, but then decided he'd be better off getting in a few hours of sleep first.

However, his mind wasn't up to cooperating. It took him down roads he hadn't thought of in years. Being a kid. Playing with his brothers. Julia. How much he'd loved her and grieved over her death. His parents, and how even after all these years, a wink from his father still made his mother blush. That made him smile.

It must have also lulled him into slumber because he'd been sound asleep when something startled him so hard he jolted upright. A crack of thunder that rattled the barn had him letting out a sigh of relief. The rain arrived within moments, pelting the side of the barn so hard water flew in between the boards. He moved his bedroll farther away from the wall in order to stay dry as the wind drove the rain through every minor crevice.

The storm was a wild one, lighting up the sky and rumbling the earth. The echoes of cracks and boom bounced off the hills as additional ones, near and far, sounded.

A particularly loud rumble of thunder was so close the hair on his arms stood, and seconds later, the distinct cracking of wood had him jumping to his feet and running for the door. A bolt of lightning lit the sky, and alarm engulfed him as a large branch snapped off the cottonwood tree beside the house. Broken side down, the house roof barely slowed the descent of the branch that was nearly as big as the tree itself.

"Clara! Billy!" He ran to the house and threw open the door.

Terror washed over him as another bolt of lightning filled the house with light. Leaves still on branches filled the doorway into Clara's bedroom.

"Clara!"

"Tom! Tom! Help!"

He was at the doorway, shoving aside and breaking off branches before they could spring back. "Are you hurt?"

"I don't think so. I can't move. There's a tree on my bed."

With no way of knowing if more of the branch was

hung up on the roof, waiting to fall, he shouted, "I'm coming to get you. Don't move!"

"Is Billy all right?"

"Yes!" Billy shouted from the darkness.

Guessing Billy's shout came from his room, Tom replied, "Stay where you are, Billy!"

Clara's room hadn't seemed this large before. From what he could determine, the tree was pretty much straight up and down, with thick branches splaying out in all directions. The hole in the roof had to be mammoth.

Blindly working his way to the bed, he shouted, "Clara?"

"I'm still here," she said. "Haven't gone anywhere."

He had to chuckle at the wit in her voice. "Why not?"

"Because I'm not a squirrel."

How a woman who lived the life she did could still have a sense of humor was pretty amazing. Then again, she was all-around pretty amazing. And likable. More than likable.

His knee bumped what he believed to be the edge of the bed. Just then another flash of lightning gave him a quick view of a long branch stretched across the bed.

"I'm going to lift the branch up, Clara, and you'll have to roll out from under it."

"All right. When?"

Having dug beneath the leaves and branches to the largest part and bracing his knees, he said, "Now!"

The branch was heavy and stout and still connected to the large base, but he finally got it up high enough he felt Clara bump into his thighs and then slide onto the floor. He let go of the branch and dropped down beside her. Grasping her shoulders, he asked, "Are you all right?"

"I think so."

He wanted to pull her close and kiss her, but couldn't, and not just because the tree could shift at any time.

"I thought the whole house was collapsing," she said.

"It's just a tree branch," he said. "A big one. We have to get out of here in case it moves."

She put her hands on the floor and started to crawl. "This way, I can see the doorway."

In his panic to get to her, he'd never thought about trying to go under the branches, which proved to be far faster and easier than working his way through the tree.

Once in the kitchen, he stood and grasped her arms to help her stand. "Are you sure you're all right? Does anything hurt?"

"Yes. No. That was just scary." She was trembling, and leaned against him. "I think that's the second time you've saved my life."

His eyes had adjusted to the light, and he cupped her face, still fighting the urge to kiss her. "Might be."

She blinked and pinched her lips together, but then grinned slightly. "I don't want there to be a third time, Tom. My luck might be running out."

The desire struck too strong to overcome. He had to kiss her, was leaning in and she was leaning toward him when a solid mass hit his thigh.

"Mom, Tom," Billy said, clinging to both of them. "What happened?"

"A branch fell on the house." Tom planted a hand on the boy's back to hold him tight against his thigh while draping his other arm around Clara and holding her against his chest. "That's all," he said. "Just a branch."

There was no going back to sleep for any of them, not even after the storm had passed. By the time the sun came up, they'd eaten breakfast and were prepared to inspect the damage. Tom was ready—actually, he needed—to get out of the house. With her bedroom completely blocked, Clara still only wore her nightgown, which was paper-thin. Every time he looked her way his blood started pounding harder against his veins.

Praying the cool morning air would chill things down, he got the ladder out of the barn and climbed onto the roof. There was a good-sized hole. Yet, truth be told, he'd expected it to be bigger. The first order of business would be to get the tree out of her bedroom.

He found several lengths of rope and a pulley in case he needed to hoist the branch back out by way of the roof.

"What can I get for you, Tom?" Billy asked, tagging along at his side.

"The saw we used to cut boards, it's hanging on the wall over there. And that other little one, it's around here somewhere," Tom instructed as he walked out of the barn. His eyes landed on the house and he sincerely hoped Clara had found something else to wear. She was fetching all the time, pretty with a remarkable figure, but wearing nothing but her nightgown had desires of doing more than kissing her firing inside him faster than a repeating rifle.

She hadn't. Instead, she'd been trying to break off

branches. Branches with wet leaves. Her nightgown was even more transparent now.

Seeing the outline of her curves, the complete shape, including the dark peaks of her breasts, the flatness of her stomach and the... He let out a growl before snapping, "Clara, get out of there."

A frown covered her entire face as she pushed aside a branch and stepped out of the room. "There's no need to—"

"You don't even have shoes on."

Standing there, wet and facing him, she pointed toward the doorway. "Because they are in there. Along with all my other clothes." Bracing her hands on her hips, she added, "If you haven't noticed, I'm wearing a nightgown."

He gave her a solid head-to-toe stare, which was enough to take his breath away, before saying, "You think I haven't noticed that?"

Her frown grew as she glanced downward. "Noticed wha—?" With a squeal, she crossed her arms over her breasts and spun around.

"Backside's about the same."

"Oh!" Still facing the other way, she put one hand on her left butt cheek, as if that was going to help anything.

He couldn't help himself and let out a bout of laughter.

"Get out! Get out of my house!"

"Can't," he said. "I gotta figure out how I'm going to get the tree out of your bedroom."

With one arm across her breasts and the other hand on her butt, she sidestepped from her doorway to Billy's and then shot inside the room.

Tom laughed again. "That's a good spot for you."

"This wouldn't be so bad if you weren't enjoying it so much!"

In full agreement, he muttered, "You can say that again."

"What did you say?"

"Nothing! Not a word!"

"Liar."

He didn't respond. No need to. He was lying. Taking the escape route they'd used last night, he crawled into the room to get on the other side of the branch and figure out his options.

"Got the saws, Tom," Billy said moments before he asked, "Why are you wrapped up in a sheet, Ma?"

Tom couldn't have stopped himself from laughing if his life had depended upon it.

Clara couldn't remember a time when she'd been more mortified, and considering all she'd been through, mortification should come easy. Someday she might be able to laugh about the day she wore a sheet, but couldn't imagine when that would be, or who would laugh about it with her. She hadn't even thought of how flimsy the nightgown was, or how wet. She might as well have been walking around stark naked.

With the sheet tied at both shoulders, covering as much as possible, she entered the bedroom to help as much as she could. Tom was sawing the fat limb that had fallen across her bed from the rest of the tree branch still standing upright in her room.

"I told you to stay out of here," he said.

"I need to help. I can—"

"Find something to do in another room."

"No, I—"

He stopped sawing. "Clara, I'm not being mean. You don't have any shoes on and I don't want you to get hurt."

No one had cared if she got hurt or not. More so, he said it with such sincerity, her heart nearly melted. "I'm sorry. I didn't think of that."

He leaned around the branch, and the smile on his face sent those butterflies fluttering inside her stomach again.

"If you wouldn't mind, you could push the table and chairs out of the way, make a clear path to the door. My plan is to tie a rope onto this tree and pull it through the front room."

"Have you ever done that before?"

"No, but there's a first time for everything."

There was nothing about the situation that was funny, or fun, but he had a way of making everything enjoyable. "I guess there is."

Accepting the chore, she went to work, moving the furniture, and whatever else he found for her to do. She also discovered why Billy liked being with Tom so much. No matter what he was doing, how hard he was working, Tom not only made it fun, he acted as if everything someone else did was exactly how it should be done. There was no arguing or demanding, just everyone working together. It made her feel good. Happy. She hadn't been happy in a very long time. More than once, she caught herself staring at him, admiring him as he worked, and she couldn't help but think about how wonderful life would be with him around every day.

She laughed, they all did, all the while they worked. Because of Tom. When the time came, Tom tied the other end of the rope to the horse and guided Billy on how to lead the horse slowly away.

With minimal additional damage to the house, the tree branch was gone. While Tom and Billy dealt with that outside, she hurried into her room, gathered her clothes and shoes and then went into Billy's room to quickly get dressed.

Tom was in her room when she entered it, standing near her bed and staring at the floorboards. He'd brushed aside a large pile of leaves, and she stepped around them to see what he was looking at.

Although there wasn't a hole in the floor, the boards were cracked and there was an indent showing just how hard that tree had hit. She covered her mouth to keep her gasp silent. All morning, they'd carried on as if it had simply been a little mishap, whereas, in truth, if that tree had landed two feet over, she would have been killed.

He looked up and she could tell by the unease in his eyes that he was thinking the same thing she was. She closed her eyes, not about to let fear overtake her now, there was no use in that, but when his arms wrapped around her, her defenses evaporated.

"It's all right," he said softly. "You're all right, and that's all that matters."

She nodded, but kept her arms around his waist and her head tucked against his chest, hiding the tears that fell. There had been many times in her life that this was exactly what she'd craved, for someone to hold her close and say she was all right and that was all that mattered.

How he'd known that, she'd never know, but a part of her would always love him for it. Love him in a secret way that she'd never tell anyone.

He held her close for some time, and she let him. Right or wrong, it was what she needed and she was tired of denying herself any sort of comfort. Tired of never admitting there were things that she needed, wanted.

When his hold loosened and he took a step back, she let her arms fall to her sides, and looked up. Her heart, as well as everything else inside her, welled with joy as his head dipped toward hers. Even though his lips only went as far as her forehead, she closed her eyes and cherished the long, soft kiss he placed there. Would cherish it forever.

His hands grasped her upper arms as his lips left her forehead. "Feel better?"

As crazy as it sounded, she felt better than she had in years. "Yes."

"Good, because we have a lot of work to do now." With a grin, he glanced at her feet. "I'm glad you found your shoes. For a while there I thought you were just trying to get out of the hard stuff."

"Hard stuff? I—"

He laughed and winked. "I know. I was just teasing."

She playfully slapped his arm. "You are very good at that, Tom Baniff. Teasing people."

"And you are very good at everything," he said. "The hardest-working woman I've ever met. The most determined one, too."

"Enough of this teasing."

"I'm not teasing." He let go of her arms, but didn't step away. "I'm serious. I have no doubt whatsoever that if I hadn't been here, you would have found a way to get that tree out all by yourself."

She couldn't be sure, because she'd never seen it before, but Tom's eyes, his entire face, held admiration. No one had ever admired her for anything.

"You're a strong woman, Clara, and I believe you can do anything you set your mind to." He reached out and lifted her chin with one finger, keeping her gaze locked on his. "Anything."

He dropped his hand and stepped around her then. She spun around, not sure what she should say.

With a grin and a wink, he said, "You could start by maybe making us some lunch. Breakfast is wearing off and we still have a day's worth of work ahead of us."

She laughed at how even his demands were more of a suggestion. "I'll think about it."

"How hard?"

"Go on," she said, waving a hand while wishing he would never have to leave. "I'll have lunch done before you have that branch chopped up and stacked."

"Wanna bet?"

Feeling as carefree as he was acting, she grabbed a branch from the floor. "No." Swiping at him like she was going to use it as a switch, she said, "Now, go on. Off with you."

He grabbed his backside as he ran for the door, like a child would trying to run away from a whipping. She laughed harder, and chased him all the way to the front porch.

The fun didn't stop there. A short time later, during lunch, Billy suggested they should just put a window in the roof so she could see the next time a tree was falling and get out of the way. Rather than tell Billy how silly that was, Tom went along with it, teasing her about sewing curtains for her new window and how she'd have to climb on the roof to wash it. It was silly talk, and utterly enjoyable, and memorable. So very memorable.

By evening, the house was fully restored, inside and out. After nearly falling asleep at the table, Billy stumbled into his room and fell onto his bed. Clara went in a short time later and removed his shoes and covered him. When she returned to the kitchen, Tom was already clearing the table.

"I'll do that," she said, grasping the bowl he was picking up. "You worked all day."

"So did you." With a grin, he let go of the bowl. "How about we help each other."

She twisted to look around the edge of the table. "Are you wearing shoes?"

"Nope," he said. "Boots."

It wasn't much of a joke, but still he laughed, and so did she.

"You should laugh more often," he said.

Not wanting the joy inside her to diminish by admitting there wasn't a lot for her to laugh about, she said, "So should you."

"I laugh all the time. I told you about the people in my town. There's always something to laugh about."

Dumping warm water into the wash pan, she said, "Tell me more about the people there."

"Well, let's see... Did I mention Wayne Stevens has a dog the size of a horse, and Wayne himself has admitted the dog sleeps on the bed with him and his wife."

"It does not."

He assured her that the dog did and then went on to tell her about other residents of the town. Some stories were funny, others touching, but one thing was clear. He truly did think a lot of Oak Grove and the people who lived there. She imagined those people thought just as highly of him. Once, during a quiet moment, she considered asking why he was after Hugh, but didn't. She didn't want to know for the exact reasons she'd told him earlier. Furthermore, she didn't want to be saddened by learning that Hugh had hurt one of the people Tom had told her about.

When the dishes were done, they went out to the porch and sat side by side like they had the last couple of nights. She would miss this. Miss talking with him. Miss laughing. And miss him. Simply looking at him was enjoyable.

They talked deep into the night, not about anything important, but things she'd remember forever. Like how he didn't like cabbage, and that he'd broken his arm by falling off a rope swing, and almost drowned when a raft he'd built didn't float.

She told him about things she hadn't thought about in years, things from when she was little, back in Iowa. The bird she'd found with a broken wing, how she'd doctored it, and watched it fly away. Or the time she'd gotten stuck in the outhouse hole and her father had to pull her out. Silly things that she'd never imagine telling anyone. But with him, it was so natural, the stories were flying out before she could stop them.

When it was time to retire, a mutual agreement neither had mentioned but somehow both understood, they rose from their chairs.

Completely understanding something else, even though neither of them had spoken of it, she said, "You won't leave without saying goodbye, will you?"

"I have to get back on the trail, Clara."

She shook her head. "That's not answering my question."

He took off his hat and spun it in his hands.

"It's a simple question, Tom."

"Then the answer is yes. I'm riding out at dawn, while you and Billy are still sleeping."

His answer was exactly what she'd thought. Hiding the hurt inside her, she said, "Well, then, let me get some food together for you to—"

"No, Clara. I've already eaten enough of your food."

"And you've earned every morsel." She started for the door. "It'll only take me a moment."

His hand grasped her wrist. "No food. No goodbye. But I will tell you this. I'll be back. I can't say when, but I'll be back. You can count on it."

Her heart leaped into her throat. She couldn't say she didn't want him to come back, but also couldn't have him coming back. Hugh would return. Eventually. He always did. Pinching her lips together, she closed her eyes, refusing to let the tears escape.

Tom lifted her hand and softly kissed the back of it. When he released it, she laid the hand over her heart and covered the back of it with her other hand, almost as if she could preserve the most precious kiss she would ever experience. She watched him walk away, and through the blur, she tried to preserve that, too.

She wanted to run after him, tell him she'd leave with him, but that would be too dangerous. For him and for Billy.

Wrestling the tree out of the house and repairing the roof had left his muscles sore, and should have had him so tired he should've fallen asleep as easily as Billy had, but that wasn't the case for Tom. Sleep was eluding him again. His thoughts were chasing each other around in his head like Billy chasing those toads last night.

He'd miss that kid, but was doing the right thing. Saying goodbye would make Billy sad, and there was no sense in that. Furthermore, he would be back. Once Hugh Wilson was tried and incarcerated. Clara would have no reason to stay here then. No one to fear finding her. No one to fear, period. Leaving without her, them, wasn't his first choice, but Clara's mind was set. So was his. He was going to find Hugh Wilson before the man had a chance to hurt Clara again. He was more determined now than when he'd left Oak Grove. The idea of Hugh even laying a hand on Clara tore at his insides harder than when Julia had died, and he didn't think that was possible.

Tom's mind eventually settled and he slept enough to be refreshed. Before the sun was up, he was, and packing his saddlebags. While he was about to toss the saddle blanket over Bullet's back, hoofbeats sent the hair on his neck standing straight. There was a chance it wasn't, but better odds said Hugh Wilson was riding in.

Tom laid the saddle blanket back over the stall wall and walked to the door. It was Wilson all right: the black-and-white paint with an arrow on its flank just like eyewitnesses had described was more than proof.

Wilson didn't glance toward the barn, merely tied the horse to one of the porch posts, grabbed his saddlebags and walked inside the house.

Contemplating his options, Tom settled one hand on the gun in his holster and watched the house door. His mind was making up all sorts of scenarios that he tried not to let take root. Clara wouldn't mention he was in the barn, but Billy wouldn't see no reason not to. The boy had hoped his father would come home soon, just so the two of them could meet. Tom had tried his best to not say anything against Hugh, or the few teachings Hugh had given the boy, even while disagreeing with some of those teachings. Most of them, actually.

When the door opened, Tom grasped the butt of his gun, but then released it when Clara was the only one to walk out. She went straight to the paint, untied it and started leading it toward the barn.

In case Hugh was watching, Tom refrained from opening the door for her, and stayed in the shadows as she walked in and closed the door behind the horse.

"You have to leave," she whispered while leading the paint into the first stall. "Now. Or as soon as I get back in the house. Quietly. I'll keep Hugh away from the windows."

"I can't do that, Clara."

"You have to."

He stepped up beside her and gently pushed her hands aside when she started to unsaddle the horse. The animal was damp with sweat and clearly fatigued. Tom didn't need any more reasons to loathe Hugh, but had them. Both the horse's condition and the fact the man had sent Clara out to see to the animal. "I have to finish what I started."

She'd already dumped grain in the feed trough and had walked over to collect the bucket of water that he'd left by the door last night. "I understand that, Tom, but please, not here. Not in front of Billy."

The saddle blanket was soaked clear through. After tossing it over the stall wall, he grabbed a rag to towel dry the horse. "Keep him in the house and send Hugh out here."

"I can't do that, Tom. I told you that. I have to think of Billy."

He wasn't sure which irritated him more: her loyalty to her no-good husband, or the fact she wore little more than her nightgown. She'd covered it with a long shawl, and wore shoes, but knowing Hugh was in the house, and had most likely seen her without the shawl on... He cursed to himself. Hugh was her husband, and had seen all she had before. Had the right to. It was him that didn't.

With his insides twisting in knots, a portion of his frustration came out as he asked, "What about when Billy's old enough, Clara? Don't you want him to have other choices besides following in his father's footsteps?"

Anger sparked in her eyes. "Arresting his father in front of him isn't the answer for that."

He clamped his teeth together until a portion of his ire eased. "I'm not saying it is. You know——"

"I know you need to leave." She was on her way to the door and didn't look back toward him. "Hugh rode all night. Give me time to feed him. He'll go to bed afterward. You can ride out then." At the door she paused, but didn't turn around. "I'm begging you, Tom—please don't stay here. Please."

He didn't waste the breath to say he wouldn't be leaving without Hugh, but he did follow her to the door, and stuck a boot in the corner so she couldn't close it tight enough to drop the crossbar latch in place. The very latch he'd repaired while she'd been sick and sleeping. Her pleading tore at him. Denying her anything tore at him, but he couldn't leave. He was a lawman and Hugh was the man he was after.

She didn't make it as far as the water trough before the house door opened and Hugh walked out. Billy was right behind him. Tom hadn't known a man's heart could sink, until his did at that moment.

"Billy tells me we have company staying in the barn," Hugh said. "Why didn't you mention that, Clara?"

Tom grasped his gun.

"Because it doesn't matter," Clara said, still walking toward the house. "He's getting ready to leave right now."

Hugh stepped off the porch. "Is he? My son didn't say that."

"He must have forgotten," Clara said.

"Maybe it's you who's forgotten things. Forgotten that Billy's my son." Hugh grabbed her by the arm. "That you're my *wife*."

"No one's forgotten anything, Hugh," Clara said. "He's just a stranger that needed a place to sleep."

Tom was about to push open the door, but Billy ran off the porch and grabbed Hugh's hand.

"He's in the barn, Pa. You'll like him. His name is Tom."

If it was anyone else, anyone but Clara and Billy, Tom would take his chances, step out and draw on Hugh. But his gut would not let him do that. Not in front of Billy. Turning, he walked over to the paint.

"I think it's time I meet this Tom. Thank him for all the work he's done around here."

Hugh was obviously talking loud enough for him to hear. Tom knelt down next to the paint and grabbed a handful of straw to rub down the animal's hind leg.

The door swung open with a bang, but Tom didn't turn around, not even when Billy spoke.

"That's him, Pa. That's Tom," the boy said with excitement. "Hey, Tom. My pa's home! I told him about fixing the barn with you, and the porch roof, and the hole in the house."

Pulling up a smile for Billy, Tom asked, "Did you tell him how good you are at splitting kindling?"

"I forgot that!" Billy exclaimed. "Hey, Pa, I can cut wood the perfect size for Ma's stove. Can't I, Ma?"

"The perfect size," she said.

Tom was still rubbing straw on the horse's leg, paying special attention to the scabs near the fetlock. The

injury was almost completely healed, which fit the timeline as to when the animal had been hobbled while tied
to the train tracks.

"I hear you're quite the jack-of-all-trades," Hugh
said. "Are you good with horses, too?"

"I've been around plenty." Tom stood and patted the
paint's rump. "You've got a good mount here."

Dressed in black from tip to top, Hugh wore guns
on both hips. Very few men wore two guns. Only outlaws and gunslingers. Or those who wanted to be one
or the other. Hugh was on the taller side. Eye to eye
with Tom, and with that gaunt look that made his eyes
beady and his cheeks sunken. Men got that look from
being in the saddle too much to eat three meals a day.
Tom had seen that look plenty of times before, as well
as the one in Hugh's eyes. Ruthlessness.

Hugh, with his hand still gripping Clara's shoulder,
pulled her closer to his side. "I know how to pick a
good mount."

The shame in her eyes almost had Tom going for his
gun, but he refused to let Hugh get his goat. However,
he did level a glare of exactly how disgusted he was
by Hugh's innuendo. Wanting to give the man something else to think about, Tom nodded toward the paint.
"What happened to him?" He purposefully didn't spec-
ify the horse's injuries.

"Got caught up in some barbed wire up in Montana,
where I was looking at some cattle to buy. The Double
Bar-S Ranch."

The lie was to give an alibi. One Tom wouldn't have

bought whether he'd already known better or not. "Montana. That's a long way to ride an injured horse."

"I didn't ride him. A cowboy there doctored the wounds, and the owner of the ranch, Will Barnett, allowed me to stay there until the horse was good enough to travel."

More lies, except that there probably was a Double Bar-S ranch owned by Will Barnett, who would say Hugh had been there. All outlaws, at least the ones who made a career out of it, had alibis and men who would cover for them. Those men were usually as crooked as the outlaws.

"Tom was just leaving," Clara said.

Tom kept his eyes on Hugh, and acted as if he hadn't heard her, or caught the pleading look in her eyes.

"Not without breakfast," Hugh said. "I'm sure that's the least you could do after all the work he's done around here."

With a quickness he wanted seen, Hugh shoved her backward. "Go start cooking. And put some clothes on while you're at it."

Clara caught her footing after a single stumble. "Hugh—"

"Don't make me repeat myself," he said with a look that dared Tom to react.

He'd like to react—was on the inside, where Tom was already seeing a bullet strike Hugh Wilson.

"Billy, come fetch some water," Clara said.

Billy took a step forward, but Hugh grasped his shoulder. "No, the boy stays here. Fetch your own water."

Tom had to fight to keep from glancing at Clara.

He wanted to let her know Billy would be fine. He'd make sure of that, but couldn't let Hugh see him react to anything.

Making sure everyone knew he was in control of everything, including the conversation, Hugh asked, "So, where're you from, jack-of-all-trades Tom?"

Chapter Six

Tom didn't blink an eye as he answered, "Kansas."

Hugh huffed out a sneering laugh. "A Jayhawker." He bowed his head slightly while shaking it as if disgusted. "Ain't never been to Kansas. Hear there's no reason to."

In the split second Hugh had broken eye contact, Tom had glanced toward Clara and gave her a look that said *Leave, now.*

She did, and by the time Hugh looked up again, expecting Tom to be insulted, Clara was gone, and Tom was far from insulted. There was already too much fury inside him for that.

"So, Tom, where you headed? When you leave here, right after breakfast that my wife cooks?"

"I'll be heading home, soon."

"How soon?"

Tom shrugged, and while keeping one eye on Hugh, walked over to pick up his packed saddlebags and bedroll off the mound of straw.

Hugh was itching for a fight. A fight that would show

Billy that the fastest gun won. Tom wasn't willing to be a participant in that game. Not in front of the boy.

"Got business in Wyoming?"

"That's the only reason I travel," Tom said.

"Seems to me, a man on a business trip wouldn't have time to help a pretty woman fix up her barn and house," Hugh said. "Unless there was something in it for him."

Tom carried his belongings to where his saddle hung on the stall wall. After flipping the bags over the boards, he tied his bedroll to the back of his saddle.

"Something fine and dandy," Hugh said.

Once the knots were tight, Tom patted his saddle. "With the number of miles I've put in this seat, there's not much I wouldn't do for a hot meal. Pounding a few nails is a small trade-off."

"But you did more than pound in a few nails, didn't you, Tom?"

"We cut wood and made poles to fix the corral and pulled the tree out of the house and—"

Hugh squeezed Billy's shoulder hard enough the boy flinched. "All that for a few hot meals?" Hugh sneered.

Flattening his hands against his thighs when they wanted to throttle Hugh, Tom nodded. "I like my meals hot. So does Billy. I think we should go in the house and eat the breakfast your wife is making while it's hot." Still not reacting to the defiant stare in Hugh's eyes, Tom added, "What do you say, Billy? You ready to eat?"

"Yes, sir!" Looking up hopefully, Billy asked, "Are you ready to eat, Pa?"

Tom didn't wait for Hugh's response. Instead he started

for the door. The man could easily shoot him in the back, but wouldn't. He was too arrogant for that. Any man, or woman, Hugh Wilson killed, he wanted looking at him. That was where he got his glory.

A mixture of anger and fear that she couldn't get under control had Clara's stomach knotted tight. She knew there was no good way for this situation to play out. Her throat trembled with each breath and her chin wouldn't stop quivering.

If only— Squeezing her eyes shut, she stopped her thoughts right there. She was sick and tired of if-onlys. Her life had been full of them, and contemplating any single one of them right now wouldn't help in any way.

After dipping her fingers in the pail of water, she splayed droplets onto the pan, hoping it was finally hot enough to start frying pancakes. As the water snapped and sizzled, she flipped the ham slices and then poured batter into the other pan now hot. The faster she got breakfast done, the faster Tom could leave.

Footsteps on the porch had her pressing her heels firmly against the floor, bracing for the next half hour or more. Hugh had been egging Tom on out in the barn, and wouldn't stop until he got a reaction. She sincerely hoped Tom's patience would win out. If not, she had no idea what she'd do. What she could do.

They entered and sat, and Hugh kept it up all right, his innuendos growing worse. Without actually saying it, he kept implying that Tom had been in her bedroom for more than removing a tree. Tom never took the bait, but she could tell it was taking its toll. The entire house felt as if time was being counted down, and with each tick, she grew more nervous.

Oblivious to the tension, Billy had dug into his breakfast, but when a quiet moment appeared, he asked, "Aren't you going to eat, Ma?"

"No, she's not going to eat." Hugh grabbed the pancake off his plate and threw it on the floor. "She's going to make me some more ham. I don't want no pancakes."

She grasped the knife on the counter, and squeezed the handle tight while getting her spiking temper under control. Tom was looking at her, and when she used the knife to slice into the ham, a ham he'd purchased, he pushed away from the table.

"Where're you going, Tom?" Hugh asked snidely. "You haven't finished your breakfast."

"I've had my fill," Tom said.

"Looks like you found yourself a little chicken, Clara," Hugh said. "A Tom-chicken." He'd been using Tom's name continuously, like it was the most disgusting word ever. "What's a chicken say, Billy?"

Tom had already reached the door and didn't slow his stride as he exited the house, closing the door behind him.

Hugh slapped the table in front of Billy. "Pock, pock! That's what a chicken says."

"Stop it, Hugh," Clara said.

"Stop what, Clara?" He swiped one arm across the table, clearing everything in its path. Dishes clattered and broke as they hit the floor. "Eating? There, I'm done."

"Pa?"

"Shut up, boy!" Hugh shouted as he jumped to his feet.

Clara shot across the room and grabbed Billy off his chair. Pushing him behind her, she said, "Leave him alone, Hugh. Go to bed. You're tired. You rode all night."

He laughed. "Go to bed? Why? So you can go out to the barn with your Tom-of-all-trades."

"Stop it."

"How many others have there been, Clara?" he asked while stepping closer. "You haven't let me in your bed since Walter died. Is this why?"

He grabbed her upper arms, and dug his fingers and thumbs deep into her flesh. She refused to show him any pain. Any reaction whatsoever. Yet she would stick to the truth. "There haven't been any others, and you know it."

"I warned you, Clara," he said, increasing his hold on her. "Over and over. You can't say I didn't."

"Tom only—"

As fast as a whip, the back of his hand cracked across her cheek. Her eyes burned and her face stung, but she still didn't react.

"Don't say that name!" Hugh shouted right before he shoved her backward.

She tried to catch herself, but stumbled into Billy. They both fell. Hadn't even hit the floor yet when Tom was opening the door.

"Stay inside!" he shouted.

Tom expected the slamming of the house door. He finished tightening the cinch on his saddle. If he didn't ride out, there would be a killing here today. As little as he'd regret seeing Hugh facedown in the dirt, he didn't want Billy to witness that. The smart thing would be to let things cool down. He'd ride as far as the ridge, then circle around and approach from the back side of the homestead. He hated the idea of leaving Clara and Billy alone with Hugh, but couldn't think of another option. Other than a shoot-out.

There was one other thing. He wanted Hugh to pay for the people he'd hurt. Death would be the easy way out. Prison, where he had to think about and remember all he'd done, was what Hugh Wilson deserved, and Tom was willing to take a chance or two in order for that to happen.

"Tom! Tom, my friend, what are you doing in there?"

Leaving Bullet in the stall, Tom walked across the barn, stopping where the open barn door left him in full view. "You're not my friend, Wilson."

"You're right—I'm not."

The glint in Hugh's eyes said it all.

Tom dived toward the mound of hay while pulling his gun. He got a shot off, and Hugh got off two. A pain in Tom's hip that went all the way down his leg said one of Hugh's bullets had hit its mark.

"Don't move, Hugh!"

Clara's voice had Tom scrambling to stand. His leg was dead weight, but he managed to get up and get to the door. What he saw sent chills down his spine.

Hugh had spun around, was now facing the house. One hand hanging at his side dripped blood, which said Tom's bullet had hit him, but in Hugh's other hand was a pistol, pointed at Clara. She stood on the porch, with a gun pointed at Hugh.

Tom reached for his pistol and cursed. It was several feet behind him, on the floor where he'd scrambled to his feet.

"Drop the gun, Clara," Hugh said.

She shook her head. "It's over, Hugh. I'm done. Drop the gun or I'll shoot."

Tom turned cold as the door to the house opened and Billy walked out.

Hugh shifted the aim of his gun, leveling it on his son. "Last chance, Clara. Drop the gun."

"Ma?" Billy said.

Tom would never know what happened first. He dived for his gun, aimed and fired, hitting Hugh in the leg, but other bullets had been fired. Relief washed over him as Clara rushed off the porch and Billy still stood upright, and then disappointment flashed inside him as Clara ran straight toward Hugh lying on the ground.

Getting up wasn't any easier this time. His hip was on fire, but Tom made his way back to the doorway.

Clara met him there. "Your leg. You're bleeding." She dropped three guns at his feet and grabbed his arm. "Can you walk?"

"Ma! Ma! Pa's bleeding!" Billy yelled. "Come quick!"

"Hugh," Tom said.

"Can bleed to death," she snapped.

Tom wouldn't mind agreeing with her, but he couldn't. Despite the anger and fear inside him, both times he'd fired, he'd aimed to wound, not kill. "No, he can't."

* * *

By the time Hugh was in Clara's bed, screaming about the pain in his hand, leg and shoulder, Tom's hip was killing him. Each step sent renewed pain. It was as if he could feel the bullet moving, digging in deeper. His pant leg was soaked with blood, and warmth splayed out with each step he took, saying it was still bleeding.

"Let me look at your leg," Clara said.

Tom stood at the kitchen table, using it to hold him up while he gathered the wherewithal to walk into Billy's room and remove his pants. He'd left her alone to see to Hugh's injuries. "No, I'll see to it," he said. "You see to Hugh."

"Tom—"

"I need him to stand trial, Clara." The bullets he'd shot into Hugh's hand and leg were minor, but the shot she'd sent into Hugh's shoulder was significant.

"That won't matter if you bleed to death before then." She weaseled herself beneath an arm, and while hooking it around her shoulders grasped his waist. "Come on—I'll help you into Billy's room. Hugh's in no danger of dying."

Hugh's screams echoed through the house.

Tom glanced toward her bedroom. "He sounds—"

"Like the coward he is," Clara said.

She was stronger than she looked, and twisted him about. Partially because he gave in and let her help him. Once he was lying on the bed, she said, "Take off your gun belt." Already pulling off one of his boots, she added, "And unbutton your pants, but don't pull them down. I'll cut up the side seam so I can fold back the material."

"No, I—"

"Don't argue with me. Not now." She'd removed his other boot and stepped up to the side of the bed. "Not today."

Unable to convince himself that he shouldn't, Tom took her hand. "Are you doing all right?"

She wrapped her other hand around both of theirs. "I'm fine. It's you I'm worried about."

Tom had the greatest urge to kiss her, and sensed she wanted the same thing.

"Ma, Pa needs you!"

She closed her eyes for a moment and sighed. "I'll be right back. Don't pull those pants down. I'm serious. You could do more harm than good."

Tom couldn't remember a time when he'd felt this useless. "I won't. Take your time. I'll be right here."

"You better be," she said with a grin as she walked out of the room.

He heard her call for Billy, but Hugh's shouting and screaming was too loud to hear much of anything else. Tom was about to crawl off the bed when Clara walked in again.

"Oh, no, you don't." She pointed a pair of wicked-looking scissors at him. "Now unbuckle that gun belt and unbutton those pants."

Clara wasn't sure what was driving her. Anger still raged inside her, a form that she'd never known before and would never forget. The moment Hugh had shifted his gun toward Billy, something inside had let loose. The truth. The destiny she'd known was always right around the corner. She'd aimed her gun straight for his heart, but at the last moment, when Billy spoke, she'd shifted it slightly and put a bullet into Hugh's shoulder instead. It was still there. And would stay there until she was good and ready to dig it out. Hopefully, his shoulder would be burning like hell by then. Which sounded nasty and mean, but that was how she felt, and she wasn't in the mood to make that change.

The compassion inside her was for Tom. She'd seen Hugh draw on him with both guns through the open doorway, but was still running across the kitchen. Tom's bullet had hit Hugh's hand, and having seen Tom roll behind the barn door, she'd put all her faith in the idea that Hugh's bullet hadn't been deadly.

She wouldn't know for sure until she got a look at Tom's injury. He'd lost a lot of blood and could still bleed out. Working swiftly, yet carefully, she sliced open the seam of his pants, all the way to the waistband, and then, as she carefully folded back the material, her heart sank at the fresh blood running out of the top of his thigh.

Wiping the blood away, she followed it backward, to a point still under the material. Carefully, because there was resistance, she eased the material back a bit farther. Unable to tell, she asked, "What do you have in your pocket?"

"My badge. My badge is in that pocket."

She snipped at the material with the scissors until she could see what she was dealing with. "Was. Your sheriff badge was in your pocket." Biting her bottom lip, she examined the badge closely.

"What do you mean?"

"I'll show you in a moment." From what she could tell, the badge was buried deep: two of the five points were completely under the skin. The good thing was, the bullet that could have gone far deeper into his leg was stuck directly in the center of the star.

"I need you to take a deep breath, and hold it," she said. With a clean cloth ready to put pressure on the wound, she waited until she heard him drawing in air. Then swiftly pulled the badge out of his thigh.

Holding the bandage tightly against the rush of blood with one hand, she held the badge up with the other so he could see it.

"I'll be damned," Tom said, taking the badge. "It stopped the bullet."

"It did, but unfortunately, the bullet forced the badge into your leg. I'm going to need to stitch the gash." She'd stitched up wounds before, but had never felt this sort of concern for the injured person. "It'll hurt."

Tom covered her hand with his. "I know, but I trust you."

"I have to do it now before—" She swallowed, not remembering a time when anything had been so difficult.

"Yes, you do," he said. "Go ahead. I won't move a muscle."

"Can you put pressure on it while I thread the needle?"

"Yes."

She slid her hand out from beneath his and willed her fingers to remain steady, both while threading the needle and then while stitching the flesh together. By the time she was done, sweat dripped down her temples and her nerves were shot. Not from Tom. He'd been an excellent patient. Hugh, however, was still squealing like a stuck pig.

"You best go see to him," Tom said as she snipped off the thread.

"He's fine."

"What's thudding?"

"The bed. I tied him to it."

"You tied him to the bed?"

"Yes. He's not trustworthy." Proud to still be holding it together on the outside—on the inside she was a mess—she gathered up her supplies. "We'll need to remove your pants now. I'll wash them and stitch the seam back together."

"I'll do that," Tom said. "You go see to Hugh."

Her hands were trembling, and she knew why. While touching him, his flesh, she'd felt an overwhelming sense of something she couldn't quite describe. Each stitch she'd taken pained her, as if she was stitching her own flesh, or Billy's. It was odd and made no sense, but the emotion inside her went deep, clear to her core, and was more than gratitude. She'd already admitted that she loved things about him, the memories she'd always have, but that didn't mean she loved him. She'd long ago lost her ability to love anyone except Billy.

She was grateful that things had turned out as they had. They certainly could have been a lot worse. So that must be what she felt. Gratefulness.

At that thought, her lungs threatened to lock up. "I—I have to clean up the kitchen first," she said, stepping away from the bed. "I'll be back for your pants."

Needing air, lots of air, she went outside. On the

porch, she grabbed on to one of the posts and sucked in several deep breaths. After a time, breathing grew easy again, something she didn't have to think about.

Billy stepped up onto the porch. "Is Pa going to be all right?"

"Yes, he'll be fine." She'd never said anything bad about Hugh to Billy, and refused to start now. Although she wanted to. Lord, how she wanted to in ways she never had before. "Did you unsaddle Tom's horse?"

"Yes."

The day had started early today. Normally she and Billy would just be eating breakfast at this time. "Go gather the eggs and see to milking the cows."

"No, I want to—"

"Go do your chores," she said sternly. "And don't come in the house until I say."

"I can't do them all by myself."

The whine in his voice and the pout on his face reminded her so much of Hugh she wanted to scream. Usually, he was excited to do things by himself. And proud. Controlling every impulse of voicing why that had changed, she turned around and walked to the door. "Yes, you can."

She took her time cleaning up the kitchen, and with each dish she picked up off the floor, each scrap of food, anger bottled up tighter inside her. When she finally walked into the bedroom to see to Hugh, he accused her of being unfaithful, of calling Tom here on purpose and of trying to kill him. He said she still was trying to kill him by tying him to the bed.

She ignored him and his threats. He may have scared

her at one time, but tied to the bed as he was, for the first time ever, she was in control, and liked it.

"Where's my son?"

"Outside doing his chores," she finally responded. The injury in his leg was little more than a flesh wound. Just above the knee, the bullet had passed through the edge of his thigh. After washing away the dried blood, she wrapped a bandage around it. "Don't bother shouting for him to untie you. He won't."

He'd yelled for Billy to untie him as soon as he'd figured out that was what she'd been doing. She'd been sly about it, pretending to bandage his hand when he'd first lain down on the bed. Instead of bandaging it, she'd used the long strips of cloth to tie his arm to the bed frame and then did the same to the other arm. That was when he'd figured it out, but it had been too late. He'd kicked and squirmed and shouted for Billy while she'd tied both of his legs, but she'd already told her son to stay outside and not come in until she said.

"You can't turn my son against me like this! Billy! Billy!"

Pressing a vinegar-soaked rag against the wound on his hand, knowing the sting would shut him up, she said, "It's sad that the only hope a grown man has is the help of a seven-year-old boy."

After much gasping and moaning from Hugh, most of which she felt was exaggerated, she tied a bandage over his hand and walked around the bed to see to the wound in his opposite shoulder.

As she cut away the material of his shirt, Hugh said, "I suppose you already saw to Tom's wounds."

She didn't respond, other than to start washing aside the dried blood with a wet rag. Two swipes showed her bullet was still there, right below the shoulder blade.

"I bet you didn't use any vinegar on him."

She felt none of the compassion doctoring Hugh that she had while seeing to Tom's wound, and that was somewhat sickening. Had more of Hugh rubbed off on her than she'd realized? The cold, uncaring and emotionless sensations inside her right now were just like him. He'd never cared about anyone other than himself.

Refusing to contemplate that any deeper, she said, "Yes, I did. He just didn't act like a child like you are."

She didn't expect his silence, but didn't worry about it, either, not even when he started talking again.

"Remember what it was like when we first met, Clara? How much fun we had?"

She remembered plenty, even things she'd told herself to forget. For a time she had forgotten certain things, even proclaimed they weren't true when Walter had suspected them. Not ready to open that box inside her, she leaned back and wiped her hands with a clean rag.

"The bullet's lodged in your shoulder blade." It would be easy enough to remove, but her mind had gone to Tom's wound. If her stitches worked loose, he'd start bleeding again. It was a long way to Kansas. With a bullet still in his shoulder, Hugh's arm would be sorer, therefore making the trip harder on him. Which, ultimately, would make the trip easier for Tom. However, allowing the bullet to remain there could cause infection and leave Hugh too ill to travel, which could make things more difficult for Tom. Torn, she said, "I can try to take it out, but might do more damage than good. You need a real doctor. A surgeon."

"Unless your Tom is a surgeon besides a lawman, there isn't one for miles and miles," Hugh snapped.

Not willing to admit Tom was a lawman or that his father was a surgeon, she shrugged.

"Get me some whiskey," Hugh said.

"There isn't any." She always kept a bottle on hand, but Tom had used it to get her temperature down.

Hugh closed his eyes and growled, "Take it out."

"You'll have to lie still."

"I am. You've tied me to the bed."

Decision made, she grasped the scissors with one hand and pressed down hard on his shoulder with the other. "And this is why. Move an inch and the wound will be worse."

Chapter Seven

By evening, Tom's leg was about as sore as it could be, and would be. The healing process had already started. Clara had stitched up his pants so neatly, including the hole the bullet had made, he couldn't even tell they'd been cut apart. But they had been. Far more than his pants had been cut apart today and all the stitches in the world wouldn't put things back to how they'd been.

That was what Billy wanted. The boy had been solemn and spiteful all day, and hosted a nasty glare in his eyes every time he looked at Clara. Tom had been the recipient of that glare, too, but ignored it. The boy had a lot of figuring out to do, more than a child his age should ever have.

Clara had told Billy to stay out of her bedroom, that Hugh was sleeping, but every chance he got, the boy was sneaking in the room. Tom had tried to stay out of it, until this final time. With a look that dared a reaction, Billy sneaked around the table while Clara was at the stove, her back to the rest of the room.

Tom reached out and snagged the back of Billy's shirt and hoisted him off the floor.

"Let go of me," he growled. "I hate you. Let go of me, you no-good lawman."

"Billy!" Clara snapped.

"I hate you, too," Billy shouted. "For shooting my pa!"

Tom didn't say a word, not even when a bout of laughter came from the bedroom. With Billy still squirming, Tom planted him on a chair at the table and kept his hold on Billy's shirt, keeping him in the chair.

Clara didn't say anything, either, just turned back to the stove. Billy squirmed and huffed, and flashed scowls at Tom with eyes that glistened with tears.

The change in Billy—from being so willing to please and helpful, to hurtful and mean—churned Tom's stomach, and he questioned if he should take Billy outside and talk to him. He'd tried to talk to him earlier in the day, but Billy had sensed that and run in the other direction.

Clara carried two plates to the table, setting one in front of him and one in front of Billy.

As soon as she set his plate down, Billy swiped it aside with his hand, sending it and the food flying. "I don't want no ham!" he shouted.

Tom was about to pull the boy off his chair and haul him out to the barn when Clara shook her head.

She grabbed Billy's arm and pulled him off his chair. "Pick that up."

"No," Billy barked. "And you can't make me."

Tom had to force himself not to intervene. He was

ready to, but once again, Clara had shaken her head. She also took a deep breath and closed her eyes for a moment.

"Yes," she said, "I can make you." Her voice was soft and her expression serious, yet sad. "But I won't, because I don't like it when people make me do something that I don't want to. Like shooting them because they were going to shoot someone else if I didn't. That was a mean thing for someone to make me do. Just as mean as throwing food on the floor."

Billy's bottom lip started to quiver, but he tried to hide it by pinching his lips together.

"I don't much care for having mean people around, because sooner or later, they make everyone around them act mean and nasty." She let go of Billy and walked back to the counter where she picked up her plate.

Billy watched her the entire time, including when she walked back to the table and sat down.

Picking up her fork and knife, she sliced off a piece of ham. With a nod, she said, "Do let me know if you want more ham, Tom. There's plenty."

Tom couldn't say if her way was better than the visits out back that he'd had when he was a child and that usually included a willow stick, but noted Billy was thinking just as long and hard about things as if he'd had such a visit.

"What about me?" Hugh shouted. "I'm hungry."

Clara acted as if she didn't hear. "There are more potatoes, too, Tom."

Going along with her, Tom took a bite of ham. "This is a tasty ham."

"Thank you," she said. "The Ryans do a good job smoking their pigs."

"Clara!" came from the bedroom.

"I added some onions to the potatoes tonight," she said, once again ignoring Hugh. "I hope you like them."

Tom already had respect for her, but felt it growing. She'd had one hell of a day, and yet sat here like little was out of the ordinary, the entire time teaching her son a solid lesson. She was an amazing woman, if only she'd see that in herself.

Hugh shouted again, and Billy, also tired of being ignored, said, "Ma, Pa's hungry."

"Did you hear anything, Tom?" she said.

Taking her clue, he shook his head. "No, ma'am, I didn't."

"Me, either. Then again, I only listen when people speak nicely and behave." She sighed. "What do you think, Tom? Aren't people more fun to be around when they behave?"

"I do agree," he said. "And these potatoes are delicious."

Billy watched them both eat for several moments before he sat down in his chair. Quiet and meek, he asked, "Can I have supper, Ma?"

Her eyes met his, but Tom knew she wasn't looking at him, but seriously contemplating her next move. It didn't take long.

"I already gave you some," she said. "When you eat that, you can have more."

Tom questioned the emotions inside him as Billy

glanced down at the floor. The idea wasn't appealing, but just as Clara must have deduced, the lesson her son needed to learn was the important thing here.

Billy climbed off his chair and scooped the ham and potatoes back onto his plate. Then he set it on the table and ate. When the plate was empty, just as she'd said, Clara refilled it.

Tom didn't doubt Billy would remember this meal the rest of his life. He certainly would.

When they were done eating, Clara fixed a plate and carried it to Hugh. Tom, having already carried his plate to the counter, nodded at Billy. The boy was clearly still full of confusing emotions, especially when it came to him, but followed suit, and helped do the dishes like they had together while Clara had been ill.

There was no talking or companionship like there had been, but Tom let that be. It would take far more than one meal for Billy to work out all that had happened, and to come to terms with how he felt about it.

He was trying to come to terms with all that himself.

Sometime later, he was standing on the porch, watching the last glow of the sun slowly fade, when Clara walked out the door.

"I would suggest you give your leg time to heal, but know it's useless, so I've already packed supplies. It should be more than enough to get you to Hendersonville." Leaning her back against the post, she continued, "It may seem out of your way, but you can catch the train there, and traveling by rail will be easier on your leg than riding."

How could she look so pretty, and be so calm and serene after the day she'd had? Because she was a strong and resilient woman. There was no other answer.

He nodded. "I'm going to Hendersonville." There was no reason not to let her know his plans. "I've been trying to figure out how to get you and Billy there, too. With only two horses—"

"Billy and I aren't going anywhere," she said. "Nothing has changed that."

"Everything's changed. There's no reason to stay here."

"Yes, there is. It's our home." She leaned her head back against the post. "This is where we were coming, my parents and I, when we left Iowa. Uncle Walter was my father's brother and wanted my father to help him run the ranch. He had several hundred head of cattle then."

He knew most of this, but let her talk.

"They were killed along the way. Late one night our horses were stolen and my parents shot. With arrows." She closed her eyes and drew in a deep breath. "Two days later, Hugh came along, and eventually, he brought me here. To where I'd been going." Opening her eyes, she shook her head. "There wasn't anywhere else for me to go back then, and there isn't now."

"With Hugh in jail, there's no reason for you to stay here." He waved an arm. "How will you survive?"

A gentle smile grew on her face. "We've managed for years, and will continue to."

Any reason he thought of, she was sure to shoot down, yet he had to try. "Clara—"

"Promise you'll let me know what happens with

Hugh. That's all I ask of you. All I need." She stepped away from the post. "You can sleep in Billy's room. I made him a bed on the floor."

Knowing there was nothing he could say to change her mind, at least not right now because she was also an extremely stubborn woman, he stepped off the porch. "I'll let you know, and I'll sleep in the barn like I have been."

In the quiet of the night, while everyone else was sleeping, Clara let her emotions loose. Tears rolled down her cheeks and onto the pillow she used to smother her sobs. The fears were as real right now as they had been while standing on the porch with her gun pointed at Hugh. Regret was there, too, and eventually, as the well inside her drained, relief came, and that was when she closed her eyes and let sleep envelop her.

The restfulness didn't last long. A nightmarish dream awoke her. She couldn't remember what it had been about, but hidden memories of how awful it had been wouldn't let her fall back to sleep.

She left Billy's bed and made her way out to the front porch and sat down in one of the rocking chairs. As her eyes settled on the barn, she couldn't help but think about Tom and all the things that had changed since he'd arrived. Including things inside her.

A smile formed as she thought about the town he'd described and all the people there. Especially Angus O'Leary and his three coffins. It was a silly thing, but a person who planned his own funeral, and wanted it perfect, was a person who wasn't afraid. Not to live or die.

That was what her problem was. She was afraid. Afraid to leave here. Hugh might have been the one who instilled that fear in her, but she was the one who'd let it grow and remain.

It wasn't hard to admit that. The hard part would be doing something about it.

She set the rocking chair in motion and leaned her head back, closing her eyes. Yes, this was home. The only one Billy had ever known, but someday, it wouldn't be enough for him. He'd need more than the teaching she provided.

When something woke her, dawn was breaking and the neigh of a horse said Tom was up. Three nights in a row he'd said he'd leave in the morning, and three mornings in a row, he hadn't. Today, though, he would, and that disappointed her. Only because she'd miss him. Miss the life he made her almost believe was out there, and available to anyone who was brave enough to go after it.

And she'd worry about him. Traveling injured and all.

Telling herself that was the strongest reason inside her didn't convince her completely, but she rose from the chair and went inside. She got dressed in Billy's room and then, as quietly as possible, started a fire in the stove before she went back outside.

Tom was leading both his horse and Hugh's to the house.

Glad to see he wasn't limping or favoring the leg overmuch, she stepped off the porch. "I'll have breakfast ready shortly."

"No, we need to get started."

"I'll get the food I packed, along with Hugh's saddlebags. I have no idea what's in them, but maybe there's evidence of whatever he did to send you after him." Afraid he might explain, she held up a hand while walking back to the porch. "I don't want to know."

In the house, she grabbed the saddlebags and bedroll Hugh had thrown on the floor in the bedroom and then gathered the food bag she'd packed. Back outside, she handed them to Tom.

"Someday, not knowing won't be enough," Tom said, tying everything behind his saddle.

"I know. But today's not that day." Resting her arms atop the other side of his saddle, she continued, "But there are some things I do know. Hugh can't be trusted. Not even long enough to relieve himself. I already mentioned his shoulder is his worse injury, but even that isn't too bad. He's going to pretend to be in a lot of pain. Don't believe him. Keep his hands tied at all times. His feet hobbled if possible, because even with his injuries, he's going to try and escape."

The wide brim of Tom's hat kept most of his face covered, but she saw the grin on his lips. He had a nice smile. One she was going to remember forever because it made her insides feel warm and light. Burying any of those feelings, she said, "It's not funny. He can't be trusted."

"I know he can't," Tom said, leaning across the saddle to look her straight in the face. "What I find funny is you telling me how to do my job. I've hauled in outlaws before."

The glint in his dark eyes made her heart flutter, or maybe it was having his face so close to hers. Either way, she didn't want it to stop. Not yet. "From what you said, Oak Grove doesn't sound like a town full of ruffians."

"Oh, you'd be surprised."

Tickled again, she asked, "I would, would I? Tell me, who was the most notorious prisoner in Oak Grove's jail?"

"Well, I guess I'd have to say that was Maggie Mc-Cary."

More intrigued by his genuine smile than the name, she asked, "A woman?"

"Yes."

"Was she an outlaw?"

"She was breaking the law."

Sure he was teasing, she smiled and challenged him by asking, "How?"

"Well, now, that's a long story." He stepped back and then walked around his horse, ducking under its neck to end up on the same side as her. "One we'll have to leave for another day."

"But there won't be another day," she said.

He took another step closer. "Yes, there will, Clara. I promise you that."

With her mind searching for a response, she wasn't prepared for what happened next.

Tom kissed her.

It was fast, his lips left hers about the same moment she realized they were touching, but it was a moment she'd never forget.

* * *

Tom questioned his sanity. He'd kept his desires under control all this time, yet standing there, staring into those eyes made a deeper shade of blue by the rising sun, all he could think about was her. All of her, and how he'd be back.

Someday soon, but right now, it was time to leave.

Spinning around, he stepped onto the porch. "It would be best if you and Billy stayed out of sight."

She stepped onto the porch and then around him to open the door. "But you may need my help getting Hugh—"

"No, I'll handle him alone from here on out." He nodded toward Billy's bedroom. "Stay in there, and keep Billy with you."

With the amount of noise Hugh made, no one could have slept through it, but Clara kept the boy in the room while Tom untied Hugh and hauled him outside. Rather than the strips of material she'd used to tie him to the bed, Tom used rope, and tied both of Hugh's hands to the saddle despite the man screaming at how badly that hurt. He also tied his feet to the stirrups.

Then with no farewells at all, Tom swung into his saddle and led the paint horse toward the trail to Hendersonville.

Hugh was far from the best company. His constant complaining got under Tom's skin as quickly as his nastiness had back at Clara's house. Here, with no one else around, he didn't need to hold his temper, but didn't need to waste the energy. Nor would he.

Stopping only to rest or water the horses, Tom kept

them moving. Shortly before the sun started to set, he found a decent spot to make camp. Once they were both on the ground, and had eaten, Tom said, "You best get some sleep. We'll head out again at first light."

"You can haul me all the way to Kansas, but you won't be able to make me stay," Hugh said.

Tom covered his face with his hat.

"Did you hear me, lawman? You ain't got any proof I was ever in Kansas. Not a single thing. They'll have to let me go, and back I'll come, right here to Wyoming and my sweet little Clara. She loves me, you know. Always has. Ever since I plucked her off the Nebraska prairie after those Injuns killed her folks."

After a moment of silence, Hugh continued, "You can pretend all you want. I know you're listening. Hearing every word I say. And you're thinking. Thinking, *By golly, Tom, he's right. I ain't got nothing on him, and Clara does love him. Why else would she have stayed in that lonely old house if not waiting for her husband to come home?* That's what you're thinking, Tom, isn't it?" He let out a snide laugh. "Hear me, Tom? I know what you're thinking."

Tom heard him, not his words but the rustling taking place. Lifting the corner of his hat, he nodded toward Hugh's feet. "That rock isn't big enough or sharp enough. You'll end up with burns on your ankles long before you cut that rope. Now, either go to sleep, or we'll saddle up and ride through the night. It's your choice."

"What rock? I see rocks over there, and there, and there, but not near my feet," Hugh said mockingly. "I see a big old moon and stars, some trees and…"

Tom stopped listening and got to his feet. Less than ten minutes later, they were back on the trail to Hendersonville. Hugh moaned and groaned, proclaiming how tired he was and that he'd go to sleep if they could stop. Tom didn't care how tired anyone was, except the horses. He kept the pace slow and a close watch on both animals. At the first sign of fatigue, he'd stop.

The horses kept going, and shortly after noon, they arrived in Hendersonville. Tom found the sheriff's office and hadn't yet dismounted when a burly gray-haired man with a permanently curled lip stepped out onto the boardwalk.

His look sized up the situation before he said, "How can I help you fellas?"

"I'm Sheriff Tom Baniff from Oak Grove, Kansas," Tom said while dismounting. "I have a prisoner I need jailed while I secure passage for us on the next eastbound train."

The other man stuck a toothpick in his mouth and chewed on it while eyeing Hugh again. Thoroughly. The badge on his chest said he was a sheriff, too, but that didn't mean he followed the law. "Sheriff Puddicombe," he finally said, holding out his hand. "Nice to meet you, Sheriff Baniff." Then with a nod, he said, "What's your prisoner's name?"

"Hugh Wilson."

The sheriff nodded. "Heard of him. Nothing I could ever go after. Just rumors."

"He robbed a train down in Kansas," Tom said.

One brow lifted as Puddicombe stared at Hugh again.

"Shorty!" the man shouted over his shoulder without taking his eyes off Hugh.

When a tall, lanky man stepped out of the office, Puddicombe said, "Take this prisoner inside and then run over to the station and tell Becker I said there'll be two more passengers. Stop at the stable on the way and have Cletus come get these animals fed, watered and ready to be loaded up." As the other man walked toward Hugh, Puddicombe added, "Keep him tied."

"I appreciate your assistance," Tom said.

"And I appreciate your dedication," Puddicombe said. "Kansas is a long ride."

"Yes, it is."

"I just had lunch at the eatery. Roast beef and green beans. It's good. Let me buy you a plate after your long ride."

Hugh was complaining about the rough treatment of the tall man named Shorty, which had Puddicombe saying, "Your prisoner will be secure. I guarantee it."

In need of sleep more than food, Tom asked, "When does the train leave?"

"Fifteen, twenty minutes, but they'll wait for you."

There were other things Tom had planned on doing while in town, like sending a wagon out to Clara's place. "When does the next one leave?"

"Not for four days, my friend."

Chapter Eight

Clara had hoped her lesson after he'd thrown his food on the floor the other day would have been a lasting one. Rather than getting better, Billy was getting worse. He was insolent and mouthy. Repeating things he'd heard Hugh say and claiming he hated her for shooting his father.

"A man doesn't do laundry!" he shouted, stomping a foot on the ground while throwing another sheet into the tub. "And that old Tom's a liar! A lying lawman! Pa didn't rob no train!"

Her hands paused on the stick she used to push the sheet into the boiling water. "Did Tom tell you that?"

"No, Pa did." Billy sent a rock flying with a hard kick. "And he said Tom was lying about it."

Clara went back to stirring the sheets in the cauldron over the fire. These sheets should have been washed yesterday, but she'd spent the day moping about. There was no other way to explain it. After Tom had ridden out, she'd felt downtrodden. Still did today, but had to get over it.

Hugh had left countless times over the years, and she'd never missed him. But she missed Tom. After only knowing him three days, she missed him. Last night, sitting on the porch alone, a few tears had fallen as the what-ifs hit her again. Then she'd played a silly game. She'd imagined what Oak Grove looked like. What it would be like to live there. What it would be like to know people who had regular lives and real jobs.

She'd never wanted to know anything about Hugh's *jobs*, and still didn't. She'd never wanted Billy to know, either, so she pointed out, "If Tom didn't tell you that, then you can't call him a liar, now can you?"

After kicking several more rocks, he asked, "Did he tell you that? Say Pa robbed a train?"

"No, he didn't."

"Did Pa tell you that?"

"No, he didn't. I hadn't heard anything about it until you just mentioned it."

"Well, I still hate Tom. He shot Pa. And so did you. I hate you, too."

"That's fine," she said. "But don't expect me to hate you." Waiting until he turned away, she said, "Tom probably doesn't hate you, either."

"He don't have no proof Pa robbed that train, either."

Twisting the sheet around the stick so she could drop it in the cold water bucket, she asked, "Why do you say that?"

"'Cause Pa told me."

Confused because she'd purposefully kept Billy away from Hugh, she asked, "When did he tell you all this?"

Having run out of rocks, Billy kicked a hole in the dirt. "When he woke me up and I told him about Tom sleeping in the barn."

She'd forgotten about that. Hugh had been alone with Billy for several minutes while she'd been putting up his horse and trying to convince Tom to leave.

"Pa said he didn't rob no friends of Tom's. He was up selling cattle in Montana. I told him he should tell Tom that." Plopping down on the ground, he muttered, "I thought Tom would listen, not shoot him."

A shiver raced up her spine so fast, she grasped the back of her neck. Hugh always used that as an excuse. Selling cattle in Montana. There was even a box of receipts inside. Each time he left her money, he left a receipt with it. She knew they were false. There hadn't been any cattle since he'd sold the last of Uncle Walter's. Yet she hadn't wanted to think about that. Hadn't wanted to know.

Someday, not knowing won't be enough. Tom had said that to her shortly before he'd kissed her and then ridden away. He was right. This time not knowing wasn't enough. She had to know that he was all right. That his leg was healing and that he'd made it to Oak Grove safely. And that Hugh was there, too, and being made to pay for his actions. How to do that, she wasn't sure. But there had to be a way. She didn't have any proof that Hugh had robbed a train, because she'd never wanted to know. If only she had, she could go to Oak Grove and be a witness.

Her heart skipped a beat at the mere idea of seeing Tom, and the butterflies returned to her stomach. No one had ever made her feel the way he had, and she wanted that back, if only for a little while. But how?

"Billy?"

"There are no more sheets," he said.

"I know." She pulled the last sheet out of the cold water and as she flipped it over the line, asked, "What was your father doing in your bedroom when he woke you up?"

Billy shrugged. "Closing the window."

Hugh used to hide things, jewelry, coins, other odds and ends, stolen stuff for sure, under a floorboard in Billy's room. That had been their room before Walter died. But after Walter died, he'd stopped hiding things there because he was afraid she'd use it to get away. He left them enough money to buy food, but nothing more. Never enough for a horse or train ticket.

Turning away from the clothesline, she started for the house. "Dump that water onto the fire."

In Billy's bedroom, she went straight to the window and opened it. The bottom board wiggled, and with hardly any effort, the flat-bottom frame board lifted up. Sure enough, there were three pouches in the space between the outside and inside walls. Two were small; one was larger and heavier.

"What did you find, Ma?"

Done hiding things, she said, "Some bags your father left here." Walking into the kitchen, she set the bags on the table.

"For me?" Billy grabbed one of the pouches, pulled it open and dumped it on the table.

Rings, watches, pins, pendants, wallets and money

clips tumbled onto the table. "No, none of this is ours." She ran her finger over a couple of the items, thinking of the people they'd once belonged to. Regular people. Good people. People like the ones Tom had told her about. "We have to give it back to who it belongs to."

As she peeked into the heavier bag, the air in her lungs grew heavy. Coins. Lots of coins. Gold coins.

"Who does it belong to?" Billy asked.

"I don't know, but we're going to find out."

"How?"

She scooped up the items and put them back in the pouch. "By taking a train ride."

"To where?"

"A town." She stopped before saying *named Oak Grove.*

Tom was so sick and tired of Hugh's mouth, of his whining, lying and overall attitude, that he dang near considered putting another bullet in the man. Just to put them both out of their misery. The only good thing about Hugh was that no one wanted to sit anywhere near him, so there was no worry that he might convince someone to untie him.

At every train depot, Hugh would put on the charm, trying to catch someone's, usually a woman's, attention. He succeeded a couple of times, but then they'd see his hands tied and legs hobbled, and go in the other direction.

Too bad Clara hadn't done that years ago. Ran in the opposite direction from him. Tom felt guilty even thinking that. She hadn't had a choice, and furthermore, he shouldn't be thinking about her the way he was. Nonstop. She hadn't done anything to encourage him to believe in one way or the other she was looking for a suitor. Not that he was a suitor.

Dagnabbit. Hugh was the one responsible for those thoughts. He went on and on about Clara and he still insinuated that more had happened than what had. Tom ignored it, but it was wearing. Partly because if his stay had been longer, something may have happened between them. The feelings he had for Clara, ones that had formed despite his efforts to hold them at bay, were like no other. He couldn't get her off his mind.

As he glanced out the window, the familiar land made him smile. That was Circle P land. They were almost to Oak Grove. It sure would be good to be home. As he watched more landmarks go by, his mind once again was on Clara. He'd never mentioned the Smoky Hill to her. How the river flowed just south of town. Billy would enjoy fishing in it. All the boys in town did. He'd have several friends here. So would she. Oak Grove was just that kind of town.

"What ya smiling so big about, Tom?" Hugh asked.

He still used his name in almost every sentence, as if trying to belittle him. It didn't. The likes of Hugh Wilson could never belittle him.

"I'm smiling because we are almost to Oak Grove." He hadn't yet stooped to Hugh's level of berating, yet couldn't stop himself from saying, "The one town you should have stayed clear of."

Hugh chortled. "Your little town means less to me than you do."

"Glad to know I'm in good company," Tom said as the train blew its whistle. "Real good company."

Not expecting a rebuttal, Hugh frowned and Tom laughed. The sooner he got Hugh tried and charged, the sooner he could head back to Wyoming.

No one knew he'd be on the train, but this was Oak Grove, so he'd barely stepped off the train, nudging Hugh to walk in front of him, when people started shouting his name.

"Sheriff Baniff!" That was Brett Blackwell with a voice as deep as a bear's cavern. Brett was just as tall and wide as a bear, too, and considering Brett's accent, that bear would be one straight out of Canada. "Good to see you're back. You sure have been missed." With a dark frown, Brett added, "This that train robber?"

"Sure is, Brett, and I'm glad to be back."

"Need help hauling him across the street?" Brett asked.

Hugh stumbled slightly as he stepped backward.

Tom laughed. "I got it, Brett, but you'll be the first I call if I do need help." And then because he did want to know, he asked, "How's the family?"

"Good. Real good. We'll plan on you stopping over at the house for supper soon," Brett said. "I'll have Wally see to your horse."

Tom nodded his response because Angus O'Leary, in his three-piece suit and top hat, had stopped right in front of Hugh. Angus met every train that stopped in town, just in case there was someone there he should know.

"This that no-good thief?" Angus asked.

"Yep," Tom replied.

Angus used his cane as a pointer to size Hugh up, from toe to head, twice before saying, "I got a coffin I'll sell him. Might have to cut his legs off, but that won't matter after he hangs."

He'd known Angus for years and had never heard the man say anything even close to that. Stranger or not.

"That's what we do to folks who hurt others around here," Angus said, poking his cane into Hugh's chest. "You remember that, lad."

Chester, the town's acting deputy, stepped up as Angus walked away. "Glad to see you, Tom. Place hasn't been the same without you." Chester glared at Hugh. "Got the cell all ready for this ruffian."

The sheriff's office and jail was across the street from the train station, and it had never taken Tom so long to cross a street before. Half the town had formed a line to get a look at Hugh, and as welcoming and kind as Oak Grove was, there wasn't a smile to be found.

When Mayor Josiah Melbourne met him on the boardwalk in front of the jail, Tom lowered his voice to ask, "Did the mail-order bride die?"

"No," Josiah said, plenty loud enough for all to hear. "But I gotta warn you, nearly every unmarried man is ready to marry her, and every one of them wants to see this outlaw pay for shooting her. We best have a guard on him twenty-four hours a day, just so someone doesn't beat the circuit judge out of a trial."

Hugh had stopped to listen and glance around at the crowd that had gathered. Over a dozen men. Tom recognized a goodly number. For the most part they were newly married to brides who'd come into the community recently.

Chester grasped Hugh's arm. "Keep moving. Your new home is right through this door and behind a solid set of iron bars."

Tom was amazed Hugh kept his mouth shut, but wasn't opposed to it. He'd never known a single person who talked as much as Hugh Wilson.

"He do that to you?"

Tom wasn't sure what Josiah was referring to until noticing the mayor was pointing at his badge. The one pinned to his chest with the bullet still stuck in the center of the star.

"Yes, but it was in my pocket at the time."

"Your pocket?"

"It's a long story," Tom said. "I'll fill you in later. Right now, Doc Graham needs to check over the prisoner while I—"

"Get a bath, a hot meal and a good night's rest," Otis Taylor said, having walked over from his barbershop next door. "Should get yourself a haircut, too."

"That all sounds good," Tom replied. Six weeks of traveling was sure to have left him looking worse for wear. "And I'll get to each one of those, Otis, as soon as I see to the prisoner."

Getting Hugh settled in a cell didn't take as long as clearing the crowd away from the building. Inside and out. Nearly every man, married or not, volunteered to take their turn sitting guard over Hugh.

Chester took charge of setting up a schedule and assigning shifts, and as soon as he walked outside to write down every name, Hugh started up again.

Tom ignored his demands and settled down in the chair behind the desk that had neat stacks of various correspondences. Chester had categorized things into piles of newspapers, letters, wanted posters, complaints and telegrams.

Certain the deputy would have taken care of anything urgent, Tom merely shuffled through things. It had been almost a week since he'd left Clara, but it felt longer, and all those hours of sitting atop Bullet and then a hard train seat had given him plenty of time to think about her. Worry about her. Another storm could have blown through, causing more damage or...

The telegram he'd picked off the pile demanded his full attention. It was from the livery in Hendersonville. The one he'd paid to deliver a horse and wagon out to Clara's so she'd have a way to get places besides walking.

The Wilson place has been abandoned. Horse and rig returned to town.

Tom was already on his feet. Opening the door, he spied Teddy White still in the crowd. "Teddy, I need to send a telegram."

Urgency filled Tom, clouding his ability to think straight, including what he should do.

Chapter Nine

$\sim\!\!\approx\!\!\sim$

With each revolution of the train wheels that took them closer and closer to Oak Grove, Clara's nerves had her sitting on the edge of her seat. The adventure of traveling, of being off the homestead, had shifted Billy's attitude. Every new sight thrilled him and that made the entire venture easier, except for her doubts and fears.

A part of her feared Billy's excitement came from the idea of seeing his father again. She made no mention of that or of a trial, and wouldn't, but would have to soon.

As soon as she'd made up her mind, they'd packed a few belongings and walked to the Ryans'. There, she'd negotiated a deal for them to take care of her cows and chickens, check on her place and loan her a horse. The Ryans had said they didn't need any payment, but she'd insisted. With little else that was truly hers, it was land she offered in exchange. There were details to be worked out, and she would upon returning. At the time, all she'd been able to focus on was getting to Hendersonville in order to catch an eastbound train.

They'd caught a train, finally. Because they'd arrived

in town shortly after one had left, they'd had to wait four days for the next one to arrive. The time delay and cost was not something she'd been prepared for. The small amount of cash the Ryans had loaned her, for she would pay them back, was being stretched so thin she could see through it.

She'd hidden the coins from Hugh's stash inside her valise, which made the bag twice as heavy as it otherwise would have been. Using just one of those coins would have made the trip easier, but she refused to do that. It was stolen money, and spending it would make her an accomplice. No one had to tell her that. Not even Sheriff Puddicombe. When the man had approached her at the livery stable, she was certain she'd be arrested, and hadn't even been able to speak.

He hadn't arrested her, not even upon learning her name, but had asked plenty of questions. She'd answered them honestly, to the best of her ability, without revealing what was in her bag. However, she'd sensed he knew, and when the train had arrived, she'd forced Billy to run in her hurry to get to the station.

He'd tripped and landed in a puddle, which had left him with a skinned knee and torn britches, and both of them traveling with mud-stained clothes. She would have had time to stitch up his trousers during any one of the long train rides or layovers in between, if she'd thought to bring along a needle and thread. Which she hadn't. Nor did she have the funds to buy a needle or thread. Still wouldn't upon arrival.

Her stomach sank as the train whistle bellowed. Billy would look like a ragamuffin stepping off the train in

Oak Grove, and truth be told, she would, too. They'd washed their hands and faces whenever possible, despite the signs saying the water in the buckets was for drinking only, but they both needed a good, deep scrubbing. The soot from the boilers covered everything, including their hair. She hadn't looked in a mirror, but imagined her hair was the same sooty gray as Billy's.

With enough screeching, clanking and hissing that she wanted to cover her ears, the train pulled into the Oak Grove depot. She was afraid to look out the window, fearful of what could be awaiting her. If Hugh's trial was already over, which it could very well be— it had been almost two weeks since Tom had hauled him away—Hugh could still be in town. Though she highly doubted Tom would allow that—he'd have him sent off to prison straightaway to protect the town— there was a chance.

There was also a chance that someone would know who she was, a slight one, but Hugh could have gotten word to someone, anyone, and they could be watching, waiting for her.

She'd been aware of that the entire way and, no matter how long the layover, hadn't ventured away from the depot in every town they'd stopped in, even those they'd had to switch trains in, including the middle of Nebraska, where they'd had to wait a full day.

Billy, with his nose pressed to the dirty window, asked, "Are we getting off here, Ma?"

Drawing a deep breath and praying for courage, she replied, "Yes."

"We catching another train?"

"No."

He turned to look at her. "This is it? This is where we're going?"

Despite everything churning inside her, she had to grin at the round spot of soot on the tip of his nose. Wiping at it with the tip of one finger, she said, "Yes. Collect your bag."

The train car had been stifling hot, and though it was hot outside, too, the wind that blew over her as she stepped onto the platform had a cooling effect.

"Howdy, ma'am." A man wearing the same type of uniform all the other depot agents had—dark blue with shiny brass buttons—touched the narrow brim of his flat hat. "Step on over there in the shade. Don't worry none about the dog. He won't hurt you."

"A dog?" Billy exclaimed. "Can I pet him?"

"Sure can. His name is Bear." Looking back at her, the man said, "Austin's Hotel and Eatery is just up the road. You have time to catch a meal before the train heads out again."

"Thank you."

"I thought you said we weren't catching another train," Billy said.

Without looking to see if the man heard him, she encouraged Billy to move into the shade. Because she hadn't responded, Billy repeated himself.

"We aren't," she whispered. Although she'd had plenty of time to consider her first order of business upon arrival, she had no idea what to do. Where to go. All her thoughts had centered around Tom.

"Look at that dog!" Billy said. "He's as big as a bear."

The dog was, and as hairy, but the brown eyes that looked up at her and the tail that thumped soundly against the boards said it was far more friendly than a bear. As Billy crouched down beside the dog, she scanned the town, her heart stopping when her eyes settled on the sheriff's office across the street.

"I say there, young lad, you've just made a friend for life. There's nothing that old dog likes more than having his ears scratched."

Clara turned, and the moment her eyes settled on the speaker, she knew it was Angus O'Leary. Tom couldn't have described him more perfectly than if he'd drawn her a picture, complete with a fancy suit and top hat. The only thing he hadn't mentioned was the old man's cane that he was now using to scratch the dog's back, or the twinkle in his eye as he winked at her.

"You must be a dog owner yourself," Angus said to Billy.

"No," Billy replied. "But my uncle Walt used to have a dog. But it got dead. So'd Uncle Walt."

"Well, there's a lot of life left in Old Bear here. You'll see that as soon as he sees a rabbit." Angus then looked at her. "You staying a spell in our little town, or just passing through, lass?"

"Staying," she said. "For a short time."

"Well, I hope it's not too short of a time." With an extremely elegant bow for a man of his age, he said, "Name's Angus O'Leary, lass, and I'm honored to make your acquaintance."

As he straightened, he held a hand out to her. Although she was a bit unsure, her response was to extend a hand to shake his. "It's a pleasure to meet you, Mr. O'Leary." That was true. She already considered him an extraordinary man.

Rather than shaking her hand, he kissed the back of it, which had her closing her eyes at how Tom had done that.

Still holding her hand, Angus stepped closer and tucked her hand around his elbow. "Allow me to escort you into our fine town."

Her stomach hiccuped, letting her know it was time to begin the next steps in her journey. The final steps. "As pleasurable as that might be, Mr. O'Leary, I merely need to cross the street. To the sheriff's office."

"Afraid that won't do you much good, lass. No one's there."

Her heart skipped several beats. "To— The...the sheriff's not in town?"

"He's in town all right, just up the road at the new town hall that Jackson Miller finished building a short time ago. It's a mighty fine sight, that new building. Inside and out. That Jackson is an artist with a hammer and nails. Even when it comes to making coffins." Shaking his head, Angus added, "He just can't seem to get the size right."

Before she could consider a response, Angus was waving his cane toward the buildings surrounding them. "No one's at the barbershop, either, not that you'd need Otis's services, or the feed mill, gun shop or livery. Most every place in town is closed today."

She hadn't considered how quiet the town was. There were no people mingling about, no riders or rigs traveling up and down the road.

"Most everyone's at the town hall, on account of the trial going on there."

She bit her bottom lip to stop it from quivering. It was a relief to know the trial hadn't ended, yet it made her tremble.

"It's been going on for a couple of days now, and won't end today," Angus said. "That's where I was until I heard the train whistle and figured I best follow Wayne, the depot agent, over here just in case he needed assistance."

She followed his gaze, toward where the depot agent was helping the porter unload several crates.

Turning about first, Angus gave her a little tug forward. "Only other person who left the trial was Rollie Austin. He owns the hotel and eatery. His wife, Sadie, a quiet young lass, is going to have a baby soon, and Rollie doesn't want her overdoing things. He'll have a bite to eat ready for any passengers needing one."

"Well, um—" She didn't want to go into the trial looking like she did, but the small amount of funds left in her pocket didn't leave her with many options.

"Come along, lad," Angus said to Billy. "You can visit Bear again later. He doesn't go far, unless he sees a rabbit of course."

"Perhaps we could just wait at the sheriff's office," Clara said.

"Can't have that, lass," Angus said.

"Why not?"

"Because I'm hungry, and I don't like eating alone."

Having no idea how much further she'd have to stretch her remaining funds, she said, "My apologies, Mr. O'Leary, but—"

"Oh, lass, do be a dear and allow a dying old man the pleasure of buying you and your fine lad a meal. It very well could be my last, and no one wants to eat their last meal alone."

Not only were his words laced with exaggeration, so was his tone. But, in the end, it was the twinkle in his aging blue eyes that made her laugh. "Oh, Mr. O'Leary, you are a darling."

He laughed and pulled her forward. "No, lass, you are the darling."

"This trial is lasting longer than a road to nowhere," Tom muttered while watching people file out of the town hall. Raymond Wolf stood in the doorway, handing guns back to those who'd given them to Wolf as they'd entered. Town ordinance refused anyone to wear a gun during the trial except for him and Chester.

"I know, and I'm almost at a loss," Josiah said, shaking his head.

That worried Tom, and so did many other things.

"I can't believe the judge allowed Hank Baldwin to be Wilson's lawyer," Josiah said. "Everyone knows Baldwin is the reason those Dalton boys got off scot-free for the train they'd robbed."

"The law says he has a right to a lawyer," Tom said, even though the words left a bitter taste in his mouth. Seeing that every aspect of the law was followed had never troubled him this much. Not ever.

"I know, but I'd recommended Ray Cabot." Josiah wasn't just the mayor of Oak Grove; he was the only lawyer. The judge had sent a request to Dodge in order for one to be assigned to Hugh.

"And as Baldwin pointed out, Cabot doesn't have any trial experience," Tom replied as his eyes settled on Hugh and his lawyer, who were whispering back and forth while waiting for the courtroom to clear out.

"Baldwin's tearing my case apart," Josiah said. "I'd like to know where he came up with all those drawings of black-and-white paint horses."

"Doesn't matter where," Tom said, just as disappointed that the unusual arrow marking on Hugh's horse wasn't so unusual. Baldwin had claimed a person needed to know they were looking for an arrow shape in order to see it, and proved it with drawings of other horses and asking what people saw in the markings, when prompted.

"I wish he'd had more in those saddlebags of his," Josiah said. "Just one item that had been stolen from one of the passengers would seal this case. Are you sure you didn't see anything at his place in Wyoming?"

Tom had kept what he'd seen at Clara's place to pertinent facts only. Although he wished he had seen something, he hadn't. Not that it would help this case anyway. "No," he said. "We know that receipt he had from the Double Bar-S Ranch isn't worth the paper it's written on."

"No, it's not, but as Judge Alfords pointed out, proving that won't prove the money in the saddlebags is the same money that slaughterhouse agent had." Josiah shoved the stack of paper off the table they stood next to into his carrying bag. "It's not even close to the same amount."

The eyewitnesses, whose descriptions of Hugh were dead-on, were also put to question. Since Hugh's face had been partially covered, Baldwin tossed out numbers of how many men had brown hair and green eyes. He also pointed out that Hugh's eyes were a gray-brown, not green, which did throw a few off. His build wasn't out of the ordinary, either, nor was his walk, which he'd disguised by claiming the wound in his leg was giving him a permanent limp.

As if knowing they were talking about him, which was a simple feat because they were, Hugh looked up. The sarcastic smile on his face fell slightly when Brett Blackwell stepped behind Hugh and hoisted him off his seat. Brett had appointed himself as Hugh's escort to and from the jail, and Tom was glad. The blacksmith was not only huge, he was swift. One wrong move and Brett would have Hugh on the ground, squished like anyone else would squash an annoying pest.

Waiting for everyone else to leave had Tom's feet itching to move. He wanted to walk out that door, too. The train whistle had sounded a couple of hours ago. Ever since he'd wired Sheriff Puddicombe in response to the message about Clara's place being abandoned, he'd been at the train station when an eastbound train had arrived. She'd boarded one with Billy, back in Hendersonville, and Puddicombe had been certain this was where she was headed.

Tom hoped so, but he also questioned why. She didn't know anything about the robbery. Hadn't wanted to know. Considering she was coming here to aid Hugh churned his stomach to the point he was barely able to eat.

He'd never been overly wide at the waist, but others had noticed how his belt was a couple of notches tighter. The small house he rented a block behind his office, which usually only hosted the necessities, now had cupboards full of canned goods and ready-to-eat foods the women of the town dropped off daily.

They claimed it was the least they could do for all his hard work. He disagreed. His hard work was proving useless.

So was his worry. Clara might not be coming to help Hugh. He just couldn't think of another reason. She'd been adamant about not leaving. That was also what worried him. That she had left. Which meant someone must have forced her and that same someone could be forcing her to aid Hugh.

"I'm going to head over to the hotel, get something to eat," Josiah said. "Care to join me?"

"No," Tom answered, stepping away from the table as Brett *escorted* Hugh through the doorway.

"I'll stop over at your place later. Maybe we can jog your memory, make you remember something, anything, that might help this case before the judge calls the court back in session tomorrow morning."

Although Tom knew that wouldn't happen, he nodded to Josiah as they walked across the room.

Before they reached the door, Angus O'Leary stepped through the opening. "Hello, gentlemen."

"Hello, Angus," Tom replied.

With a grin that was even wider than usual, Angus said, "Just the men I was looking for."

Tom attempted to step around the old man, but then

a sixth sense had him grasping Angus's forearm. Cautious, because he hadn't told anyone, Tom chose his words carefully. "Did anyone get off the train today?"

The twinkle in Angus's eye had Tom holding his breath at the flare of excitement deep inside him. The only other person who knew what Sheriff Puddicombe's telegram had said was Teddy White. Though Teddy also owned the newspaper and was dedicated to his profession, he was just as dedicated to holding back information that no one else needed to be privy to.

With a nod toward the front of the room, where Judge Alfords was reading through the testimonies that Abigail White had been assigned to write, word for word, each and every day, Angus lowered his voice. "We need to talk. The three of us. Now."

Abigail had been given the task because, as Teddy's sister and the newspaper's writer-reporter, she could write faster than people could talk, ensuring not a single word would be missed. The judge reviewed her report after each session. Tom didn't know if that was to make certain she hadn't missed anything or for the judge to make sure he hadn't missed anything. One thing was clear: although her attitude had changed somewhat since Teddy had gotten married and had a baby last Christmas, Abigail was not known for keeping secrets of any kind.

"Let's go to my office," Josiah said.

Tom held back, waiting for Angus to follow Josiah out the door. Then, while the other man was a few steps ahead of them, he asked Angus, "Did someone get off the train today?"

"Never fear, Sheriff. All are safe when Angus O'Leary is near."

A shiver had the hair on Tom's arms standing on end. He liked straight-out answers, not riddles, but he also knew Angus. The old man wasn't going to say anything more until they were behind closed doors.

That happened relatively quickly, considering Josiah's office was only a short walk up the street, and once behind closed doors, when Tom discovered Clara was right next door, at Rollie's Hotel, he almost shot right back out the door. Would have if Angus and Josiah hadn't stopped him.

"Just sit down, Sheriff, and let me tell you what I think," Angus said.

"I don't have time—"

"In this instance, you need to make the time," Angus said. "Because if you don't, none of this will end up as it should."

Flustered, Tom wrenched off his hat in order to scratch his tingling scalp. Needing to know if Clara was all right, how she looked, had his entire body itching to move. Huffing out a breath, he said, "Stop talking in riddles, Angus, and tell us what you know."

"As I said, I arranged for a room for her and her son," Angus said. "Poor little lass is down to her last few pennies."

"I'll pay for the room," Tom said, digging in his pocket.

"That's not what I'm saying, Sheriff," Angus said. "I don't want your money. Furthermore, you can't pay for her room."

Tom opened his mouth to argue, but Angus pointed

his cane at him. "If you do that, that too-smart-for-his-own-good lawyer will try to convince the judge you've been hiding her out the entire time, waiting until the end of the trial to bring her in as a witness. And that could put anything she has to say in jeopardy."

Josiah, who'd been extraordinarily quiet until then, said, "He's right, Tom. In fact, if Baldwin gets wind that Wilson's wife is in town, and that we know about it, he'll accuse us of withholding witnesses, evidence."

Growing more agitated, Tom paced the floor. "We don't know she's here to testify. She didn't say that." Questioning if he'd missed Angus mentioning that, Tom asked, "Did she?"

"No," Angus answered. "If she'd tried, I'd have stopped her. All she told me was that she was here to see the sheriff."

Tom's heart skipped a beat. "She's—"

"There's no other reason for her to be here," Josiah said, rubbing his chin. "And we need to think through what we are going to do about it."

"There's nothing to think about," Tom said. "She doesn't know—"

"Sit down, Tom. Maybe that'll help your thinking," Josiah said.

"My thinking? There's nothing wrong—"

A sting on his shin had him spinning about to look at Angus, whose cane had just whacked his leg. Angus patted the seat of the long sofa he sat on.

"Right now, the only person who knows who she is is me," Angus said. "Wayne knows a woman and child arrived. So does Rollie, but they don't know her name.

I told her she could use my room, as I've been known to do a time or two when I see a down-on-their-luck traveler."

That much was true. Angus considered himself a one-man welcoming committee, yet Tom couldn't see the justification of the secrecy the other two seemed to be so intent upon.

"Having met her while chasing down that thief has made you unable to see the forest for the trees."

Tom shook his head at Angus's latest riddle.

"I agree," Josiah said. "From the moment that robbed train rolled into town and we learned of the misdeed, you've insisted that the law settle this entire escapade, Tom, and I agreed. Still do." Josiah slapped a hand on his desk. "I've built this town. When I said I'd bring in twelve mail-order brides, I did it. And if I say I'll bring in a dozen more, I'll do that, too. So when I said we'll see that robber put away, I meant it, and that's exactly what we are going to do."

Josiah stood and scratched the side of a jowl as he walked around his desk. "You might think she doesn't know anything, but she might. Things she didn't want you to know."

A few things the other two had said had Tom thinking, and realizing he might be too close, too involved, to clearly see all aspects. But Clara didn't know anything. She was too intent on not knowing anything Hugh did. Just so she wouldn't have to admit any of it to Billy. However, only a short time ago, he'd been questioning if someone else had forced her to come to town. That could be the case. He didn't want to admit it, but it could be.

"Now, as I see it, we, especially Tom and I, can't have anything to do with this situation." Josiah pronounced *situation* as if it was an obscurity. "The fact that a woman got off the train today is an insignificant piece of information that doesn't matter to us at all."

Looking directly at Angus, Josiah said, "In fact, when she walks into the trial tomorrow, simply because she heard it was taking place, no one even notices her. She is the one who asks the judge if she can speak. Offer whatever information she may have. None of us know anything about it or her."

A smile formed on Josiah's face. "Then, when she states her name, we can claim the other side was hiding witnesses." A frown then appeared. "I wish you would have taken her somewhere else besides the hotel, Angus. Your house, perhaps. Maybe you could—"

"I live at the hotel, Josiah," Angus pointed out.

"Oh, that's right. You do," Josiah said. "My concern is that Baldwin and Judge Alfords are both staying at the hotel, too."

Tom was listening, but his mind was on Clara. He couldn't pretend she wasn't in town. Couldn't pretend to not recognize her if she walked into the courtroom.

"If I'd taken her anywhere else, more people would know she's here," Angus said. "I told her to stay in my room. The boy, too. He was so worn-out from all their travels, the poor little lad fell asleep as soon as his belly was full and his mama had scrubbed him clean."

Tom tried not to let anything show. Clara had to be just as exhausted. Just keeping up with Billy had worn him out those first few days while she'd been ill. That boy could buzz circles around bees.

"All right," Josiah said. "Keep her there, and the boy. Until tomorrow morning. We just have to hope that Rollie or Wayne don't say anything to anyone."

"They won't," Angus said. "They're both too worried about their wives and the babies they're carrying to care about anything else. They're only attending the trials to get their minds off their wives for a while. If you ask either of them, they probably can't tell you a thing that's been said in that courtroom."

Tom didn't believe that, but he did agree that both Rollie and Wayne were keeping close tabs on their wives. Just as he would if—

Tom shot off the sofa, startling the other men as much as the route of his thoughts had startled him.

"Did you remember something?" Josiah asked, looking hopeful.

"No," Tom said. Then, trying to come up with something to explain his actions, he said, "But Angus needs to go out the back door. We don't want anyone knowing he's been in here talking to us so long."

"I agree," Josiah said. "Now, we all just have to hope that Wilson's wife is here on our behalf and not his."

Chapter Ten

She'd had some long nights in her life, long, scary, lonely and downright frightful, but Clara had never not slept a wink. Trying to justify why that had happened, she told herself it was because she'd taken a nap after Angus had kindly escorted her and Billy into his hotel room—rooms, actually, since he lived here. He had a small sitting room adjacent to the bedroom hosting the bed she and Billy had spent the night in.

The past several days had been long, and sleepless, for both her and Billy. She hadn't realized how tired he'd been. After eating and taking a bath yesterday afternoon, he'd climbed upon the bed and had yet to wake. A smile tugged at her lips at how he'd been amazed at the bathtub, and how he'd said taking a bath that way wasn't so bad. She'd agreed. If there wasn't so much on her mind, she might have enjoyed the bath she'd taken a bit longer.

Turning from the window that showed a sky turning shades of pink from the morning sun, she glanced at the bed and her still sleeping son. She'd been exhausted, too. Still was, but her nerves wouldn't let her sleep any more than they'd let her relax in the tub.

She wanted to see Tom so badly, like a hunger that couldn't be satisfied. But she knew she couldn't, and that had her twisted in knots.

Upon his arrival last evening, Angus, bearing a tray of food, had asked her to once again dine with him. Their conversation had been interesting, and confusing at the same time. Angus had a way of talking in riddles almost. Saying things that had hidden meanings. Silently, but with exaggerated hand gestures and expressions, he'd encouraged her to explain what she thought he'd been trying to say, without actually saying it.

It was so confusing and frustrating. At times, not knowing what he was trying to get across had made her head pound, but eventually, it all became crystal clear.

No one could know she was here. Not until she walked into the courtroom and asked permission to speak to the judge. Angus didn't want to know why she was here or what information she wanted the judge to know about. She could relate. She'd spent the last eight years not wanting to know. And was now aware of how frustrating that could be to others.

Not knowing.

She also now hated the position that had put her in.

Angus, in his not-so-subtle I-can't-tell-you-so-figure-it-out-but-don't-tell-me way, had also relayed that she wasn't to have anything to do with Tom. Not look at. Not talk to. Not even slightly acknowledge they knew one another. She couldn't blame Tom for wanting that. He was a sheriff. She was an outlaw's wife.

She closed her eyes tightly and held her breath at the tears that burned and fought to be released. That was part of why she was so exhausted. All this fighting happening inside her. Once this trial was over, and Hugh was sent to prison—oh, how she prayed that would be the outcome—she would head straight home and never, ever leave her house again. Life had been easy there compared to this.

There she'd only ever had to worry about Hugh riding up the road. Since leaving she'd had to worry about every person she'd encountered.

"Up already?"

She wiped the moisture off her lashes before turning about. Dressed in his elegant three-piece suit, Angus was peeking through a crack in the door. He, everything about him, made her smile. She crossed the room and pulled the door open. Pointing toward the top hat on his head, she whispered, "Do you sleep in that?"

Frowning, he touched his hat. "This? Heavens no, lass. That would damage it beyond repair. Furthermore, this hat is brown." He then smoothed the sides of his jacket over his sides. "And, if you care to notice, this suit is brown as well. I wore a black one yesterday." With a grin, he plucked the handkerchief from his breast pocket. "This one is yellow—gold, actually. Yesterday's was red."

"Forgive my lack of attention to detail," she said with a nod. "I had not noticed. I do apologize."

"No harm done." With a wink, he continued to whisper, "Tomorrow's will be blue." Stuffing the handkerchief back in the pocket, he added, "And white."

"Oh, Mr. O'Leary, I shall never forget you."

With another one of his elegant bows, he said, "Nor I you, lass." Straightening, he gestured into the sitting room. "May I have a word with you this fine morning? Where we won't disturb the young lad?"

"Certainly." She stepped into the other room and pulled the door shut. "I can't believe he's still sleeping."

"It'll take him time to catch up on all the sleep he's lost, I'm sure."

"But when he does…" She shook her head while glancing around the room and stopping when her insides flinched. Billy wouldn't be confined to this room today. He would be in a courtroom, where his father was on trial. Sickened by the thoughts, she grasped the back of the chair pushed up to the small table in the center of the room.

"I've a favor to ask of you, lass," Angus said.

"A favor of me?" She shook her head. There was a tiny sofa near the window, barely as long as she was tall, yet last night, Angus had insisted that it was perfectly large enough for him to sleep upon. "You've already done more favors for me than I'll ever be able to repay."

"Oh, lass, life isn't about repaying favors. It's about doing them."

His ability to make her smile was uncanny. "Whatever it is, Mr. O'Leary, I will gratefully grant your favor."

"I'm thinking the young lad there doesn't need to attend any functions that may be on your agenda this fine day. With that in mind, I'd like your permission, your favor, to ask Mrs. Blackwell, Fiona Blackwell, if the lad Billy could spend the day at her lovely home, romping and roaming and chasing bullfrogs with her two fine lads, Rhett and Wyatt."

Although grateful at the prospect, Clara was about to claim she couldn't put anyone out of their way, especially not knowing how Billy might behave, when Angus raised a hand.

"Now, before you decline, lass, let me assure you that Fiona is married to Brett, the blacksmith, who is so big he makes Wayne's dog, Bear, look like a newborn pup, and Fiona knows a thing or two about raising lads. Little intimidates her. Brett's size doesn't even scare her, and he's scared a lot of people in his days."

"Mr. O'Leary, I wish I could, but Billy…" She glanced toward the bedroom. She certainly didn't want Billy in the courtroom with her, but at the same time— "He's never spent any time away from me." A fraction of a thought made her recall there had been four days when she'd been ill, and though not away from her, Billy had spent that entire time with Tom.

"Then don't you think it's about time, lass?" Angus said. "Nothing grows as well under a tree as it does in sunshine."

As she was searching the hidden meaning in that idiom, Angus leveled a pleading look upon her.

"Please, lass, it's the only favor I'll ask of you."

She huffed out a breath, only because she had to force herself not to laugh at his antics. "You know I can't say no to you, don't you?"

"No, lass, but I can hope." He patted the hand she

still had on the back of the chair. "I'll be gone for a while now. Need my morning shave. And then I'll pop over and talk to Fiona."

He then pulled a cloth off the top of a tray sitting on the table that she hadn't even noticed. Stunned, she could barely look away from the muffins, boiled eggs and assorted tiny bowls of jams.

"I took the liberty of seeing you had some breakfast. The tea's still hot and the milk's still cold. See that you and the lad eat it all while I'm gone."

He was already at the door, and before he opened, she asked, "Mr. O'Leary, are you—?" She glanced at the food and then back at him as stories her mother used to share when she was a young child popped into her head. "Are you some sort of leprechaun?" Glancing between him and the food again, she added, "A big one, with more magic?" How else could he have done all this, getting dressed, the food, without her hearing him? Even with the door closed, she'd certainly heard his snores last night.

His laughter was soft and musical and filled the room. "Aw, lass. I'm no leprechaun. Just an old Irishman." Then before he slipped out the door, he whispered, "But the world is full of magic, lass. If you go looking for it, you'll find it."

Tom was up early, and had to force himself not to go to the hotel. He'd tried to convince himself it was just for breakfast, but the smarter, more rational and level-headed man inside him couldn't be convinced. That had to be the lawman part of him. The part that knew a lie when he heard one. Even a silent one coming from within.

The eggs and bacon that he fried for himself and ate tasted like sawdust, and had him rubbing his stomach while the food sat inside him, congealing into a solid lump. The rest of his insides were just as out of sorts. The idea of seeing Clara had him grinning one second and frowning the next. She shouldn't have to do all this alone. She'd been alone practically her entire life. He shouldn't have left her alone, but he'd had to. Hadn't had a choice.

Didn't this time, either, and there wasn't a dang thing he could do about it. Any action he took to assist her could cause Hugh to get off scot-free. In fact, the only hope there was for Hugh to get charged was that Clara had some incriminating evidence. The lawyers were both scheduled to give their summations today, and the judge would make his ruling.

No one else had gotten off the train: he'd acquired that information without rousing suspicion. That hadn't helped much. Him, that was. Deep inside, he had this hope, this wish, that she was here because of him. That shouldn't be. But something had happened to him back there at her ranch. He'd started to feel again. Deeply.

Burying those thoughts, Tom cleared off the table, washed his plate, cup and fork, and then pushed the hot pan and coffeepot to the back of the stove. It was time he headed to his office. He had no desire to listen to Hugh squawk about being set free today, but didn't have a choice in that, either. Hugh had driveled on every day, so today would be no different, except for the fact that his nonsense talk might come true today.

Then what? Would he insist Clara leave with him? Would she leave with him?

Tom wrenched open the door and slammed it shut behind him. Talk about buying the cart before the horse. He hadn't even seen Clara and was already fretting about her leaving.

Crossing the field that separated his house from the sheriff's office, he told himself that the lawman inside him needed to take over. Make him see things in one way and one way only. The right way. The way of the law. Without feelings. Because a lawman would never, not for a single moment, forget that Clara Wilson was a married woman. Married to an outlaw who had robbed the good people of Oak Grove.

Later that morning, while walking into the town hall, Tom was pretty proud of himself. He hadn't looked up the street toward the hotel since stepping foot in his office. Nor had he searched the crowd for her, the one following him into the room. Most everyone in town, men and women, had filled the seats every single day, and would today, too. They had a stake in the outcome. This was their town, and though Julia, the mail-order bride, hadn't been part of the town then, she was now, and if there was one thing Oak Grove community members were proud of, it was making sure everyone was taken care of.

As he followed Brett, who was once again escorting Hugh to his seat, Tom remembered how Brett's wife, Fiona, had gotten bit by a rattlesnake shortly after she'd arrived in town. The women had banded together to take care of Fiona night and day. They'd also moved her into Brett's place because the house Josiah had put her in wasn't furnished. The women had almost tarred and feathered Josiah about that, too.

The mayor had learned a lesson on that one, and hadn't been quite as strict when it came to the other mail-order brides as he had the first few.

A bit of a shiver tickled Tom's spine. He certainly hoped Josiah didn't order another dozen brides. As far as he knew, the only two not married of the original twelve were the two who had been on the train that was robbed: Julia Styles, the woman who had been shot in the side but was doing fine now, and another, older woman, Bella Armentrout, who had shot one of the robbers. The other ten women were married and now integral parts of Oak Grove, almost as if they'd always been here. As well as a few others. Brett's bride, Fiona, hadn't been part of the first or second batch of brides who had arrived. She'd come to town on her own, with her two sons in tow, and so had Hannah, Teddy White's bride, whom the women had flocked around like mother hens, sewing clothes and nappies for the baby long before she'd been born. Doc Graham's new bride wasn't one from out east, either. Sylvia had been here for some time. Her husband had deserted her a few years back, leaving her and a small boy to fend for themselves on a run-down chunk of property that had flooded out this spring.

The Oak Grove women had come together then, too, not just for Sylvia, but the others who'd been flooded out. They'd taken food, blankets, clothes, furniture, anything anyone could spare to those who needed it.

As he took his seat in the front row, nodding and greeting those around him, including Brett, who'd taken a seat directly behind Hugh, Tom couldn't help but wonder how they'd all respond to Clara.

"Sheriff."

He turned to his right, and nodded as Steve Putnam sat down next to him. "Steve." Leaning forward a bit, he nodded again. "Mrs. Putnam."

"Hello, Sheriff," Mary said. "Hope you're well today."

"Same to you, ma'am," Tom replied. Mary had been one of the first brides, and Steve was rarely seen without her. Actually, she'd gone to Steve's ranch the day she'd arrived in town. Josiah had been hot under the collar when he'd discovered that. And when he'd learned Mary and her sister Maggie were making and selling tonic stronger than the whiskey Danny and Chris Sanders sold over at the Wet Your Whistle Saloon.

"Sheriff."

Tom once again nodded a greeting. "Jackson, Mrs. Miller," he said as Maggie Miller sat down next to her sister and Jackson beside her, taking up the last seat in the front row.

Something different about the women caught his attention, and he leaned forward again, to look past Steve. He'd been gone several weeks, and though he'd seen them since arriving home, he hadn't noticed they'd grown. Or maybe it had more to do with the fact that before meeting Clara, he'd never really noticed women—other than the fact they were women, or in Mary and Maggie's case, looked alike. Leaning back, he said to Steve, "I guess congratulations are in order."

"Thanks," Steve said before he leaned closer to say, "I won't be offended if you're hoping they both don't have twins."

Tom grinned while saying, "As long as they don't start making and selling tonic, I don't have a concern one way or the other." Remembering the stunned look on Clara's face, he added, "Your sister-in-law is the only woman I've ever had to arrest."

"I bet that was hard," Steve said.

Honest, and because there were things about today making him feel the same way, Tom said, "Like shooting a horse with a broken leg… Even though you know it has to be done, it guts you."

The judge entered through the side door that Abigail White sat next to. Nodding at her, Alfords walked over behind the desk facing the room. The room went quiet as everyone turned to face the front of the room. Men removed their hats and set them on their laps, while women did the same with their gloves, all of which would later be used to fan themselves when the heat grew as the day went on. With two raps of his gavel against the desktop, Alfords said, "Ladies and gentlemen, court is now in session."

Judge Alfords was still making his opening speech, reminding the spectators the rules of order, when the door in the back of the room opened. Tom told himself not to turn around, not to even glance over his shoulder, not to… It was too late. His curiosity was greater than his intelligence.

Disappointment plunged his excitement clear to his boots as he watched Angus quietly close the door. While walking to the only empty seat in the house, a chair along the back wall, Angus acknowledged him with a wave.

Tom gave a single-finger wave in response and turned back to face the judge as Alfords asked if the lawyers were ready to begin.

The only witness left to testify was Bella Armentrout. Josiah had been saving her for last. She'd gotten a good look at Hugh because he'd snatched a cameo pin off the front of her dress.

Josiah stood. "We are, Your Honor. At this time I'd like to call Miss Bella Armentrout to the stand."

The judge turned to Hugh's lawyer. "Any objections?"

"No, sir," Baldwin said, half standing, and taking his seat again in one easy movement.

"Miss Bella Armentrout, please step forward," Alfords said.

A hushed mumble came over the room, as well as the screeching of several chairs moving as the woman made her way out of her seat to the aisle that had been left open by the rows on either side of the center of the room. Since she was not a small woman, in breadth or height, chair legs once again scraped the floor. Her skirts rustled and her heels clicked a steady beat as she walked forward, past Josiah's table and the one Hugh and Baldwin sat at.

Due to the fact Tom had hauled Hugh in and therefore had to testify, which he'd done several days ago, Chester was the one swearing people in, and did so for Miss Armentrout.

After Alfords had asked her a few preliminary questions, he nodded to Josiah. "Mr. Melbourne."

"Thank you, Your Honor," Josiah said, stepping around his table. "Miss Armentrout, can you recall exactly where you were sitting on the train on the day Judge Alfords just referred to?"

"Yes, I can," Miss Armentrout said loud and clear, and with a glower toward Hugh.

If he'd been more sure of today's outcome, Tom may have smiled about then. Hugh Wilson should have known better than to irritate this woman. A rattler would have the sense to head back to its den if she leveled those eyes on it.

Baldwin cleared his throat, as if that might make Miss Armentrout cast her eyes the other way, and at that same moment, Steve Putnam bent closer.

"How'd you like to wake up next to that?" Steve whispered.

Tom had heard such remarks before, but never put much thought behind them. Until now. Steve wasn't being rude; he was merely comparing a woman to his wife, who he thought was the most beautiful woman on earth. That was how it should be. Every husband should think that. Even Bella Armentrout's, when she did marry. As those very thoughts formed, Tom had to pinch his lips together, partly because Mary elbowed Steve so hard he grunted.

It was Josiah who finally broke Bella's glare by asking her to further explain. She did, saying that Miss Julia Styles was sitting on the bench seat beside her, and that they were in the very middle of the train. That there were three bench seats behind them, and three in front of them, with the exact same number on the opposite side, and that was where the slaughterhouse agent had been sitting. Directly across the aisle from her. She then went on to describe what happened, how the train blew its whistle several times before stopping, and that three men, with kerchiefs across the lower halves of their faces and guns drawn, boarded the car before the train had rolled completely to a stop.

She described them all, and her descriptions matched the two who had died as well as Hugh precisely.

With urgings from Josiah whenever she paused, Bella Armentrout continued, saying the shortest of the three had gone to the back of the train while the one with red hair stayed near the front, and the tallest—she let it be known she was referring to Hugh with another glower his way—had walked to the center. All three had started demanding that people empty their pocketbooks and bags of any valuables and drop them in the canvas bags each man carried. When she claimed neither she nor Miss Styles had any money, Hugh had reached down and plucked the cameo, which had been her mother's, right off her dress, tearing the material in the process.

She stated he then turned his attention to the slaughterhouse man, who had slid a flat leather bag under his bottom. The robber had told the man to get up but the man had refused. The bandit had then cocked the gun, saying he'd warned him.

The slaughterhouse man pulled out a gun, but the outlaw fired first. The man's gun had gone off, too, but he was already dying, the weapon falling from his hand. Other shots started going off. She wasn't sure from where. She said Julia Styles was screaming, as were others, and then the robber had turned and shot Julia. Bella said that was when she'd reached into the front of her dress and pulled out her gun.

"It's just a little Colt derringer, and I knew I only had one shot. That man," she said, while pointing at Hugh, "was already running for the door at the front of the train, and I knew my little one shot wouldn't hit him, so I shot the man running behind him. The shorter one. Right in the back of the knee. Other people were shooting, too, and the short man fell to the floor. The redheaded robber had been shot, too. He was stumbling out the door. And that man—" she indicated Hugh again "—shot him in the back, making him fall off the train. Last thing I saw, he was jumping over the robber he'd just shot."

A low muttering spread through the room and Judge Alfords let it settle before he said, "Go on, Miss Armentrout."

"That's about it," she said. "I didn't see him grab the loot bag from the other robbers as some say happened, nor did I see him cut the hobbles off that poor black-and-white horse as others did, but that robber's face was this close to mine." She held up a thumb and forefinger, showing a short distance. "Close enough that I got a whiff of his nasty breath, and close enough that I'd know those beady, sunken eyes anywhere."

The murmurs spreading through the room were

louder this time. Tom glanced at Judge Alfords, expecting him to raise his gavel at any time, and then back to see Baldwin and Hugh bending their heads toward one another, whispering.

When the room finally quieted, Alfords asked, "Mr. Melbourne, do you have any more questions for Miss Armentrout?"

Josiah nodded toward the witness before saying, "No, Your Honor."

Alfords glanced toward Abigail White and waited for her to flip a piece of paper onto a growing stack and position her pencil over a new sheet before he asked, "Mr. Baldwin, do you have any questions for this witness?"

Pulling his jacket over his stomach as he stood, Baldwin walked around his table before saying, "Yes, Your Honor."

"Your witness, then," the judge said.

Baldwin walked all the way to the front, stopping right next to Miss Armentrout's chair. In Tom's mind, Baldwin would do better staying several feet away. The look on Bella's face said the lawyer's closeness didn't intimidate her, but it did irritate her.

Frowning and rubbing his beard, Baldwin asked, "Miss Armentrout, you just claimed you'd know the eyes of the man who robbed the train you were on anywhere, didn't you?"

"You heard me," she replied. "You were sitting right there."

Baldwin gave her a sarcastic smile. "I was, but I didn't hear you say what color his eyes were."

"Because I didn't," she said. "But if you want to know,

they were green. Not a dark green, more on the lighter side, but green."

The air Tom had been holding slipped out of his chest as a heavy sigh.

"Your Honor," Baldwin said, "with your permission, I'd like to have Mr. Wilson step close enough for Miss Armentrout to tell us, the entire courtroom, what color his eyes are."

Before the judge could answer, a request came from the back of the room.

"Excuse me, Your Honor, but may I approach the bench?"

Tom, recognizing the voice, spun around so fast his chair nearly spun with him.

Chapter Eleven

Clara's entire being shook from the inside out, and she tried her best, her very best, to not look at the man who sat on the center edge of the front row. If her eyes met Tom's she might not be able to speak. There had been several times while the witness had been speaking that she thought about standing up and stating her request, but had held out, waiting for the moment that felt exactly right.

That was what Angus had said. That she'd know the exact moment. Of course, he'd said it in an idiom that she'd had to decipher, but eventually had. Just as she'd waited until the sound of chairs being shuffled about while the witness had walked forward would disguise her entrance. It had worked. Other than Angus, only one person had noticed her, a man who'd left his seat and gestured for her to take it.

An entire herd of cattle could come through the door right now and no one would be able to hear them. Hugh had jumped to his feet, and a huge black-haired man who had to be Brett Blackwell had instantly grabbed Hugh's shoulders, shoving him back into his seat.

The lawyer was shouting for the man to release Hugh, while the judge pounded his wooden hammer against his desk, shouting for the lawyer to get his client under control and the room to come to order.

Needing a small amount of support to keep her upright, and knowing she still couldn't look toward Tom, Clara glanced sideways, toward Angus. With a wink and a nod, he flipped his cane forward.

Her feet felt frozen to the floor, her entire body paralyzed in place, to the point she could barely shake her head.

Angus flipped his cane again.

Praying for strength and fortitude, Clara took a small step. Then, because she was still upright, she took another one. And another. They grew easier then, each step, and they became more forceful. As she walked past the rows of chairs, the room got quieter. By the time she stepped between the two tables, even the lawyer shouting at Brett Blackwell had gone silent.

Hugh, however, shouted something about her not being there. She didn't hear exactly what he said because the judge had shouted even louder.

"Mr. Wilson, I will hold you in contempt if you don't quiet down!" The judge pounded against his desk loudly.

Clara took a final step that brought her directly in front of the judge, trying not to flinch as his hammer rapped the top of his desk a final time.

In the silence that followed, her own breathing echoed in Clara's ears.

Leveling a serious stare on her, the judge asked, "Do you know the consequences of interrupting a court that is in session?"

Blinking at the moisture blinding her, she shook her head. "I apologize, Your Honor. I've never been in a courtroom before."

He leaned closer to his desk. "Who are you?"

Swallowing and hoping her voice wouldn't crack, she said, "My name is Clara Wilson." Embarrassed, yet knowing she had to explain, she tilted her head slightly toward the table Hugh sat at. "The defendant is my husband, Hugh Wilson."

The shouts behind her made her pull her shoulders up and duck her chin, bracing herself for the unknown.

Standing up, the judge pounded his hammer against the desk again. "Order! There will be order in this court!"

It took time, but the noise finally quieted.

"Your Honor, a wife cannot testify against her husband," Hugh's lawyer said.

Lifting her chin, she looked straight ahead. "I'm not here to testify against him, Your Honor."

The mumbles this time weren't nearly as loud, and easy to speak over. "I'm here to give you this." Lifting the valise she'd carried with both hands, she set it on the judge's desk and unhooked the clasp. "I have no idea where any of it came from, but I found it in my son's bedroom, and none of it belongs to us." She then spread the sides of the bag wide so the judge could see inside.

His eyes grew wide as he glanced from inside the bag to her.

Without a word, she pulled harder on the side of the bag, and glanced down at the thing she'd shifted to the very top a short time ago while sitting in the back of the courtroom.

The judge reached inside and pulled out the cameo.

"That's it! My mother's cameo!" Miss Armentrout shouted. "Turn it over. I scratched her death date on the back."

Hugh shouted again, but was muffled so quickly that Clara wondered if Brett Blackwell had done something to quiet him.

While the judge was looking at the back of the cameo, Clara said, "I'd also like to mention, Your Honor, that Hugh's eyes are sometimes light brown, or a grayish color, but they turn green when he's mad. Which is what color they probably are right now. Green." Looking away for the first time, she glanced toward Miss Armentrout and said, "A light, unforgettable shade of green."

"They're green all right!" A deep voice echoed off the ceiling. "A hideous green."

Chatter broke out across the room, but without Hugh's shouts, the judge didn't use his hammer as he spoke over it. "Thank you, Mr. Blackwell."

Then, when the room fell silent, the judge sat down in his chair. After a moment of staring at the bag, and then her, he asked, "Is there anyone here who can prove you are who you say?"

She nodded. "Yes, Your Honor." The lump was too large to swallow, so her voice did crack as she said, "Sheriff Tom Baniff."

* * *

Tom dropped his hat onto his seat and stood. He had to plant his feet firmly on the floor in order to not step forward. He'd seen Clara's hands trembling as they clutched the handle of the valise while walking past him, and how she'd flinched every time Hugh had shouted, but it was the break in her voice when she'd said his name that had him wanting to rush forward. That couldn't happen. She'd worked too hard, timed things too perfectly, for him to destroy it by giving away the impression he knew her better than he'd testified to.

Clasping his hands behind his back, Tom said, "That is correct, Your Honor. I was at Mrs. Wilson's home when I apprehended Hugh Wilson."

Judge Alfords settled an almost understanding gaze on Clara. "You're the wife who shot him?"

Tom's heart sank. He'd had to include that in his testimony, knowing Hugh's lawyer would have accused him of hiding relevant information if he hadn't.

Her back stiffened and her chin rose as she said, "Yes, Your Honor. Right after Hugh had shot Sheriff Baniff, he turned his gun on me. I had a gun, too, and he told me to drop it. I refused, and told him to drop his. He then turned his gun on my seven-year-old son, and told me he'd warned me. I'd heard that before, and knew what it meant, so I shot him." After a brief pause, she added, "In the shoulder because I didn't want to kill him in front of our son."

Tom didn't think his heart could go any lower, but it did while wishing she hadn't said that last line.

"I see," Judge Alfords said.

A buzz of excitement and shock filled the room, and Tom shifted his gaze to Josiah, willing the man to do something, say something.

It was Hugh's lawyer who spoke instead. "Your Honor, we knew nothing about this witness. We should have been told! I motion for a mistrial. A mistrial!"

"Shut up, Mr. Baldwin, or I will hold you in contempt!" Alfords said while slamming his gavel against his desk.

Tom's gaze was locked on Clara again, noting the way her shoulder shook, and how she raised one hand, swiftly swiping it across both cheeks.

"In light of the evidence Mrs. Wilson has provided, the court will take a recess." After checking his watch, Alfords said, "We shall reconvene at two o'clock this afternoon." He then picked up the gavel, but before bringing it down on the desk, which would officially release everyone, he said, "Sheriff Baniff, please escort Mrs. Wilson from the room."

Tom's hands never shook, ever, but they did right now. He flexed his fingers, and wrapped them around the brim of his hat while walking forward. As he stepped up beside Clara, Alfords leaned forward.

"Take her out the side door, Tom, to the hotel," the judge whispered. "If there's not a spare room, she can use mine, number four."

Tom nodded and gently wrapped a hand around Clara's elbow. She didn't look up at his face and he didn't look down at hers. At the side door, while pausing long enough to open it, he noted the pained look and the tears in Abigail's eyes as the reporter attempted to smile at Clara.

Outside, with the door firmly closed behind them, Tom said, "Just breathe, Clara, and put one foot in front of the other."

She glanced his way and he tightened his hold, stabilizing her as she stumbled slightly. The tears cascading down her face almost made him trip, too. Taking his own advice, he forced his feet to keep moving.

The hotel wasn't far, and once there, he rang the bell with one hand while keeping the other on Clara.

Rollie's wife, round and walking slow, came through the doorway behind the desk. "Hello, Sheriff," she said shyly.

"Mrs. Wilson needs a room," he said.

If the name surprised her, it didn't show. "Number six is open," Mrs. Austin said, taking a key off its wall hook. "Top of the stairs on the left."

"Thank you." Tom took the key while turning Clara toward the wide staircase.

He waited until they were halfway up the steps before asking, "Where's Billy?"

"With Brett Blackwell's wife," she answered quietly.

"Do you want me to go get him?"

"Not quite yet." Drawing in a breath, she said, "I don't want him to see me yet."

"All right, and don't worry about him. Fiona's a good person. She won't let anything happen to him."

"That's what Angus said, but I'll have to go get him soon. He doesn't know why we're here."

Tom sucked in air quietly. The entire town, including the children, knew about Hugh's trial. Billy probably did by now, too.

Finding the room, he unlocked the door and opened it wide for her to enter. He didn't want to, but had to release her arm as she crossed the threshold.

Without turning around, she said, "Thank you, Tom. I'll be fine now."

There wasn't much time. Josiah would want to discuss what had happened, and try to guess how the judge would rule things. Others would want to talk to him, too. Knowing all that, and that he'd have to be available, he entered the room and closed the door. He didn't speak, or think, just stepped forward and wrapped his arms around her. She stiffened at first, but then spun about and wrapped her arms around his waist.

It shouldn't feel this right to hold her, but it did, even as it pained him.

He held her tight, and rubbed her back when the sobs racking her had her trembling. She cried, quietly, but hard, for several minutes before her shaking calmed to slight quivers. Then she released him and stepped back.

Unsure what to do, he eased his arms from around her, but set them on both of her shoulders while asking, "What can I get you? What do you need?"

She shook her head and attempted to smile. "Nothing. Thank you."

He hadn't forgotten how pretty she was, and was just enthralled by it all over again. It left him tongue-tied, yet he felt as if he had to say something. The dress she had on was pale blue, with white lace circling her neck. "You...you look n-nice. That dress. It's—"

"Not mine." She wiped her cheeks dry. "Angus brought it to me. Apparently, Otis's wife is a seamstress."

Tom nodded.

She was nodding, too, and at the same time, they both said, "Martha."

Her soft giggle and how she closed her eye for a moment was memorable. All of her was unforgettable. It was so good to see her again. To touch her.

"You didn't tell me about her."

He shrugged. "I've never had a dress made."

She giggled again. "I suspect you haven't." Bowing her head slightly, she took another step backward.

Reluctantly, he removed his hands from her shoulders. There was so much he wanted to say, so much he wanted to ask, but didn't know where to start.

"How's your leg?" she asked.

"Fine. How's yours?"

"Fine."

"That's good." He looked around, trying to come up with something else to say. Talking with her before had been easy. Back at her place when they'd sat outside on the porch, watching the sun go down. He'd missed that, and thought about it, every evening since leaving her place.

A knock sounded on the door. He looked at her, and waited for her nod before he walked to the door and opened it.

Of all people, he didn't expect to see Judge Alfords. "I'd like a moment to speak with Mrs. Wilson, Sheriff." Glancing around him to Clara, the judge asked, "Alone?"

Tom turned to Clara, waiting for her response. Judge or not, if she wanted him to stay, he was staying.

She nodded. "Yes, Your Honor." With another gentle smile, she said, "Thank you, Sheriff Baniff."

Alfords walked into the room and Tom glanced one last time at Clara, who gave another slight nod. With little else he could say or do, Tom stepped out of the door and pulled it shut behind him.

Angus stepped off the last step and then rested both hands heavily on his cane while saying, "Is the lass doing all right?"

"Appears to be," Tom said, trying not to sound like his mind and body were completely out of sorts. The effects of holding Clara were still living inside him.

"She's a hearty lass, Sheriff," Angus said. "You go on and do what you have to, being the sheriff of this fine town and all. I'll be here. Right here."

The noise floating up the stairs indicated the hotel was filling up with people from the trial, and it was his job to keep the peace and order. A choice he'd never regretted until he'd had to put it up against Clara. Hearing his name being called below, he nodded to Angus. "Thanks. I appreciate all you've done for her."

With a twinkle in his eyes, Angus looked at the door to Clara's room. "It's been my pleasure."

Tom turned and started down the steps, only to pause when Angus spoke again.

"You know, Sheriff, it's a funny thing."

"What's that, Angus?" Tom asked.

"How we don't even realize how much we love songbirds until we hear the right one sing."

He didn't have the time or fortitude to contemplate Angus's riddles right now, so Tom merely nodded again and walked down the steps to where a crowd had formed—of mainly women.

"How is she, Sheriff?" Mary Putnam asked.

"Oh, the poor dear." Martha Taylor wiped both eyes with a handkerchief. "I can't imagine what she's been through."

"Can I see her, Sheriff?" Maggie Miller asked. "Having been arrested by you, I know how hard it is for a woman to be in jail."

There were other women, asking about Clara and demanding she not be arrested.

He held up both hands. "Ladies! Ladies!" When the questions slowed, he said, "Mrs. Wilson is busy right now, but I assure you, she will not be arrested, so there's no need for all of this."

"No need!" Martha pushed her way past the twins to stand directly before him. "You're wrong, Sheriff. There is plenty of need. That woman needs our help and support."

"With what?" Tom asked.

"Everything!" Martha insisted. "After all she's been through, she needs folks to let her know we care. That we can help her with whatever she needs."

"I'm sure she'll appreciate hearing that, but right now you all just need to go on about your business." As the women started talking among themselves, he added, "I'll make sure Mrs. Wilson knows that you all want to meet her."

Josiah stood behind the women and waved a hand for

Tom to join him. Walking that way, Tom said, "Go on, now, ladies. The best thing for Mrs. Wilson right now is for all of you to go about your business." He wasn't sure if that was the best way to go about things or not, but didn't know what else to do.

He started across the foyer as some of the women filed out the door, and others walked into the dining room with their husbands, only to be stopped short by Abigail White.

"You will tell her that the women want to meet her, won't you?" Abigail asked.

Tom had never liked thinking the worst of people, but Abigail had been known to write some very unflattering articles about people, and he wouldn't have that happening to Clara.

Abigail shook her head. "I'm not here as a reporter, Sheriff Baniff. I'm here because if anyone were about to shoot my niece, Teddy and Hannah's little girl, Dorie, I would shoot them." Tears fell down her long and narrow face. "And not in the shoulder. I would shoot them dead." Lifting her chin, she continued, "Even threatening to shoot a child is not right, Sheriff. Not right at all."

"No, Abigail, it's not," Tom said. "It's not right at all."

"I just want you to know how I feel, because if Hugh Wilson does not go to prison, I might."

Tom's blood ran cold. "Abigail—"

She'd already turned about and was walking out the door. Of all the people who lived in Oak Grove, he'd never have expected such justification from Abigail. He took a step to follow her, but someone grabbed his arm.

"Judge Alfords say anything to you?" Josiah asked quietly.

"No," Tom replied, watching Abigail as she turned up the boardwalk. "He's talking with Clara now." He couldn't keep calling her Mrs. Wilson. She was Clara to him, and deep down, he didn't want her to be associated with Hugh Wilson in any way.

"I sincerely hope it's not ruled a mistrial," Josiah said. "Wilson will get off for sure."

Tom's blood was turning colder. This town would never be the same if that happened. May never be either way.

The hotel room was small, hosting one chair, a bed and a dresser. The judge had suggested she take the chair while he sat on the bed, setting her bag on the mattress beside him. Then he explained he needed to ask her some questions. She'd agreed, and he'd asked several questions about how long she'd been married to Hugh, and about Uncle Walter's homestead and Billy.

His only response to most of her answers was a nod, and ask another question, until he pulled the bag to his side and sighed.

He was a tall, thin man, with curly dark hair and bushy brows that rose as he asked, "Do you know what a mistrial is, Mrs. Wilson?"

"No, not really."

"It can occur when evidence, which could be considered unfair to the defendant, is improperly presented during the trial. Either side, the prosecuting or the defending, can request a mistrial. It's up to the judge to decide to grant the motion, or let the trial continue."

As her stomach knotted, she nodded. There would be nowhere she and Billy could go if Hugh wasn't convicted. Nowhere at all.

"That's you," she responded.

"Yes, it is, so you see, my reputation, my life's work, is on the line as much as the defendant's is. If I know evidence was purposefully withheld to sway the outcome of this trial either way, I can't, in good conscience, make an innocent or guilty ruling."

"So it would be a mistrial."

He nodded. "Yes. Now, I need to ask you some questions. I can't swear you in, but I need you to tell me the truth."

Her throat was on fire, so she nodded.

"Did Sheriff Baniff ask you to bring all this here?"

"No, I didn't find it until after he left." Tom was the last person to blame for all this. She had to make the judge see that. "Sheriff Baniff never told me why he was after Hugh. Actually, he never told me he was after Hugh." Rushing on, she explained how she'd been ill when Tom arrived, and that after waking up, she knew he was a lawman, but that he'd never actually told her. She explained about the holes in his vest, and how she'd known Hugh was robbing places and people, but never asked because she didn't want to know. It was a terrible thing to admit, but it was the truth.

"How did you know to come here? To Oak Grove?"

"Because th-the sheriff told me this is where he was from. That it was a nice town and the people here. He never said this is where he was bringing Hugh, but after they left, my son, Billy, was mad. Upset. And said that Hugh hadn't robbed a train. That was the first I'd heard about a train robbery. Hugh must have assumed that Tom had told Billy and wanted him to think Tom was lying. When Billy told me that Hugh had been in his bedroom, I knew why. Years ago, Hugh used to hide stolen property in there, but had stopped because he was afraid I'd find it and use it to leave." She didn't bother saying she'd had nowhere to go.

"Go on."

"With Tom there, Hugh must have decided to hide things again. He didn't worry about the money in his saddlebags because he had a receipt for money." Sighing, she added, "He always had receipts for the money."

"So after finding this—" he nodded toward the bag "—you left to come here."

"Yes."

"When did you arrive?"

"Yesterday afternoon. I was going to go straight to the sheriff's office, but…" She didn't want to put Angus in jeopardy.

"But?"

"A man was at the train depot."

"I need the entire truth, Mrs. Wilson. It's imperative and will determine my decision. What man?"

She swallowed. "Mr. Angus O'Leary was at the train station. He explained that no one was at the sheriff's office and invited Billy and me to come to the hotel as his guests. My son was very tired, and hungry, so I agreed. After we ate and cleaned up, both Billy and I fell asleep. When I awoke, it was late, so I decided I'd take that bag to the sheriff's office in the morning."

"Did you?"

"No. I decided to take it to you instead."

"Why?"

She pinched her lips together to hold back the truth, yet that was exactly what the judge needed to hear. It was hard because she hadn't even admitted it to herself. But it was the truth. The whole truth. "Because I didn't want to embarrass Tom. Didn't want him to think that he had to help me." Tears stung her eyes and her throat burned as she pushed out the words. "I'm an outlaw's wife. I don't deserve respect or help from a lawman." She pressed the back of her hand to her nose as she sniffled. "I don't deserve respect from anyone. I had to do it myself. Just like I've had to do everything else. That's just how it has to be."

He leaned forward and patted her knee. "No, Mrs. Wilson, it's not how it has to be. You deserve respect, and assistance. What you did took courage. More courage than a lot of men have."

That wasn't true. She was a coward. Had been for years and years. "Did I ruin everything?" Swallowing a sob, but unable to hold back the tears, she asked, "Will Hugh go free?"

"I have to know that how you presented this information wasn't orchestrated by someone else before I can determine that."

"There was no one else. Just me."

He took her hand. "I need to know one more thing." She nodded.

"Since arriving in town, when was the first time you saw Tom Baniff or Josiah Melbourne?"

"When I walked into the courtroom."

"You're absolutely sure of that?"

"Yes." She held up a hand as she'd seen the witness Bella Armentrout do earlier. "I swear, Your Honor."

His bushy brows were pushed up again, as they had been several times while talking, and he rubbed his chin while looking at the bag beside him. "I need to keep this for the time being."

"I don't ever want to see any of it again," she said. "Ever."

He smiled. "I meant the bag, ma'am. I'm assuming that is yours."

Heat tinged her cheeks at her own ignorance. "Oh, yes, it is."

"I'll see you get it back." He wrapped his fingers around the bag's handles. "Tom Baniff is a good man. Well respected and well liked. If I forget, he'll make sure you get it."

The lump that formed in her throat this time threatened to cut her air completely off.

Picking up the bag, the judge stood and walked to the door. There, before opening it, he said, "I'd be remiss if I didn't mention one other thing. As a judge, I also grant divorces, Mrs. Wilson, and will be in town until tomorrow morning."

Chapter Twelve

"I asked to speak to you and Josiah separately for a reason, and I'm sure you know that reason, Tom," Judge Alfords said.

Tom took his hat off as he walked into the judge's hotel room. "Yes, I believe I do."

"Please, have a chair." Alfords closed the door and waved to the table in the corner near the open window. "As you also know, I just finished speaking with Clara Wilson. Just left her room."

Tom sat down, and although there was no need to answer, he said, "I do."

"Did you know she was coming to town?"

He'd hoped for questions he could answer honestly while leaving a few things out. That would leave more of a chance of Hugh being convicted. Since that wasn't the case, Tom said, "Yes, I did."

Alfords's face fell.

Tom set his hat on the floor and rested both arms on the table. "I didn't know when, but I knew she'd arrive soon."

"You asked her to come. To bring this evidence?" Alfords gestured toward the bag sitting on the bed.

"No, I didn't ask her to come, and I didn't know about any of that." Knowing this meeting would go quicker if he simply provided the information, Tom continued, "When I left her place, I went to Hendersonville to catch the train, but before boarding, I asked the livery to send a horse and rig out to Clara's place. My thinking was, if she had a way to get there, she might go to Hendersonville. If not, with a rig, she could at least get to her closest neighbor without having to walk the ten miles one way."

Withholding how much it bothered him to leave her and Billy out there all alone, he continued, "When I arrived here, there was a telegram from the livery, saying Clara's place had been abandoned, so the driver returned with the horse and rig. I then sent a telegram to Sheriff Puddicombe in Hendersonville and he replied saying Clara and Billy had boarded an eastbound train and he thought she was coming here. Both of those telegrams are in my office."

The judge laid both hands flat on the table. "I know you'd like this to get over as quickly as possible, but I have specific questions I need to ask, and will ask that you answer without providing any more information than what I request."

"All right," Tom said, knowing the judge had his reasons.

"Did you know Clara Wilson had arrived in Oak Grove prior to her walking into the courtroom this morning?" the judge asked.

"Yes."

Once again, the judge appeared disappointed. "How?"

"Angus O'Leary told me last night, said he'd put her and Billy up in his room because they'd been hungry and worn-out."

"Is Angus known to do such things?"

"Yes, ask anyone in town. If there's a passenger down on their luck, they usually get a meal and sometimes a bed, compliments of Angus."

"Did you go see Clara Wilson? Talk to her?"

"No."

"Did you give Angus any advice as to what you thought he should tell Clara to do?"

"No, I did not. Matter of fact, I asked him if she was here to testify and he said he didn't know. That she hadn't said that." Tom laid both of his hands on the table, as if to show he wasn't hiding anything. "In fact, Judge, I went to bed last night and woke up this morning wondering if Clara was here to testify on behalf of Hugh Wilson."

The judge closed his eyes briefly as a smile formed. "Thank you, Tom." Letting out a long sigh, he said, "I hope my conversation with Josiah goes as well as this one has."

Tom couldn't lie. "I do, too, Judge. I do, too."

Five minutes later, Tom had the opportunity to make sure that happened, but couldn't take it. In order for the judge to make the decision only he could make, he had to have the truth from everyone.

"What did he ask you?" Josiah asked again. "We have to make sure our stories are the same."

It would be easy to tell Josiah exactly what to say,

how to answer the judge's questions, because everyone knew how Josiah could bend things to go in the way he wanted them to. He'd done it with the mail-order brides, and in other situations.

No, it wouldn't be easy, because it would be wrong, and he'd fought against wrongdoings too long. Committing one would never be easy for him. "Just tell the truth and our stories will be the same," Tom said. "That's what the judge needs. The truth. Not calling a mistrial if there was intentional wrongdoing would damage all Alfords has done in the past and the future. He can't wager that and neither can we."

"I'm not saying I won't tell the truth," Josiah said, puffing out his barrel chest. "I just want to make sure Hugh Wilson gets his due."

"And he will." Tom had to believe that. His gaze had gone to the top of the stairs again, where Angus had entered Clara's room. That had been before he'd met with Judge Alfords, and Angus hadn't yet exited.

"I hope so," Josiah said. "Why did Alfords ask to speak to Baldwin before me?"

"He needs to hear all sides of this before he can make his decision." Tired of waiting, Tom slapped Josiah's shoulder. "Just tell the truth. I'll see you later."

Taking the stairs two at a time, he reached the top in only a few seconds, and knocked on her door just as swiftly. Angus opened the door and planted a hand on Tom's chest to stop him from entering the room. Clara sat at the window, her back to him.

"She's crying," Angus whispered. "Doesn't want me to know, but she's crying."

Little made Tom nervous, and a crying woman had never bothered him before, but this woman did. Because it was Clara and he had no idea what to do for her. "Go get some lunch," he told Angus. "I'll stay here with her."

Angus gathered his cane from near the bed and headed out the door like he hadn't eaten in years.

Tom closed the door, and with no idea what to do next, took his hat off.

"You can leave, too, Sheriff," she said without turning around. "I'll be leaving soon to go check on Billy."

Hugh had called him Tom a thousand times, acting as if it was the most disgusting word on earth, and it hadn't disturbed him. Not once. Clara calling him Sheriff left a sting like no other dead center in his chest.

"I'm not here as a sheriff," Tom said. "I'm here as your friend."

"I don't have any friends."

"Sure you do," he said. "There's Mrs. Ryan."

"She's my neighbor, not my friend."

"Well, you talk to her, don't you?"

"Yes, and I talk to you, too, but you aren't my friend, either."

Not completely sure he was handling this correctly, or if he even knew how, Tom sat down on the bed. "So what would I need to do to become your friend?"

"Nothing, because you can't."

"Yes, I can. I can do anything I want." That sounded like something Billy would say, but he didn't regret saying it because it made Clara turn around.

Her eyes were red and her cheeks tearstained, which made something powerful rise up inside him. He wanted to hug her again, hug her until all the pain covering her face disappeared. And stayed gone forever.

She shook her head as a tiny smile formed and then disappeared. "I believe you can do anything you want, but I can't. I can't do anything. Not do it right." She rose to her feet and threw her arms in the air as she walked past the bed. "I ruined it. Tom. I ruined everything. Everything."

"No, you didn't. You provided evidence that—"

"Has caused a mistrial." She covered her face with both hands. "Hugh will go free."

He stood, and pulled her hands off her face. "We don't know that. The judge hasn't decided."

"But he will, and it's all my fault. I should have stayed home." Her eyes were full of sadness. "I just…I just thought of all the people you told me about, and wondered if those things I found had belonged to them." She blinked as a tear slipped out of her eye. "I'd never done that before. Never thought about the people Hugh robbed. But I should have! I—I just never had a name or a face to put with them like I did this time."

Full of guilt because it was his fault that had happened this time, he rubbed his thumbs over the backs of her hands while saying, "That wasn't why I told you about the people here."

"I know." Her voice shook, yet the sadness in her eyes had been replaced with a glint of anger or frustration. "I also know I never thought about the others because I didn't want to know. Thought if I didn't know, I could pretend it wasn't happening, but it was, and pretending it wasn't was wrong."

"You're being too hard on yourself, Clara."

"No, I'm not. I haven't been hard enough. If you know something is wrong and you don't fight against it, then you become part of it. And then you become stuck, stuck forever."

"But you did something."

"And it wasn't soon enough, was it? If I'd done something before, that girl wouldn't have been shot. That agent wouldn't have been killed. And they aren't the only ones." She spun around, breaking the hold he'd had on her hands. "If I hadn't been so selfish."

"Selfish? You weren't being selfish, Clara."

"Yes, I was." She walked to the window and pulled aside the curtain. "And people were hurt because of that."

"People were hurt because of Hugh, not you. And you weren't being selfish. You were afraid. Afraid for you and Billy. No one would ever blame you for that."

"Maybe not, but they will pity me for it. Pity me for being the outlaw's wife. I've seen pity before. Seen it on Uncle Walter's face. On Donald and Karen Ryan's faces. I even saw it on the judge's face."

She sounded so sad, so sorrowful, Tom couldn't stop himself. Nor could he think of anything else to do. He crossed the room and spun her about. "Pity's not a bad thing. It just means people feel sorry for you."

"I don't want people to feel sorry for me. I don't— I thought— Oh, it doesn't matter!"

She twisted, trying to break his hold, which only made him increase it. In the process of that, she ended up against him, her face looking up at him.

There was something in her eyes that he couldn't

quite read but it made the memory of kissing her strike. That little fast kiss he'd placed on her lips before riding out had haunted him at times. Right now it made him wish it had been longer, more intense, and that he could tell her pity had not been on his mind then.

Maybe he shouldn't have kissed her then. And for sure shouldn't now. She was a married woman. Kissing her wasn't right. But damn it, at this moment, he didn't want to worry about what was right or wrong.

Her breath mingled with his, and she didn't pull back or look away. An inch more and their lips would touch. Undeniable heat flooded his veins, making his pulse race, and an exhilarating bout of craving raced across his stomach.

At this moment, he wasn't a lawman, but a man who was totally engrossed by the woman in his arms. It was impossible to ignore the allure any longer. Her charm and beauty, as well as her strength and courage, had won him over in ways he'd never imagined.

Slowly, deliberately, he closed the space between their lips. There was no awkwardness, just a perfect merger that made his heart leap. Her lips were incredibly soft, and sweet. So sweet. His palm cupped the back of her head as the pressure between their lips increased. Then, as if of their own accord, their lips began to move in a timeless, effortless dance.

Kissing Clara, really kissing her, was like nothing he'd ever imagined. Who could have known what it was like to experience something this precious, this perfect?

The end, the parting, was just as perfect. He folded both arms around her shoulders and held her tight to his chest, just savoring the connection of her body against his. Her arms, wrapped around his waist, tightened as she rested a cheek on his shoulder blade, the tip of her nose settled into the hollow of his neck. It could have been minutes, or hours, they stood there. He truly had no idea, for time had no meaning.

She was the first to move, lifting her head to look at him. Tom held his breath as her eyes met his, because he could see the sadness returning. And regret.

Then her eyes shifted to his badge, and a tear slipped down her cheek.

Like a cold front, bitter and frosty, the lawman in him returned, cynically reminding him that he was on duty. Was always on duty. She was here because of him. He'd been the one who'd ridden in to her homestead and shattered the only life she'd ever known. And was making it worse.

Judge Alfords could grant a mistrial.

Furthermore, there was nothing right or justifiable in his actions. About kissing her.

She put her hands on his chest and pushed, forcing him to break his hold. Then she spun around. "You need to leave."

Regret washed over him with as much force as a flash flood from spring rains. "Clara, I—" He had no idea what to say.

She couldn't take much more. Couldn't take much more of anything. Though she kept trying not to look at it, not to see it, the star on his chest kept flashing before her eyes, and the bullet stuck dead center in it.

A clear reminder of how her actions had almost gotten him killed. Turning to him, she pointed to her chest. "No, I." Thudding her chest with her finger, she continued, "Me. *I* should have done this in the beginning. Told you to leave the moment you walked through the door of my house."

"You fainted the moment I walked through the door of your house."

Thoroughly flustered, and with a heart still racing from his kiss, she pushed him out of the way and stomped past. "You know what I mean. The first time I saw those holes in your vest, knew what you were, I should have told you to leave."

"That wouldn't have made any difference."

"Yes, it would have."

"I would have still caught Hugh. He would still have been brought here to trial."

"But I wouldn't have been compelled to follow."

"Why did you? Why did you come here?"

Because of you. The words were almost out when she clamped her lips shut. He couldn't know the truth. She didn't want to know it. Yet of all the things she hadn't wanted to know, all the things she'd refused to believe, this one wouldn't be denied. Wouldn't stay buried deep inside with so many others. "I already told you," she said.

"What if I don't believe you?"

Twisting just enough to see his face, his eyes that had never belittled her, never insulted her, and that weren't now, she shook her head. "Then you can believe whatever you want."

"What if I said it was because you didn't want to see Hugh go to jail?"

Her heart sank, leaving her chest hollow and aching. Needing to disguise that, she narrowed her eyes to make it look like she'd been insulted, not hurt. "How dare you?"

"There are a lot of things I dare."

There probably were, but hurting someone just because he could wasn't his way. He wasn't that callous or heartless.

"Such as daring to make you see the truth," he said.

She already knew the truth, and had been lying about it. To everyone, including herself. She wanted Hugh found guilty and put away for his misdeeds, but she'd wanted that for years and had never done anything to make it happen. She wanted those stolen items returned to their rightful owners, which could prove impossible because she didn't know whom they belonged to or how long they'd been in Billy's room. The truth, the real reason she'd forced her two milk cows to walk ten miles to the neighbor's place, borrowed all they had to loan, and hauled Billy to Oak Grove, was that she'd wanted to see Tom.

She told herself it was to make sure his leg had healed, but that was just an excuse. He'd changed something inside her. The way he'd treated her, and Billy, had made her contemplate all the things inside her and all the things she'd wanted but thought she could never have. He'd kept telling her she was a strong woman, could do whatever she wanted to, and that was true. But no matter what she ever did, she'd still be who she was—an outlaw's wife. That would never change. Tom wasn't only a lawman, he was a respected man, an upright citizen, and as much as she wanted him to be her friend, wanted him to be more than that, she could never have it. Befriending her would tarnish him. Ruin all he stood for. Just as the judge had said not declaring a mistrial would do to him.

"You were tired, Clara, tired of the life you and Billy had, and you decided to do something about it," Tom said. "That's why you came here. That took courage. I don't even know how you managed it. But you did. And I'm proud of you for that."

"Don't be." Not about to take the chance he might wiggle the truth out of her, she said, "I have to go check on Billy."

"Well, I am proud of you, whether you want me to be or not." He picked his hat off the bed and put it on his head. "Other people are, too. And I promised a few of them that I'd introduce them to you."

Taken aback, she shook her head. "What? Who?"

He shrugged, and grinned. "Half the town, at least half, maybe more."

She pressed both hands to her stomach as it flipped. "I can't."

"Yes, you can. Afterward, you'll have time to check on Billy before court is called back in session."

Stalling simply because she had to, she said, "I need to wash my face first."

Tom waited patiently at the door while she washed her face with water in the porcelain pitcher and washbasin sitting on the dresser, and then checked her hair. She didn't want to leave the room, but had to. Because if she didn't, he'd stay here with her, and that could prove more dangerous than living with Hugh ever had been. Another kiss like he'd just given her, and she'd be begging him to become much more than her friend.

Taking a deep breath, she walked to the door.

"There's nothing to worry about," Tom said while opening the door.

"Other than a mistrial," she said as all the fears she'd had earlier, and some new ones, settled deep inside her.

The dining room was full of people, and her stomach flipped again as the occupants of each table leaned closer to one another, whispering, including the two women sitting at the table with Angus. They were certainly twins, which meant they were Mary Putnam and Maggie Miller. She had no idea which was which, or which husband sitting next to them was Steve or Jackson. During the long journey to Oak Grove, she'd thought about each and every person Tom had told her about, and at one point or another, had thought about how wonderful it would be to meet them.

It didn't seem so wonderful now. Downright frightening was how she'd describe this moment.

"Sheriff!" Angus shouted, waving his cane in the air. "Over here! Bring the lass over here."

Tom had a hold of her elbow, and gently urged her forward. "Looks like Angus saved us a seat. That's the Millers and the Putnams sitting with him."

"Which is which?" she whispered in return.

"The man with dark hair on the right is Steve Putnam. The lighter-haired one is Jackson Miller. I'm assuming their wives are the ones sitting next to them."

Clara was so busy staring at the table across the room, she nearly bumped into the woman with tight red curls who'd stepped in front of them.

"Oh, that dress is perfect on you," the woman said. "I knew it would be."

Clara knew this was Martha even before Tom spoke.

"Clara, this is Martha Taylor," he said. "Martha—"

"I know who she is, Sheriff." Smiling brightly, Martha continued, "You just let me know if you need anything. Anything at all."

"Thank you, Mrs. Taylor. I'll return the dress—"

"Return? Not on your life. It's my gift to you. And you just let me know if you need anything for that adorable young Billy. I can whip something up lickety-split." Martha stepped aside then. "I'll let you have your lunch. Angus or the sheriff can show you where my shop is. It's right by the barbershop that my husband, Otis, owns." She pointed to the bald man standing at the table beside them.

"Ma'am," Otis said. "It's nice to make your acquaintance."

"Yours, too, Mr. Taylor."

Clara had no idea how she'd been able to sound so normal. She certainly didn't feel that way.

Others nodded at her and said hello as Tom guided her toward Angus's table. She responded and was overly thankful that Tom hadn't stopped to talk to anyone else.

"Sit here, lass." Angus pointed to the empty chair next to his, and then pointed to the one next to her chair. "Sheriff, got room for you, too?"

"Thank you, Angus," Tom said, taking his seat after holding hers while she sat.

"I ordered lunch for you, too," Angus said. "Roast beef and potatoes. Rollie will bring your plates right out." Patting her hand, he continued, "Let me do the honors. This here is the dear lass Maggie, and that's her husband, Jackson. Then we have Mary and her husband, Steve."

The others said hello, as did Clara. There wasn't time for more because Angus was already talking again, explaining that Jackson had stolen Maggie from right beneath his nose, and how Steve kept Mary hidden for a month at his ranch so no one else could marry her.

Both Maggie and Mary had long black hair that hung freely, and Maggie tucked several locks behind one ear as she said, "Angus, stop. You'll frighten her away before we get a chance to talk."

That didn't happen. Clara was soon so engrossed in the conversation and the occupants of her table, her face hurt from laughing, something she didn't even know was possible.

A split second later, all that happiness disappeared.

"Sheriff, I need to talk to you before court reconvenes."

The man, whom she already recognized, introduced himself as the mayor, and then Angus assured Tom he'd escort her over to see Billy and have her at the courthouse in plenty of time to hear the ruling.

As Tom walked away, Clara felt the room closing in on her.

Chapter Thirteen

Tom sat in the same chair he had every day since Hugh's trial had started. Josiah had said he'd told the judge the truth. Tom hadn't questioned what that truth entailed. He was better off not knowing. However, he'd be doing a whole lot better if Clara had arrived. The room was almost full, Brett had already delivered Hugh to the table, but there was no sign of Clara and Angus. Jackson and Maggie had taken seats in the row behind him, leaving the two seats between him and Steve for Clara and Angus.

He should have escorted her over to see Billy himself. But that would have meant shirking his duties, and he couldn't do that. No matter how twisted it left him, he couldn't do that.

Judge Alfords entered through the side door and Tom took another long look around the room. His gaze went past Jackson and Maggie, who were also looking, and past Steve and Mary. Steve shrugged and shook his head. Saying he didn't see them, either.

The room quieted and Alfords started his opening speech. Tom twisted as unobtrusively as possible, glancing toward the back of the room. Jess Radar, one of Steve's hired hands who'd been instructed to direct Angus to the front of the room, shook his head.

Where was she? Angus was old, dang it. Duties be damned, he should have escorted Clara himself.

When hushed whispers started floating over the room, Tom shot his glance to the front of the room. Alfords was shuffling some papers. So were Josiah and Baldwin. Tom searched his brain, wondering what the judge had said that he'd missed, but there was nothing to remember. His mind had been elsewhere.

"With that said…" Alfords let his gaze settle directly on Hugh.

With what said? Tom cursed under his breath, fully infuriated with himself. He'd never not heard, not listened when a judge had been talking. Not paid full attention while in a courtroom. Even while berating himself, his gaze had gone to the back of the room.

Alfords started talking again, and Tom forced himself to face forward and listen.

"…fully prepared to render my decision."

The room went completely silent: not a soul appeared to be breathing. Tom wasn't. His lungs were locked tight.

"I will not be granting the motion to declare a mistrial."

The air in his lungs rushed out, and once again, Tom turned to the back of the room. Once again, Jess shook his head.

Alfords waited until the room quieted down before

he told Hugh to stand. Hugh refused at first, causing some commotion, which was handled quickly. The judge then started reading off the charges against Hugh, and pronouncing a guilty verdict after each charge.

The courtroom erupted as Alfords pounded his gavel a final time. Brett took control of Hugh with ease and Chester cleared a pathway for Brett to haul the prisoner back to the jail. Tom followed as far as the door. Then, glancing left and right, he headed toward the blacksmith shop. The Blackwells lived just beyond it, and that had to be where Clara still was.

He made it across the street and onto the boardwalk when someone stepped out from under the awning. Sliding to a stop, Tom grabbed Angus by both arms. "Where is she?"

"I figured it was safer for us to listen outside the side door, just in case that outlaw went free."

That might have been a good plan, but not what he wanted to know. "Where is she?"

Angus nodded across the street. "She just entered the hotel. Said she wants to talk to the judge."

Tom spun around, but Angus grabbed his arm. "Only the judge. No one else."

"What? Why?"

"Don't know. Didn't ask. Figured she had her reasons."

Clara turned away from the hotel's open doorway and let out another sigh of relief. Remorse swam inside her, but she couldn't talk to Tom, not right now. Hugh had been found guilty. She'd thank the good Lord every night for that. Every night. But that didn't solve all her problems. In fact, Hugh was now the least of her worries.

With little idea of what to do, she hurried toward the steps and the room she'd been assigned earlier. She had no means to pay for it, so shouldn't be using it, but she had to have a moment to contemplate things.

A moan or groan had her pausing on the first step. Backing down, she glanced around the corner, into the dining room. The sound came again and she entered the room, scanning it thoroughly.

A door on the far side was slightly cracked, and the sound, which definitely sounded like someone in pain, appeared to be coming from there.

Clara crossed the room and carefully pushed the door open wider. It appeared to be a parlor, perhaps the family residence of the owners, Rollie and his wife, Sadie. Stepping farther into the room, listening, Clara peeked around the doorway. Her heart leaped into her throat and she rushed forward.

"Mrs. Austin? Sadie? Are you all right?"

The tiny blonde woman was bent over, clutching her stomach. As she lifted her head, shock and fear covered her face. "Doctor!" she gasped. "Baby!"

Clara glanced toward the door, hoping someone would walk through it. People must be on their way here. "I'll get the doctor," Clara said, "but let's get you comfortable first. Is the pain subsiding? Can you walk?" It had been years since she'd given birth to Billy, but she remembered certain things.

Sadie let out a long breath. "I think it is." Shaking her head, she said, "It came on so fast."

"I know," Clara said. "And it hurts."

"I didn't expect—" Sadie sucked in another breath.

"It's going to be fine, but don't hold your breath. That makes it worse."

Sadie nodded and breathed and nodded again. "I think it's going away, but I—" She glanced down to the floor.

A puddle confirmed everything. "Your water broke. Where's your bedroom?"

Sadie pointed to a door nearby. This edge of the parlor was behind the staircase, which was the only reason Clara had heard her. "I'll help you in there. We'll go slow."

"Sadie! Sadie!"

"In here!" Clara called. "Hurry!"

Rollie Austin rushed into the room a moment later, and as soon as he saw his wife, he pressed both hands to the sides of his face. The top of his head was bald, but the ring of black fuzzy hair that surrounded his head turned into muttonchops that connected to a bushy, black mustache. "Oh, my. Oh, my."

"We'll need the doctor," Clara said. "But need to get her into the bedroom first."

"Oh, yes, yes, hurry. Hurry," he said, running to Sadie's other side.

The pain had passed, and Sadie didn't need much help walking into the bedroom.

As soon as they entered the room, Clara said, "I'll go get—"

"No." Sadie grabbed her arm. "Please let Rollie go get the doctor."

"Yes, yes, I'll go get the doctor." Rollie spun around and ran through the door, only to dash back into the room a second later. "I love you, Sadie." He kissed his wife on the lips. "Love you so much."

"I love you, too," Sadie said. "And I'll be fine. I promise."

Rollie raced back out the door, and Sadie said, "Will you close that, please?"

Clara did and then wrapped an arm around Sadie. "Where's a nightgown? We'll get you out of this dress."

Sadie pointed to the dresser. "His first wife died in childbirth. He's so worried."

"You are going to be fine," Clara said. "Just fine."

"I know you don't know me, but would you mind staying with me? I don't want Rollie seeing—"

"Of course I'll stay, but perhaps you'd feel more comfortable with one of the other women in town."

Sadie shook her head. "I'd like you to stay. I think I'll do better with a stranger. I'd be so embarrassed to have someone I know—" Her soft words stopped as she looked at the nightgown Clara had pulled out of the drawer.

"I understand," Clara said. "Let's get you into bed."

Tom didn't care if she wanted to see him or not—he had to know she was all right. Just a quick glance would be enough. He was about to step through the hotel door when Rollie ran straight into him.

Catching Rollie before he tumbled to the ground, Tom asked, "What's wrong?"

"Doctor. Need doctor."

Tom's entire body went hard. "Why?"

Rollie was shaking his head and trembling. "Sadie. Baby." Both hands grasped Tom's vest. "I'm not ready for this. Sadie's so tiny. So sweet and shy. And tiny. So tiny."

Knowing the history of Rollie's first wife and their child, both dying during childbirth, Tom said, "Calm down, Rollie. I'll go get Doc Graham, but have you seen Clara Wilson?"

"Who? Oh, yes, yes, she's with Sadie. And yes, yes, go get doctor. Please. Go get doctor."

Other people were gathering around and Tom turned to the person right behind him. "Angus, send someone to get the doctor, and then send someone over to the saloon and bring a bottle of whiskey for Rollie. He's going to need it."

Tom then ushered Rollie into the hotel and through the dining room to the door that led to the family living quarters. "Where are your boys, Rollie?"

It wasn't until Rollie fell onto the sofa in the parlor that he answered. With his eyes on a door that must be the bedroom, he said, "They're at the Blackwells. I didn't want them underfoot for Sadie while I was at the trial."

All the boys in town enjoyed being at the Blackwell residence. "They'll be fine," Tom said. "You sit right there. I'll check on Sadie."

"Please do, and tell her I love her."

Tom nodded at the same time he knocked on the bedroom door. A moment later, it opened a crack. Relief flooded over him to see Clara.

Keeping the door closed except that tiny crack, she said, "We need the doctor."

"He'll be here in a minute. How are you?"

"I'm fine. Sadie's the one having a baby and I have to help her get her nightgown on." Glancing toward the sofa, where Rollie sat holding his head with both hands, she said, "Keep him out of here." There was a soft mumble in the background before Clara said, "And everyone else."

She closed the door before he had a chance to respond one way or the other.

A second later, she opened the door again. "Except the doctor."

The door closed again, and Tom turned about. Rollie's head was now hanging between his knees.

Tom paced the room, wondering what was taking the doctor so long, while keeping everyone else out. Which wasn't easy, since practically every woman in town tried to convince him Sadie needed her assistance. He agreed that she might, but stated that Clara was with Sadie and until Doc Graham said so, no one else could enter the room.

Most agreed readily; others took more convincing. Especially Martha, but she readily found a purpose when he asked her to go let Fiona Blackwell know what was happening and to keep Rollie's sons at her place until otherwise notified. The last thing Rollie needed was those two rambunctious boys racing about.

Nelson Graham finally arrived. Turned out he'd been called to the jailhouse. Hugh was claiming infection had set in in his shoulder.

"There's no infection," Nelson said. "And knowing it was his wife who stitched him and you up is comforting. I'll be glad for her assistance with Sadie."

Tom had nearly forgotten that Clara had been the one to doctor him and Hugh. Pride welled inside him as he said, "She's good, Doc. Real good."

With a glance toward Rollie, Nelson said, "Don't leave him alone, and keep him out here, no matter what you hear."

Looking at Rollie, who'd now flung himself backward and was staring up at the ceiling and mumbling, Tom said, "I won't."

Nelson nodded as he knocked on the door and then entered the bedroom.

Tom stationed Angus behind the front desk to let people know the dining room was closed and to inform the hotel guests of where they could find an evening meal.

When Clara stuck her head out the door and informed him they needed a pot of boiling water, Tom did it himself, knowing Rollie, who had downed half the bottle of whiskey that had been delivered, couldn't manage the task.

Evening arrived, and Rollie, glassy-eyed and stumbling, was wearing out the carpet with his constant pacing. He was wearing out Tom's nerves, too. He was a lawman, and there was no law that stated this was a part of his duties.

If he agreed with what Josiah said about never marrying, he'd never be in the same position as Rollie. Josiah had stopped in early, excited at how well the trial had turned out. Tom was pleased that Hugh had gotten his due, a life sentence for the crimes he'd committed, but was also wondering what that meant for Clara and Billy.

That was where his thoughts had been when a pain-filled scream had filtered through the closed bedroom door. Rollie had dropped to his knees, head bowed and hands clasped.

Josiah had shaken his head and smiled. "We're the smart ones, Tom," he'd said. "Staying clear of women. Never getting married means you never have to go through something like this." With a nod toward Rollie, Josiah had added, "Look at him. It's not worth it. Anything that will bring a man to his knees is just not worth it. Of course, you already know that. Like me, you know you're not a family man. We're committed to taking care of the entire town rather than a select few. Sure can't do both."

Josiah had left before another pain-filled scream sounded, and though he normally took all Josiah said with a grain of salt, Tom had to admit there was an ounce of wisdom in the mayor's words. Perhaps more than an ounce.

It was late—had to be, the sun had long ago set—when Sadie's baby finally made her entrance. A little girl, red and wailing, who wasn't overly happy to leave her nest. "You did it," Clara said to Sadie while taking the baby from Nelson Graham. "Just a couple more hard pushes and it'll all be over."

"You have been excellent help, Clara," Nelson said. "Almost as good as my wife."

"Thank you, Doctor," Clara said while cooing to the tiny baby as she washed her with the now tepid water. Nelson had explained that Sylvia, his new wife, was his assistant, but she was feeling under the weather and didn't want to pass anything on to patients this week. Clara hadn't voiced her thoughts, but from what the doctor explained, she had to wonder if Sylvia was pregnant. The two of them were probably just so busy taking care of everyone else, they hadn't realized it yet. Or maybe just didn't want to tell anyone.

She couldn't help but wonder what it would be like to live in Oak Grove. There were so many people getting married, having babies, living lives that were indeed the kind she'd dreamed of more than once. Those thoughts, as all others, had her thinking about Tom. He was always on her mind. He'd be such an amazing father. And husband. No door would keep him out while his wife was having a baby. It was funny how she just knew things about him. Perhaps because he was the exact opposite of Hugh in every way.

Cradling the clean and swaddled infant, she waited until the doctor signaled he was finished before she carried the baby over to Sadie. "Here she is, your precious daughter." Laying the baby in Sadie's arms, Clara whispered, "She has all ten fingers and toes. I counted."

"Thank you, Clara. I don't know what I would have done without you."

Clara ran a hand over Sadie's head. "You would have had a baby girl, just like you did." Then she said, "Let me get everything cleaned up. Then I'll let Rollie in."

That happened a short time later. As Clara opened the door, three men turned her way. She wasn't surprised to see Rollie, or even Tom, who made her heart skip a beat, especially the way he glanced toward the third man.

Judge Alfords.

Rollie's long legs nearly tripped over themselves twice as he rushed across the room. "Can I see them now?"

"Yes," she said, her eyes once again on Tom. Judge Alfords nodded and walked out of the room.

The door closing behind her startled her slightly, but understanding Rollie and Sadie needed privacy, she stepped away from it. Tom met her in the center of the room, and a great desire to have his arms wrap around her washed over her from head to toe. He was the strong one, not her. Strong and righteous and handsome, so very, very handsome.

"How are you?" he asked while taking her hand. "You must be exhausted."

"I'm fine," she said. "Sadie did all the work. I just held her hand."

He let go of her hand and she regretted her words. She hadn't meant it to sound the way it had.

"Judge Alfords waited to talk to you because he's leaving early in the morning."

She nodded, nearly having forgotten that she'd wanted to talk with the judge. "I do want to talk to him."

"I told him you'd be along shortly. That I wanted to talk to you first."

He seemed a bit unlike himself. Like he was nervous, which put her nerves on guard. "Why?"

"Uh—well, to tell you that Billy's upstairs. I sent Angus over to collect him when it started getting dark. Figured Fiona would have her hands full with her boys and Rollie's for the night."

That was Tom. Knowing what she needed without being told. She'd wondered about Billy, more than once, but had also known Tom would think of him. She'd never had that before, and shouldn't have grown so used to it so quickly. But she had. "Thank you."

"And, well, I wanted to know if you need anything else. If there's anything I can do for you."

He was so wonderful, so caring, so him, and giving in to the desire to still be held, be kissed again by him would be so easy. Therefore, she shook her head. Life had never been easy and wouldn't start being so now. "No. Thank you, but there's nothing." Standing here, talking to him, was only making the desires inside her stronger. "I'd better go see the judge so he can get some sleep."

"I'll show you to his room."

He took a hold of her elbow and the desire to simply lean closer to him sprang forth. She knew what room the judge was in, but she was selfish enough that she wanted Tom to stay at her side a bit longer. She'd seen him through the side door of the courtroom, and the way he kept looking to the back of the room. She'd also seen the empty seat beside him, and had wished she'd been able to sit there. But knew she couldn't. She had to stop all this before it became too late. Hugh may have been found guilty, but it wasn't over. Not for her, and may never be.

They'd arrived at the judge's door and she drew in a breath for fortitude.

"Would you like me to come in with you?" Tom asked.

"No, you must be tired."

"Not at all."

He had the ability to make her smile with hardly any effort whatsoever. "Well, you should be. I am."

"I'll wait and see you upstairs afterward."

Though his words were innocent, they sent a warmth throughout her body that she hadn't experienced in a very, very long time. Shaking her head, she knocked on the door. "No, please don't wait."

The judge opened the door and she slipped inside without waiting to hear Tom's response. He was just too kind, too good, too respected for her.

"Please have a seat, Mrs. Wilson. You've had quite a day."

"Thank you, Your Honor."

"I'm glad you requested a meeting. When I heard about Mrs. Austin, and that you were helping her, I was afraid if we waited until morning, there might not be time. I'm leaving on the first train, along with, well, with your husband, to see he arrives in Leavenworth."

"That's where he's going?" She'd heard of Leavenworth, the prison there. Everyone had. It was an outlaw's worst nightmare.

"That's my recommendation, and I intend to see it's fulfilled."

"Is it appropriate for me to thank you for your decision today?"

His smile softened his aged face. "Yes."

"Then thank you." As the truth bubbled up inside her, she admitted, "I believe you saved my life today."

"I believe Tom Baniff did that by arresting your husband and bringing him to see justice was done."

She closed her eyes to gather her emotions. "T— Mr. Baniff already saved my life twice. I'd requested there not be a third time, but I guess he didn't listen."

"Or he did. Knew what needed to be done and did it." With another gentle smile, he said, "That's the kind of man Tom is. One of the best I know. As a man and a lawman. This town is lucky to have a man of his caliber. Far luckier than most. Without Tom, Oak Grove wouldn't be the safe, friendly place it is."

Everything he'd said, she'd already thought about. This town was lucky to have Tom, and wouldn't be the same without him. Others felt that way, too. The doctor had talked about how not only the serenity, but the progress of Oak Grove, rested on Tom's shoulders.

"I agree." Too unstable to continue talking, and thinking, about Tom, she said, "I wanted to talk to you about—"

"Forgive my interruption, but before we get to that, I have something I need to tell you about. It concerns those coins you brought in."

As she'd feared. It wasn't over. Might never be. Hugh had always said she was an accomplice by being married to him. "All right."

"If you had tried to spend one, just one, you'd have been arrested."

"I assume they were stolen." Everything had always been stolen. Hugh never acquired anything legally. She shrugged. "They weren't mine to spend."

"They're also fake. The government's been looking for them for years. Those coins were made to dupe the Indians. Over ten years ago a governmental official decided to have fake gold coins made and given to the Indians in exchange for land in Nebraska. It was an underhanded deal that few knew about, and no one was ever prosecuted for it because the coins were robbed from the Indians, and they'd never surfaced, until today." He lifted his bushy brows. "There is also a five-hundred-dollar reward for their recovery."

There was a buzzing noise in her ears. "Reward?"

"Yes, reward. Add that to the five hundred the slaughterhouse put up for the capture and conviction of the man responsible for murdering their agent, you have one thousand dollars coming your way. I'll see that it's delivered to you."

The buzzing in her ears was louder, and she pressed a finger in each ear, trying to make it stop. It didn't, and this was impossible. "One thousand dollars?"

"Yes, one thousand dollars. Enough for you and your son to start over."

So much had happened, and it all seemed unreal.

"You didn't know about the reward on your husband, did you?"

She shook her head.

"Well, now you do." He shuffled some papers lying

on the table. "Now, let's get to the reason you wanted to see me about. I'm assuming it's a divorce."

It was late, she was tired, and so much had happened that her mind didn't want to function properly. "Yes, but I don't know much about them. What I need to do."

"I do, and I already took the liberty to draw up the papers, that is if it is what you want?"

She nodded, and admitted, "I never wanted to marry him in the first place." There was more she'd have to admit someday, but those things were still too hidden deep down.

Judge Alfords explained everything thoroughly, including how Hugh, now as a convicted felon, no longer had any rights. Not concerning her, or Billy. The judge also explained that he'd have to file the paperwork at the county seat before the divorce was final, and that he'd do that as soon as possible and notify her. Before she left the judge's room, he also reminded her to take her traveling bag. It was now empty, and she was thankful for that. Was thankful for so many more things than she'd ever been before.

Including that Tom had followed her request and wasn't waiting for her. She was depending on him too much, and had to stop.

The lamp in her room had been left lit, and turned down low. Billy was in the bed, and his clothes had been folded and set on the chair. So were her things, including her nightgown. She hadn't used the nightgown since leaving home. Sharing the room with Angus last night, she'd slept in her dress—as Angus had pointed out this morning when he'd brought her the one from Martha.

With a thousand dollars, she could pay Martha for the dress. Pay the Ryans the money she'd borrowed. She'd hoped they'd want to buy some of her land, but they'd insisted upon just loaning her the money instead.

The thousand dollars would allow her to pay for this hotel room, too, and make the travel home easier for her and Billy. A pang shot across her stomach. Ignoring it and the cause of it, she crossed the room and set her traveling bag on the floor.

Quietly, she slipped off the dress from Martha and draped it over the chair before putting on her nightgown, blowing out the lamp and crawling into bed beside Billy.

He moaned slightly and then twisted to look at her. "Is it time to get up?"

"No. Go back to sleep," she whispered, kissing the top of his head.

"I was hoping it was morning." His yawn belied his words. "I had more fun today than I've had in my whole life."

Her smile was interrupted by her own yawn. "That's good."

He flopped onto his back and closed his eyes, but rather than going to sleep, his eyes popped back open as he kept talking. "Wyatt and Rhett showed me where they bury the fish guts after fishing. We didn't dig them up 'cause their pa says things that are buried need to stay buried. Brett, that's their pa, said I can go fishing with them someday. And we rode their pa's horses. They're big, like him. It was just in the corral, but it was fun. And we played hide-and-seek and checkers and I ate something called dessert. It sure was good. You ever have dessert, Ma?"

"Yes, I have, and I'm sure it was good." Although Billy was excited over his day, sadness crept around inside her at all the things he'd missed out on back home. The only children he'd ever played with were the two Ryan girls who were older than him. And though she made sweets when possible, for some reason, she'd never called them dessert.

"I told them I'll come back tomorrow. I could've slept there like Kade and Wiley but Angus said you needed me here." After another yawn, he asked, "What did you need me for?"

"I missed you," she whispered. "I hadn't seen you all day."

"Oh." After a pause, he asked, "I can go back tomorrow, can't I?"

She had no idea what tomorrow would bring, so merely said, "We'll see. It's late now. Close your eyes and go back to sleep."

He snuggled up against her side. "We played good guys and bad guys, too. You ever play that?"

"No, I haven't."

She'd thought he'd fallen asleep when he spoke again.

"They said there's a robber in jail. That he robbed a train and shot people."

Her stomach clenched.

"Is that Pa, Ma? Is that who they were talking about?"

Chapter Fourteen

It wasn't far to his house, yet it was the loneliest walk Tom had ever taken. He'd waited on the street corner until he'd seen the light go out in Clara's room, just to be sure she'd finally made it to bed before he'd headed for home.

In all his years, he'd never had so many things weighing so heavily on his mind. A fair number of them had to do with Clara. What she would do now that Hugh would be spending the rest of his life in Leavenworth.

Chester had offered to escort Hugh to the prison, and so had Brett. Tom had thanked them, but declined. It was his job and he'd do it. Taking Hugh where he belonged wasn't what was so troubling. The train trip there and back wasn't too long. He'd be gone three days at the most. What troubled him was if Clara would still be here when he returned, and if he could ask her to stay.

That wasn't his place to do, especially when he didn't have anything he could offer her. A splattering of regret washed over him as he stopped on the stoop of his house. It was small. A front room and a bedroom. Not nearly enough room for a husband, wife and child.

He opened the door and stepped in. Other families lived in smaller places; he'd seen them. As the sheriff, not only of the town but of the surrounding area, he'd visited most every ranch, farm, home and business in a hundred square miles of Oak Grove. Glancing around at the rough-hewn boards making up the unpainted walls, he sighed. True, this was not what he'd want for his wife, but it wasn't the size of the house or the way it was built that was the issue. He could find a new house, build one that would have plenty of room. However, he couldn't marry. It wasn't because of what Josiah said, although seeing what Rollie had gone through tonight did cement what he'd already known. A wife needed her husband.

Clara needed that. If Hugh had been home instead of out robbing trains and people, she would have had a very different life. A life she deserved. A home. A husband who was there with her.

In some ways, being a lawman was as bad as being an outlaw. Because he'd had to testify in this case, things had been different, but usually, when there was a prisoner behind the bars, he slept in his office. Ate there, too. That was why this little house had suited him just fine. Traveling had suited him, too. Wherever and whenever needed.

"And will continue to," he said aloud, as if that would solidify his thoughts. Convincing himself it would, he went to bed.

It didn't, of course, and he tossed and turned all

night, unable to get comfortable with either the lumpy mattress or his thoughts.

Morning came just as scheduled, and he walked the short distance to his office while the sun was still rising and the morning birds were just starting to sing their songs. The chirping reminded him of Angus. Yesterday the old man had spouted one of his many idioms, something about not loving songbirds until hearing the right one.

Tom shook his head. He had no idea what kind of bird was singing. Had never taken the time to pay attention or notice. Just like he'd never noticed women before Clara. "Damn it," he muttered. That was what Angus was talking about, and the old man knew that Clara had him tied up in knots. Tom increased his speed. No one else could know. No one. He had to make sure of that.

The town, his town, wouldn't look upon him the same way if they knew how Clara affected him. Josiah had pointed that out more than once: a married man had too many of his own worries to take proper care of a community.

Tom opened his office door, and Chester sat up on the cot he'd been sleeping on in a cell exactly like the one next to it. Except, unlike Hugh's cell, Chester's wasn't locked and the door was open.

"He give you any trouble?" Tom asked. Hugh had sat up, too, and was scratching his head with both hands.

"Nothing I couldn't handle," Chester replied while pulling on his boots. "Other than his constant complaining."

Tom knew all about that.

Chester tossed the single blanket over the cot before leaving his cell. "Says his arm's hurting."

"It is," Hugh said. "That backstabbing wife of mine waited too long to take the bullet out. She gave me blood poisoning."

Ignoring Hugh, Tom said to Chester, "Doc said it was fine."

"Yep," Chester said. "Just fine."

"No, it's not," Hugh said. "She was too busy doctoring you, Tom, to see to my wound in time. It's blood poisoning."

Tom picked up the coffeepot and carried it to the door so he could dump the old grounds around the side of the building. "Then you won't have to worry about it too long, will you?"

Chester nodded. "That's what I told him. If it was blood poisoning, he'd already be six feet under, or well on his way."

Tom walked outside and around the building. After emptying the pot, he went to the well and rinsed out the pot before filling it with fresh water. His thoughts weren't on Hugh; they were on Chester. He was married, and had two children. A daughter and a son. But he only filled in as deputy when needed. His regular job was at the hardware store.

More focused on what was going on inside him than around him, Tom skidded to a stop as he rounded the corner of his office.

Clara and Billy were walking up the boardwalk. She was wearing the same dress as yesterday. The blue one that Martha had given her. She smiled slightly, but he could tell it was only for show. He said nothing, did nothing, except stand there and watch them approach.

"Hi, Tom," Billy said when they stepped beneath the awning of his office.

"Morning," he replied. Billy had been mad at him when he'd left their place, but last night had acted happy to see him. Children were like that. Got over things far more quickly than adults. "You're up early."

Clara was holding Billy's hand, and as they stopped before him, she placed the other against her stomach. She also swallowed hard.

Concern leaped inside him. Whatever she had to say wasn't easy for her.

"Is there something you need?" he asked.

"Yes." She glanced down at her son. "Billy would like to say goodbye to his father." Lifting her gaze to him, she asked, "Would that be possible?"

He wanted to say no, but couldn't. Clara would have considered Billy's request long and hard before coming to this conclusion. Even though he wished otherwise, Tom nodded. "But he can't go in alone."

She shook her head and then nodded. "I already told him that. I'll be with him the entire time."

Tom shook his head. "I meant the two of you can't go in there alone." Not wanting her to think he didn't trust her, he added, "By law." That wasn't a lie. He was the sheriff and he made the laws when needed.

"That's fine," she said. "We understand."

Tom then stepped over and pushed open the door, while nodding for her and Billy to enter. Hugh was spouting off about something, but stopped momentarily.

The silence didn't last long. "What do you want?" Hugh shouted. "Here to gloat? Don't get used to it, Clara. Others will learn about what you did. I warned you about that. About this. Not even your precious Tom will be able to save you."

Although anger filled him, Tom was also proud of Clara. How she'd kept her composure. With her chin up, she placed both hands on Billy's shoulders and guided the boy a few steps closer to the jail cell.

With a steady, calm voice, she said, "Billy wanted to say goodbye to you."

Hugh's lip curled as he glared at her, never once glancing down at the boy.

Keeping his eyes on the trio, Tom walked over and set the coffeepot down. Not only did Clara deserve so much more than Hugh Wilson, so did Billy.

"Why'd you lie to me?" Billy asked. "Why'd you tell me you didn't rob that train?"

Hugh still didn't pull his nasty gaze off Clara. "Your mother's lying, son. I didn't rob any train."

"Ma didn't tell me," Billy said. "Rhett and Wyatt did. And Kade and Wiley."

A bout of fury raced over Tom. Billy's face was pained as he stared up at his father. Sympathy for Billy swarmed inside him, too. The entire town had been talking about the train robbery for months, so it wasn't surprising that Brett's sons and Rollie's would talk about it, too.

"They're lying, too," Hugh said.

Tears formed in Billy's eyes. "No, they aren't. They're my friends."

"You don't have any friends," Hugh said. "Just like

your mother. She thinks Tom's her friend, but Tom's already got what he wanted from her."

It took all Tom had to stay still.

Clara slid her hands off Billy's shoulders, down onto his chest, as if protecting him. "Say goodbye now, Billy."

"'Bye," Billy said. Then, as Clara turned him and her around, he glanced over his shoulder. "I'm glad you ain't gonna be my pa no more."

"Me, too," Hugh sneered.

Chester slapped the jail cell. "Sit down!" As he walked away from the bars, Chester shook his head. "That idiot doesn't even care about how many people he's hurt, or what he's losing."

Tom agreed, but kept silent.

Clara didn't. "He never has cared, Mr. Chadwick." With another forced smile, she then said, "Thank you, Sheriff."

Tom crossed the room and opened the door, then followed her and Billy outside. He searched for the right words, but concluding there probably weren't any for what the boy had just experienced, he laid a hand on Billy's shoulder. "You're one brave boy. I'm proud of you."

Looking up at him, Billy wiped at both eyes with his fists, before saying, "You're my friend, aren't you, Tom?" Scrunching up his face, he wiped his nose on the back of his hand. "I know I acted mad at you. I'm sorry about that, and I'm not mad at you anymore."

Tom knelt down in front of the boy. "Yes, I'm your friend. I consider you a good friend. And it's all right to get mad. Everyone does. It's just never all right to hurt someone when we're mad at them. Not even their feelings. And thank you for apologizing. That really is a good friend."

Billy smiled and nodded. Tom was about to stand up, when Billy asked, "You wouldn't lie to me, would you, Tom?"

The desire to throttle someone had never struck Tom as hard as now, when he wanted to lay into Hugh for how badly his words had hurt Billy. "No, Billy, I won't. Good friends don't lie to each other. Good people don't lie."

Billy wiped at his nose one more time before asking, "Rhett and Wyatt and Kade and Wylie are my friends, too. Don't you think they are?"

Tom gave him a full smile, hoping it would help ease Billy's troubled little mind. "Yes, they are. I'm sure they are hoping you'll be visiting them again today."

Billy's eyes lit up as he smiled. "I told them I'd be back today. I like playing with them."

"That's good. Be a good friend to them and they'll be good friends to you."

Billy nodded again, but then frowned. "Can I ask you something else?"

"Of course."

"If I don't tell them that…" He glanced toward the office door. "…that he's my pa, is that lying?"

It certainly wasn't right that this little guy had so much to deal with at his age. Tom would have liked to say that would be fine, but he couldn't. He'd just vowed not to lie, and he wouldn't. "Well, if they ask you directly, and you say no, then that would be a lie."

Billy gnawed on his bottom lip as it started to quiver.

Tom squeezed the little shoulder still beneath his hand. "I'll tell you what I'd do if I was in your shoes."

Hope filled Billy's eyes as his head bobbed up and down.

"I'd tell them that he was my pa, but that now he's in a place where he can never hurt anyone ever again."

Astonishment covered the boy's entire face, making his eyes shine as he smiled. "I could. And I could tell them I was there when you arrested him. You arrested him just like when we were playing good guys and bad guys yesterday. And…and I could tell them that Ma helped."

Billy's excitement made Tom smile. "You surely could," he said. "And you could say you helped, because you did. You took good care of Bullet. Every lawman needs a well-cared-for horse to help do his job."

"That's right! I did!"

The way Billy leaped forward and wrapped both of his little arms completely around his neck filled Tom with something he'd never felt before. It filled his heart with light brighter and warmer than the sun ever had. He put his arms around Billy and hugged him tight.

"Thank you, Tom. Thank you."

Releasing Billy, Tom had to clear his throat before saying, "You're welcome. And in case I didn't say it before, thank you for taking such good care of Bullet."

With his shoulders square and his chest puffed out, Billy said, "You're welcome."

Tom stood then, and the tears that rolled out of Clara's

eyes faster than she could wipe them away made him want to hug her as tightly as he had Billy.

Some might not call what had just happened a miracle, and maybe it wasn't, but to Clara, it was the most magical, the most wonderful, moment she'd ever witnessed. She'd been at her wits' end while walking out the door, wondering how on earth she could help her son understand life. Understand that he hadn't done anything wrong, yet was being blamed, and paying for Hugh's actions.

Unable not to, she stepped forward and stretched up on her toes to kiss Tom's cheek. Before stepping back, she whispered, "Thank you. I'll never be able to repay you for what you've just done."

He shook his head, and she pressed a finger to his lips. He would deny having done anything worthy of repayment. That was who he was.

As she removed her finger, she whispered, "Just say 'you're welcome.'"

He nodded. "You're welcome."

After wiping the moisture off her cheeks one last time, she took a hold of Billy's hand. "Ready?"

"Yes," he replied. "Can I go over to Rhett and Wyatt's now?"

Billy's smile made her so happy she couldn't stop smiling, even while saying, "No, it's too early. Most everyone is still sleeping. But maybe later."

Billy accepted that easily, and as they started walking, Tom fell into step beside her.

"I'll walk back to the hotel with you."

Though she didn't mind in the least, she said, "That's not necessary."

"Yes, it is," he replied. "I have to haul some breakfast back to the prisoner and Chester. And remind Judge Alfords the train doesn't stay long this early in the morning. Most folks in town use the whistle as a signal it's time to start their day." With a grin, he added, "It's better than a rooster."

"I'm sure it is." Appreciating how he'd refrained from using Hugh's name, she said, "Judge Alfords said that he's traveling to Leavenworth today."

"That's correct. I'll be traveling with him."

Her heart took a tumble. "Must you?"

"Yes, I must. It's my duty."

His commitment to everything he did was just a small part of what she admired about him. "I understand that." She bit her bottom lip for a moment, not entirely sure it was her place to say more, but she had to. "I'm just concerned about your safety. You will be careful?"

He gave her one of those quick little winks that sent her heart into a flutter.

"I always am." He was looking forward again, but his profile showed he was no longer smiling. "I'll be gone about three days. If you need anything during that time, you can ask Chester. He knows where I keep—"

"We'll be fine." She'd had to stop him. Her entire life she'd been depending on someone else to provide for her, and had to stop. Yet, not wanting him to think she wasn't grateful for his kindness, she said, "But thank you. I appreciate the thought."

They took several more steps before he asked, "What are you going to do now? If you don't mind my asking?"

"I don't mind you asking, but I don't have an answer. I'm not sure." She did need to figure that out. Actually, she had a lot of things to figure out.

"May I ask a favor?"

He didn't sound like himself, and that made her stop walking. "Of course. Is something wrong?"

"No. I—I just would appreciate it if you and Billy were still here when I return."

She drew in a deep breath, trying to tell her heart that it was putting more into his words than was there.

"We'll still be here," Billy said before encouraging her to agree. "Won't we, Ma?"

She squeezed Billy's hand and started walking again. "Yes, we will still be here." In that, they didn't have much of a choice. She was broke. Until the reward money arrived, she couldn't go anywhere.

"Good," Tom said. "It shouldn't be more than three days, and remember what I said about Chester. He'll help with anything you need."

"Thank you, again, for the offer." She left it at that. There was still too much unknown to say more.

They crossed the street and entered the hotel, at the same moment a loud crash echoed off the ceiling. She and Tom shared a look as they all three hurried into the dining room.

Judge Alfords was the only one there, and he gestured toward a swinging door. She hadn't been in there, but knew that door led to the kitchen.

"Rollie's on his own this morning," the judge said,

stopping near a table. "I was just on my way to check on him. Hoping to have some breakfast, or at least a cup of coffee, before that train arrives."

Another clatter had Clara waving toward the table. "You men sit down. I'll go help Rollie." Nodding toward the judge, who'd saved her life as much as Tom had, she added, "You'll have breakfast, complete with coffee, shortly. I promise." Still holding Billy's hand, she said, "You can help."

Opening the kitchen door, she nearly gasped aloud. She most certainly had never seen a kitchen in such disarray.

Rollie, staring at several broken plates, said, "I was just trying to get a cup." Looking up, he shook his head. "I ran this place by myself before Sadie came along, but I'm all thumbs this morning. Can't seem to do anything."

"Don't worry, Mr. Austin," she said, unbuttoning her cuffs. "Billy and I are here to help." She plucked an apron off a hook and slipped it over her head while snagging a cloth to grasp the handle of the coffeepot that was boiling over on the stove. "How is Sadie this morning? And the baby?"

"I need to go check on them," he said. "They were both sleeping when I left them, but that was more than half an hour ago."

"Then go check on them." She rolled her sleeves out of the way and tied the apron strings behind her back. "Billy and I will see the judge gets his breakfast."

Rollie's stare at the door was full of longing. "But I

need to make three meals for the sheriff, too, and my helpers won't arrive for another hour or more."

"Billy and I can handle four meals." She glanced at her son. "Can't we?"

"Yes!"

She smiled at him, all the while knowing Tom's talk had given her son a desire to be helpful, be a good friend. "Go on now, Mr. Austin, and do let me know if Sadie needs anything."

His face lit up. "Oh, Mrs. Wilson, you are a godsend. A pure godsend."

"I'm just glad to help, but could I ask a favor?"

He was on his way to the door. "You name it!"

It was silly, but it was her first step in changing who she was. "Could you call me Clara, please? I'd greatly appreciate it."

"And I'd be honored, Clara."

She nodded and waved the cup she'd taken off the shelf toward the door. "Wonderful. Now go see to your wife and daughter."

The door swung on its hinges from his hurried departure. After filling two cups, she handed them to Billy. "Be careful, these are very hot, but carry them out to Tom and Judge Alfords."

"I'll be careful, Ma," he said, taking a cup in each hand. "And I won't spill a drop."

She opened the door and waited until he was well clear of it before letting it swing shut. Turning about, she surveyed the room, taking in the supplies and cooking utensils. Including the broken plates on the floor. First things first. She gathered three pans and set them on the stove to start warming, and then picked up a broom.

When the door opened, she said, "Grab that dustpan near the back door and bring it here."

The pan appeared near the pile she'd swept up, but the hand holding it wasn't Billy's.

Tom looked up. "I'm here to help."

With one sweep, she filled the pan and then bent down and clutched the handle in front of his hand. Eyeing him directly, she said, "No, you aren't." Pulling the dustpan from his grasp, she stood. "Don't argue with me, Tom. You, Judge Alfords, this entire town has already done more for me than anyone in my entire life." She crossed the room, dumped the pan in a rubbish pail, and set it and the broom aside. Turning about, she pointed around the room. "This I can do. Cooking a few meals is the least I can do."

His gaze locked on her, and the silence echoed in her ears, but she stood her ground.

Then, with a wide smile, he winked. "All right. I've missed your cooking."

Happiness exploded inside her so fast her cheeks burned. "Then go sit down. It'll be done shortly."

She sliced off several pieces of ham, and while they were warming, mixed up batter for pancakes and greased a skillet to fry the eggs. She also filled a bowl with butter and a small pitcher with syrup, and had Billy carry them out to the other room.

He was as excited as her, and she kept him busy with other small jobs, carrying knives, forks and spoons, salt and pepper, and a bowl of sugar, out to Tom and the judge.

It was as if the world wanted everything to go right for her because by the time she'd loaded plates with ham and eggs, and others with pancakes, Rollie returned.

"Sadie and the baby are doing fine," he said. "Just fine."

"That's wonderful news. I'm so glad." She nodded toward the tray on the table in the center of the room. "I have tea and scrambled eggs ready for Sadie. You can deliver that to her while Billy and I take these to the judge and sheriff. Once Tom's done eating, I'll have plates ready for him to take to the jail."

"How will I ever thank you?" Rollie asked.

"We'll talk about that later." Her mind had been laying out a plan all the while she'd been cooking. A solid plan that made her feel good about herself. Her abilities. And her future. "Right now, you need to go eat breakfast with your wife. I made enough for you, too. And we have to carry these out to the dining room."

Chapter Fifteen

If he'd had a choice, Tom would have taken more time to say goodbye to Clara, but the train was due and Chester deserved his meal to be hot upon delivery. About the same time he and Judge Alfords had swallowed the last bites of their tasty breakfast, she'd arrived at the table with two baskets, stating the larger one was for Chester and the smaller one, for the prisoner.

Alfords had thanked her for the meal and as he'd left the table, said he'd be at the sheriff's office shortly. Tom had waited for a moment alone with her, but as Alfords had walked out of the dining room, Josiah and Angus had entered. So had Miss Bella Armentrout.

While Josiah had started talking, saying now that the fiasco was over, everything could get back to normal, Angus, always observant, had figured out Clara was cooking this morning. Upon hearing that, Miss Armentrout stated she wasn't much of a cook, but certainly knew how to wash dishes, and started clearing the table. Tom was happy to see that Clara would have help this morning. He was also glad to know Angus would keep a close eye on her. Just as he had since she'd arrived.

Tom picked up both the baskets and thanked her.

"You're very welcome," she said, and then walked around the table, stopping near him. "You will remember which basket is which?"

If he was a suspicious man, he might have questioned why, but there was no need with her. "Yes, I will."

She nodded, but then a hint of worry filled her eyes. "And you will be careful?"

"Yes." There were too many around to say much more. Not exactly certain what more he would say if they were alone, he merely said, "And you remember that Chester can help with anything you need."

"I will." Her smile was back, and brighter than he'd seen before. "See you in three days."

"You can count on it," he replied, and then because he had to, he headed for the door.

The spring in his step felt good, but knowing she'd put it there concerned him. Hugh had been convicted, would soon take up permanent residence at Leavenworth. That had the potential to change her life, and would, but it wouldn't change his. Despite all the happiness that kept flaring inside him, he had to remember who he was. What he was.

Walking into his office was a clear reminder of that. Wesley Riggs was there, the sheriff from the Carlyle area southwest of Oak Grove, along with a couple other men wearing deputy badges. There were also two wild-eyed men in the other cell beside Hugh's. No matter how many were caught, there were always more men out there set on breaking the law.

"Hey, Tom." Short, with dust from traveling turning his brown hair several shades of gray, Wesley gestured toward the cell. "Been chasing these two for over a week now. Cattle rustlers." Wesley then gestured toward Hugh. "Hear that's the train robber you went after." With a nod toward him, Wesley asked, "He do that to you?"

There was no need to look down, at the star on his chest that still held Hugh's bullet. He'd ordered a new one, but it hadn't come in yet. Tom set the baskets on his desk. "Where are the rest of them?" Seasoned, he knew it took more than two men to rustle cattle.

"Already got their due," Wesley said. "If there's anything left of them, we'll pick up the carcasses on the way back home. Need to let our horses rest up for a day. Caught these two after dark and rode the rest of the night to get here." He nodded toward the men in the cell. "The short one's bat-shit crazy. And quick. Already dodged three of my bullets." With a glance at the bullet-centered star, Wesley said, "I'd have killed any man who'd done that to me."

Reality struck Tom. That was the reason he'd become a lawman, and remained one. If all lawmen were as quick to kill as the outlaws, this country would never be tamed. The law proclaimed justice, and that was what he worked toward, and why. Carlyle was a small settlement with more saloons than houses, and would remain that way as long as Riggs was in charge.

"Hear Alfords is in town," Riggs said. "Good thing. I can let him know we need him over in Carlyle."

Tom gestured for Chester to come get the food baskets while he walked around his desk. "Alfords is heading to Leavenworth with me today."

"Hear that, too," Riggs said, while glancing at the cells. "Don't mind waiting a week or more. Give these fellas time to contemplate their future." As Chester took the checkered cloth off the top of one basket, Riggs said, "My boys and I will head over to the hotel for some grub, then grab some shut-eye."

"You can come back here to sleep," Tom said, with a glance toward Chester that conveyed an order to see that happened. He didn't want Riggs and the others anywhere near Clara, or even wandering around town. "My house is out back. You can use it."

"Appreciate that," Riggs said, walking toward the door with his deputies following.

The train whistle bellowed as Riggs opened the door.

Under its shrill, Chester said, "I'll send Brett to the hotel if they aren't back by the time the train leaves."

Tom nodded. That was why Oak Grove was prospering. Because the entire town knew what it took to make peace, and keep it.

"Why are there two baskets?"

In answer to Chester's question, Tom pointed toward Hugh. "The little one's for him."

Chester had already unloaded the bigger basket containing a platter of eggs, ham and pancakes, along with containers of butter and syrup, and Tom didn't even try to hide the grin that formed as Chester took the cloth off the second basket. There was nothing but a plate with two pancakes, somewhat on the burnt side.

Clearly remembering how Hugh had tossed pancakes on the floor back at her house, Tom accepted the small amount of triumph Clara deserved at preparing this final meal for Hugh. He picked up the plate of pancakes and walked over to slide it through the bars. "Eat up, Wilson. We'll be heading out in five minutes."

"What's this slop?" Hugh said, staring at the plate. "They're burnt, and I hate pancakes." He shoved the plate back through the bars. "I have a right to a decent meal. One like his."

Tom smiled at how Chester was making a show of sticking a thick chunk of ham into his mouth. "No, you don't," Tom said. "You lost all your rights the minute you were convicted. Eat what you have or not. That's your choice."

"I'll eat it, if you don't want it," one of the other prisoners said.

"Me, too," the other piped in.

Turning his back to them, Hugh asked, "Do I at least get a fork?"

Chester glanced into the basket and shrugged. "Guess not."

Busy, but enjoying every moment, Clara found the hours went by swiftly, yet, somehow, the days didn't. Every time she thought about Tom, which was continuously, disappointment that it was still days before he'd return filled Clara. The nights were even longer.

As she lay in bed, there was nothing to take her attention off her thoughts.

With Sadie recovering, and Rollie wanting to be at her side, he'd offered room and board and wages to her and Billy. Even though it was only pennies, Billy was as proud of his earnings as she was of hers. It felt good to know she was legitimately earning what she was receiving. That it was in no way connected to Hugh. She tried not to think about him. Wanted to just forget everything about her past. But unlike so many things she'd buried deep in the past, this time things wouldn't stay hidden. They kept popping up like weeds in a garden.

"We don't ever have to leave, do we, Ma?"

She was afraid her tossing and turning had also been keeping Billy awake.

"I don't want to," he said. "I like living here. I like my friends. I like Angus, and Mr. Austin, and Brett, and, well, a whole bunch of people. Mr. Chadwick paid us boys a penny each to sweep out the jail cells now that those outlaws are all gone. And Mr. Gallagher gave us each an extra licorice stick 'cause we were so well behaved while spending our pennies at the mercantile."

"You told me that." Even as she smiled, she had to warn him, "And you remember what I said, don't you?"

"Yeah, that I can't spend all my money on candy."

"That's right."

His sigh was filled with contentment rather than exasperation. "I won't. Wanna know why?"

"Why?"

"Because I wanna show it to Tom. I bet he'll be proud of me. And happy that we swept out the cells. That's what Mr. Chadwick said, and I believe him. You believe him, too, don't you, Ma?"

Even with all the uncertainty filling her, she was confident about a few things. "Yes, I do. Tom will be proud of you."

"He'll be proud that I did what he said, too. I told my friends that Pa had robbed that train, but that he wouldn't ever do that again 'cause Tom and me and you were the good guys and he was the bad guy. That's when I told them we're going to live here, forever and ever. I wasn't lying, Ma." After a quiet moment, he asked, "Was I? We don't have to go back to Uncle Walter's house, do we?"

As hard as she tried, she couldn't figure out a way to answer that.

"I'm sure the Ryans are taking good care of Nellie and Bess," Billy said. "Those cows probably already made friends with the Ryans' cows. And Mr. Ryan said he'd go fetch the chickens, so we ain't got nothing to worry about. Do we?"

Wanting him to never have to worry, she said, "I'm sure Nellie and Bess are fine, as well as the chickens." With her own conscience twisting inside her, she said, "But we did say we'd be back for them."

"Couldn't we write them a letter? Tell them we like it here?"

"That was our home for a long time. Won't you miss it?"

"Heck, no. There was nothing to do there. No one to play with."

Clara could relate to how he compared Uncle Walter's

homestead to Oak Grove. She held many of the same opinions. Although she'd called it home, it had felt more like a prison.

"We don't have to worry about strangers here, Ma." There was a tremble in his voice. "You remember them, don't you? The ones who rode with—"

"Hush, now," she said, wrapping both arms around him. "You're right—we don't have to worry about strangers." While hugging Billy close, trying to ease his fears, her own filled her with the speed and fury of a flash flood. Her being here, in this quaint, peaceful little town, could cause more destruction than the river had this spring. Everyone still talked about how the river had flooded a few months ago and how the town had come together, under Tom's guidance, to keep everyone safe.

His bullet-centered badge appeared before her eyes, and she pulled her eyelids open, hoping to chase the image away, but it wouldn't leave. That badge may not be enough to protect him from another bullet shot his way because of her. Hugh had never worked alone. There had always been others, and as soon as they learned what had happened, they'd come looking for her. Their revenge would include Tom. That scared her like nothing ever had.

Over the next couple of days, the fear inside her grew like a snowball rolling down a hill. She kept it hidden, but that didn't stop it from becoming so large it consumed her, while awake and sleeping. The nightmares were the worst. Those of Tom gunned down and the entire town blaming her, rightfully so. And blaming Billy. That nearly gutted her.

She pretended it didn't. Kept a smile on her face and went about as if she was the happiest person on earth, cooking and cleaning at the hotel, making friends, even attending a quilting club meeting with Fiona Blackwell.

That was where she was, midafternoon on a sunny day, when the train whistle sounded and shortly afterward, Billy burst into Martha's dress shop, along with Fiona's boys, Rollie's two sons and Dr. Graham's son, around the same age as the others.

"Sheriff Baniff's back!" Kade yelled.

"He sure enough is, Ma," Billy exclaimed. "Tom's back. Saw him with my own eyes!"

Trying to conceal her face from glowing as brightly as Billy's, or turning red from his casual use of Tom's first name, Clara said, "That's nice." Then, knowing she'd never be able to sew a single stitch with her trembling hands, she added, "I suspect I should go see if there are any passengers needing something to eat."

"I'll be along shortly to help with the dishes," Bella said. "I'm almost finished with this block."

The club was sewing a quilt for the young bride who'd been shot. She'd agreed to marry Jules Carmichael and the wedding was set for next Saturday. Julia had just announced her decision last night. However, the quilting club was almost done with the quilt because they'd known Julia would decide on one of the many men hoping for her hand in marriage. Clara hadn't realized how many bachelors lived in and around Oak Grove until she'd started cooking at the hotel and feeding most of them.

"No hurry," she said to Bella. The boys had already

left the shop and her feet were itching to move just as fast as theirs had. "I can manage."

"I know you can," Bella said, "but I also need to get ready for my afternoon walk with Josiah."

The mayor and Bella spent every afternoon together, and that may be part of the reason why Clara had a hard time convincing herself things couldn't change. No one had thought the mayor would ever get married, but it appeared he was thinking along those lines.

If the mayor could marry, then maybe Tom— She stopped her thoughts right there and responded to the others as they bade her farewell. Stepping out the door and onto the boardwalk, she willed her heart to stop racing at the prospect of seeing him. The sheriff's office was on the other side of town, giving her no reason whatsoever to walk anywhere near it on her way to the hotel, which was only three blocks up the street.

The boys, all six of them, were clustered together a short distance ahead, near the opening between the saddle shop and the hardware store. When they saw her coming, they took off between the buildings, laughing and squealing. The church was back that way, as well as the open meadow they liked to play in, but their antics had her curious and a bit suspicious as to what they'd been doing. They'd captured a little bull snake yesterday and brought it into the hotel to show her. One of the girls who helped serve food during the supper hour had dropped two bowls full of stew at the sight of it.

Eyeing the ground closely as she drew nearer, Clara felt her heart leap into her throat when someone stepped out of the opening between the buildings. She pressed a hand to the base of her throat as her eyes quickly raced upward from the pair of men's boots, her entire insides bursting when her eyes connected with his. She had never felt such joy, such happiness, at seeing someone. The desire to run forward and leap into his arms, kissing him and hugging him, filled every ounce of her being.

Trying to conceal that was nearly impossible. This was the man who made her believe there was goodness in the world. Hope. Love. Swallowing hard, she tried to keep her smile small. "Hello, Sheriff."

"Hello, Clara," Tom replied. "It's good to see you."

Her cheeks were nearly hot enough to fry eggs. "It's good to see you, too."

He had both hands in his pockets and was rocking back and forth on his heels. "Billy said you were down at Martha's dress shop."

The desire to reach out and touch him, just to make sure he was real, and fine, and right before her, was driving her insane. Unable to keep them still, she used both hands to smooth her dress over her sides. "I—I was. We—they are sewing a quilt for Julia." Suddenly, she couldn't stop talking. "She's marrying Jules Carmichael next Saturday. Announced it just last night. Well, actually the mayor announced it, but Julia and Jules were there. As were many others. The quilt is beautiful. A unique pattern I've never seen before." His smile said he knew she was jabbering, so she forced herself to stop before she looked like a babbling fool. "I thought I'd better check to see if any of the train passengers are hungry."

The wind had whipped several strands of hair across her face, and her chatting had made a clump stick to her lips. She reached up to remove it at the same time he did. He was faster, and after pushing aside her hair, he clasped her hand.

"I was the only passenger to get off the train," he said. "And I could use a cup of coffee."

The warmth and gentle strength of his hand sent a tender wave of calm throughout her system. At ease, tranquil, she said, "I can make a fresh pot."

"That would be wonderful," he said.

He released her hand, but held her elbow as they started walking. Feeling much better, far more relaxed, she asked, "How was your trip?"

"Non-eventful," he replied. "Which was nice."

"I'm sure it was, after everything." She bit the end of her tongue, chiding herself for referring to all that had happened.

"How were things here?"

"Good. Busy." She went on to tell him about working for Rollie, and about the snake incident yesterday. They were both laughing when they crossed the main road to the hotel.

"Tom! Heard you were back!" Josiah stepped out of his law office. "I'm anxious to hear how it went."

As Josiah stepped onto the boardwalk, Angus appeared, almost as if out of nowhere. "Mayor," Angus said. "I need to speak with you."

"Later, Angus. I have to meet with Tom right—"

"That will have to wait," Angus said. "It's about my

will. Never know when I'll keel over. I'm not getting any younger, you know."

There wasn't a person for miles around who wasn't curious as to what would happen to his money when Angus did finally have that funeral he'd planned, including the mayor, who hoped the town would be the beneficiary.

"I'll catch up with you later, Tom," Josiah said, waving for Angus to enter the law office.

"Nothing's changed," Tom said, urging her forward by pressing a hand on her lower back.

She liked how he did little things like that. It made her feel protected. Her stomach hiccuped then because she knew there was nothing she could do to protect him.

Tom had looked forward to this moment. He'd known he'd be happy to see Clara. Thankful, too, that all was well. But he hadn't imagined how right it would be. He'd just said nothing had changed, and it hadn't. Nor would it. The ride home had given him plenty of time to think. About him. About her. Even about Billy.

When he'd been at her place, he'd wanted to convince her to leave, to understand her strength and resilience could be put to use elsewhere, making a better life for her and Billy. He'd also vowed to go back and get her, and would have, too, if she hadn't come to Oak Grove on her own. She was here now, and so was he, and he had no idea what to do.

"Have a seat," she said. "I'll go make that coffee."

"Sheriff," Rollie said, walking out of the door on the far side of the dining room. "So glad to see you're back."

"It's good to be back," he said, watching Clara walk away. It was good to be back, but that didn't change the fact that he wasn't what Clara needed. She needed a man who didn't have to come back because he'd never left. Wasn't delivering outlaws to prisons or chasing them down.

"How will I ever thank you?" Rollie asked. "Not only for catching that bank robber, but for what you did for me the other night, and how you brought Clara here, to Oak Grove, just when we all needed her the most. Sadie feels the same way." Holding both hands out, he said, "Your meals are free from now on."

"Thanks, Rollie, but that's not necessary."

"Oh, but I must do something."

Tom glanced toward the door Clara had entered. "You already are," he said. "You're helping out Clara and Billy. He told me that you're paying him for his work."

"I most certainly am, but it's the other way around. Clara and Billy are helping me out. Billy's a good boy. I'm hoping some of it rubs off on Kade and Wiley."

"I guess it all depends on which side you're standing when you look at things," Tom said.

"I suspect so." Rollie nodded toward the door. "Clara making you something to eat?"

"Just some coffee."

After glancing toward the living quarters, Rollie said, "I'm on my way over to the mercantile while Sadie and the baby are sleeping. Do you mind?"

"Not at all," Tom answered. "Go ahead." He didn't even wait to see if Rollie left the dining room before he walked to the kitchen and opened the door.

"I'll bring the coffee out to you," Clara said, setting things on a tray. "I have some cherry pie. Thought you might like some."

He'd have given anything to be able to hug her out there on the street, and again right now. Thoughts along those lines had lived inside him night and day since he'd left town. He'd considered both sides of things, the ins and outs, the good and bad, and ultimately ended up in the same spot every time. Damned if he did and damned if he didn't. The one thing that held true was history. He was thirty years old, and in all those years he hadn't needed the things she made him think about. Therefore, he must not really need them, and could survive without them. Furthermore, he had no right to believe she wanted any of the things he'd been contemplating.

During the train ride home, he'd thought about a lot of things. Including how she'd blushed when he'd winked at her before leaving. That reminded him of his parents, and the love they'd shared. That was when it had hit him. He loved Clara. Loved everything about her. So much, he wanted her to be happy, safe, and cared for far beyond anything that he wanted.

She'd just gotten rid of one husband, and probably didn't want anything to do with the idea of another one. In fact, she was still married. He'd meant to ask the judge about that, but had never worked up the courage. It had been the first time in his life that had happened, but truth be told, it was none of his business. No law was being broken, so there was no justification for him to even inquire about how she'd go about divorcing Hugh.

"It looks good," he said. The pie probably did. He really hadn't noticed because, unfortunately, they most likely wouldn't have much privacy, so he needed to get right to the point. The reason he'd told himself he had to find her as soon as he arrived in town. "I told Judge Alfords that I'd let you know about the reward money."

She spun around and walked to the stove, and he could swear he'd seen the shine completely leave her eyes.

"It's still yours." He'd been glad that the judge reminded him of the reward the slaughterhouse had put up. She'd more than earned it from all those years of putting up with Hugh. It had been interesting, too, the way the judge made sure Hugh knew who was collecting the dead-or-alive reward on his head. "The confirmation of his conviction has been sent to the slaughterhouse's lawyers and they'll notify Micah Swift at the bank when to expect the funds to pay you."

She still hadn't turned around, so he continued, "Alfords said he'd contact you about the reward for the coins. He said the government is slow when it comes to releasing money." He hadn't known anything about that reward, but she deserved it, too.

After pouring coffee into a cup, she turned about and carried it to him. Her hand shook slightly as she held out the cup. "I don't want either of those rewards."

He took the cup and set it on the table. "Why not? They're yours."

"No, they're not." She stepped around the table and

ran a hand along the edge, never looking up at him. "You captured Hugh. I didn't. And as for the other one, maybe the government should give it to the Indians for tricking them in the first place."

"I can't accept rewards," he said. "No lawman can. As for the other one, the government will never do that."

"Well, I can't accept it, either."

"Why not?" He rounded the table and took her shoulders, twisting her so she had to look at him. "That money can change your life and Billy's."

"Maybe," she said. "But not really." She was shaking her head. "The only people who can change Billy's life and mine are Billy and me." She shrugged. "With or without money."

He understood the truth in her words, but not her refusal. She'd earned that money. Most people were standing at his door to collect their reward before the ink was put to paper. She had to see reason in this. He had to make her see it. "Clara—"

She held up one hand and backed away from him, out of his hold. "I've thought about this, Tom. Ever since Judge Alfords told me about it, and I can't take it." She rubbed her cheeks with both hands. "It feels wrong, and I'm tired of feeling wrong. From now on, I'm going to earn what I receive."

"But you earned this."

"No, I didn't. If I'd told you where Hugh was. If I'd—"

"But you didn't know."

"Exactly." She huffed out a breath and walked around

him. "Because I didn't want to know. I was too weak. Too scared. Too selfish."

"No—"

"Yes, I was. I was petrified every time I saw someone riding up the road. And not just because I thought it might be Hugh or one of the men he rode with. I was afraid it might be the law, and that they'd arrest me. All I could think was what would happen to Billy?" She'd paced to the stove and turned back. "Well, I know what would have happened to him. The same thing that happened to my parents and to Uncle Walter."

There were no tears on her face, in her eyes, just a cold anger he hadn't seen coming from her before.

"There," she said, tossing her hands in the air. "I've said it. I've known who killed my parents and Walter for years, but didn't dare say it. Hugh. The father of my son killed them. He acted like they were accidents. That my parents had been attacked by Indians and that Walter had fallen in a ravine, but I knew that's not what had happened. It wasn't Indians. It was Hugh's friends. I recognized them. Had seen them in the town we'd passed through two days before, and he'd been with them." She closed her eyes and growled slightly. "And I heard the shot that killed Uncle Walter."

His insides were twisting themselves into knots, aching for her. She'd been through so much and deserved a peaceful, uncomplicated life from here on out. "You were only protecting yourself," he said. "By not saying anything—"

"By not saying anything, I let it go on. And on. And still would be if you hadn't shown up."

There was anger and accusation in her tone, enough to slightly curdle his stomach.

"By not saying anything, I was letting people die," she said, pacing the floor again. "And now I have to make sure it doesn't start up again. I can't ever again let someone I love die on account of me."

"Nothing's going to happen to Billy." Wanting to chase those thoughts as far from her mind as possible, he said, "We were talking about your reward money, Clara. The money you deserve because—"

"Don't you see, Tom?" She'd stopped right before him. "That money's blood money, and will connect me to Hugh as much as any money he stole. I won't take it. No one can make me."

She was so strong in her conviction, in her belief, that he had to agree with her, at least partially. "You're right. No one can force you to take it." He grasped her hand. "But you're also wrong. Nothing is going to happen to Billy. Or you. Trust me, Hugh's in prison. It's over."

Shaking her head, she whispered, "That's where you're wrong, Tom. It's not over. It'll never be over. Not for me and Billy, and that's why we have to leave here."

Stunned, for he sincerely didn't expect to hear that, he asked, "Leave? And go where?"

"Home." She lifted her chin, but it quivered as she spoke. "That's the only place I'll ever belong."

Frustrated because that was the last place he wanted her to go, he said, "Clara, you need—"

"I need," she said firmly, seriously, "to get as far away from you as possible."

Chapter Sixteen

Days later, Clara was still sick to her stomach. She hadn't meant to blurt it out like that, but as she'd stood in the kitchen, with Tom holding her hand, her thoughts and feelings had gotten all mixed up. She'd thought long and hard about the reward money before he'd come home, and had decided not to take it, but it wasn't until that moment in the kitchen with him that she fully realized what had happened to her during all the time she'd been trying to figure out what to do with her life and how to go about it.

She'd fallen in love with Tom.

Although she'd never known just how strongly a woman could love a man, she did now. It was undeniable, and powerful, and all consuming. Every time she caught a glimpse of him. Every time she thought about him, she thought she might break inside. But she couldn't. She couldn't give in, couldn't start to tell herself that even a few days in his arms would be worth what would eventually happen. For it would happen. Hugh had warned her. His threats had always come true in the past. And they would again.

Because she loved Tom, would always love him, she couldn't let that happen to him or to the people of Oak Grove, who had been so good to her. Whether she divorced Hugh or not, her past wouldn't change. Everyone she'd loved had died because of her. Therefore, she couldn't love anyone ever again. Getting as far away from Tom as possible was the only way to stop the feelings that grew stronger inside her every day.

Although Sadie was up and about and the baby was doing fine, Rollie had asked her to stay on cooking, earning a wage, until the baby was old enough for Sadie to return to the kitchen. He didn't say how long, and Clara didn't ask, but figured it would only be a few more weeks.

She was being selfish in that aspect, too, because seeing Tom, even from afar, was better than not seeing him at all. Which in itself was dangerous, for she wouldn't be able to keep seeing him for long. Within three weeks, she'd have enough money for her and Billy to travel home and pay back the Ryans what she'd borrowed.

A heavy sigh left her chest. She'd told Billy last night that they'd be leaving in a few weeks. He'd been talking about going to school here when summer ended, and she couldn't let him get his hopes up for that. He'd been furious, and said he wouldn't go, but this morning, upon seeing the other boys, had run off to play like every other day.

"Clara! Clara!"

Turning, she watched Sadie walk into the kitchen.

"These were just delivered for you." Sadie held up two envelopes.

There was no mystery in whom they were from.

Judge Alfords. Clara covered the bread she'd just set to rise with a cloth. "You can set them on the table."

"I can finish in here while you go read your letters," Sadie said. "Altina is sleeping. She's such a good baby."

"Yes, she is," Clara agreed.

"And you are the best employee we've ever had." Sadie handed her the envelopes. "Go read these and relax a bit. You make me feel guilty doing so much."

Clara took the letters. "Don't feel guilty. You just had a baby."

"Weeks ago, and because of your help, I'm fine now." Sadie waved a hand toward the door.

Clara left the kitchen and went upstairs to her room. She'd written to the judge, asking him to decline the reward on her behalf. This would be his response.

The first letter was from Judge Alfords, but it made no mention of the reward. Instead it held a divorce decree, releasing her from all connections to Hugh. The judge had also penned a letter explaining the second decree concerned Billy. It stated that if the time ever came that she remarried, her new husband could legally claim Billy as his child, giving him a new last name.

A sense of finality washed over her, but so did sorrow. There was only one man she'd ever consider marrying, and she couldn't do that.

Setting that envelope aside, knowing she didn't have the wherewithal to go down the path her mind wanted to, she picked up the second one.

It was a letter from Karen Ryan.

Clara had barely made it through the opening pleasantries when she heard someone shouting her name.

Jumping off the bed at the urgency that rippled her spine, she ran to the door.

"Clara! Clara, come quick!"

Hitching up her skirt, she ran for the stairs and started down them. Sadie stood at the bottom, wringing her hands together.

"What? What is it?"

"It's Billy," Sadie said, glancing toward the doorway.

Racing down the last few steps, Clara asked, "What's happened? Where is he?" As she leaped off the bottom step, she saw Kade standing in the doorway with a dirty, tearstained face.

Clara's heart clenched. "Where's Billy?"

"Sheriff Baniff carried him to Dr. Graham's house."

Without waiting for the boy to say more, she ran out the door and all the way to the doctor's office. Others stood outside the doctor's house, including Brett and Fiona.

"They'd tried climbing the bell tower on the church," Fiona said. "Tom's in there with him."

Clara started to step around the couple, but Brett took a hold of her arm. "Tom said you should wait—"

"Like hell." She twisted out of his hold and bounded up the steps, throwing open the door.

A scream she recognized as Billy's came through a doorway on the other side of the room just as Sylvia Graham grabbed her by both arms.

"Let go," Clara shouted, trying to get away from the woman who wasn't any bigger than her.

"No," Sylvia said. "Billy's going to be fine, but his

leg is broken. The sheriff is holding him down while Nelson sets it."

Billy screamed again and Clara fought against Sylvia's hold. She'd never not been able to get to her son when he needed her. "Please! Please, let me go to him."

"In a minute," Sylvia said. "Billy will be stronger with the two men in there than you. Clara, look at me. Tommy broke his ankle last spring, so I promise Billy will be fine."

Clara knew Tommy still walked with a limp from the broken ankle, and understanding that not that long ago Sylvia had felt the exact way she did right now, Clara wrapped her arms around the other woman.

"He's going to be fine," Sylvia whispered. "Just fine."

Tom kept one eye on the door, praying that Clara wouldn't barrel through it at any moment. He'd seen a lot in his life, but never a leg twisted around like Billy's had been. Having just left Wolf's gun shop, he'd grabbed a hold of Wyatt to ask what was wrong as the boy had run across the street, shouting for his pa. Tom's stomach had landed in his boots when Wyatt had said that Billy was hurt.

The story he got from the boys was that Billy didn't want to leave Oak Grove so was going to hide out in the bell tower, and the rest of them would bring him food. Of course, all six of them had to try climbing the church bell tower first. Even Tommy, who had already broken one ankle so badly he'd walk with a limp for the rest of his life. When this was over, and Billy was fine, he'd give all six of those boys a talking-to, might even make them spend a night in jail, just so they'd think twice about pulling a stunt like that again.

"That's it," Nelson said. "You can let him up a bit now, but keep him still while I tie on some slats to hold it in place."

Tom may never have been more relieved. Holding Billy down while Doc twisted his leg all the way back around and then set the bone had hurt him dang near as bad as it had Billy.

He'd released the pressure holding Billy down, but the boy didn't let go of his arms. Instead he squeezed them harder.

"That hurt, Tom," Billy said, tears still falling.

"I know it, buddy," he said, resting his forehead against Billy's. "And I'm afraid it's going to for a while longer. Doc Graham has to bandage it up yet."

"It already feels better, though," Billy said.

"That's good," Tom answered, rising up slightly.

"We don't have to tell Ma about this, do we?"

Tom had to smile, and nod. "Yes, we do. Matter of fact, she already knows." Having heard her earlier, he added, "She's out in the other room."

Billy's head slumped farther against the pillow. "Can someone with a broken leg ride on a train?"

Tom's insides hardened as he said, "Yes." Then, wanting to hear it from Billy, asked, "Why?"

"Ma says we gotta leave here, Tom, and I don't want to."

Not willing to express his thoughts on that, Tom said, "Climbing the bell tower wasn't a good idea no matter what your mother said. And you'd better never try it again."

"I won't. I promise." With eyes full of sadness, Billy asked, "You aren't mad at me, are you, Tom?"

He was mad, but not at Billy. Standing up, just to put a bit more authority behind his words, Tom said, "I'm disappointed that you tried such a stunt, and I'm sad that you're hurt, but I'm not mad."

Billy nodded and wiped at his eyes with both fists.

"All done," Doc said. "The break was just above the knee—that's why it looked so bad. Luckily, it was a clean break. But he'll need to stay in bed for at least a week, to make sure that bone reattaches." Looking down at Billy, Doc continued, "And you'll need to wear these splints until I say. A good six weeks at least."

"I will. I promise."

Doc nodded before glancing at him. "I'll go get his mother now."

That gave Tom a moment to brace himself. He hadn't seen Clara since she'd said she had to get as far away from him as possible. To say that had gutted him was an understatement. It had completely disemboweled him. But shouldn't have. He'd already decided that he wasn't what she needed and he should have been glad that she'd felt that way, too.

But he wasn't. He wasn't glad about anything.

The door opened and her tear-filled eyes met his for a moment before she rushed to Billy's side. Tom stepped aside and kept his thoughts and opinions to himself while Nelson explained the accident and the break, as well as the healing requirements.

"I'll ask Brett to have Wally bring a wagon over from the livery to haul Billy to the hotel," Nelson said.

Tom thought about following him out, but couldn't make his feet do it. Seeing her, the desire to go to her, hold her, tell her Billy would be fine, was twisting his insides into knots. That irritated him. He shouldn't care about her. Shouldn't love her. She'd said she wanted to be as far away from him as possible, but not other men. Every single man in town ate at the hotel, some of them three meals a day, and they gushed about her cooking. He'd heard it, seen it, and it made him mad as hell. If she wanted to leave, then she already should have.

A couple of minutes later, the doctor was back. "There are a few boys out here who want to see the patient. Is that all right?"

"Yes," Clara said.

With his frustration building, Tom waited until the boys had walked into the room, as meek as he'd ever seen them, yet full of empathy for their friend. Then he walked to the foot of the bed and pulled Clara into the other room.

"This wouldn't have happened if you'd gone home already," he hissed. "Why haven't you?"

Anger snapped in her eyes, which was fine with him. She could get as mad as she wanted and it still wouldn't outbeat the fury inside him. If she was gone, Billy wouldn't be hurt and he wouldn't have to look at her, wish she cared as much about him as he did her.

Keeping her voice low, she answered, "Because I promised Rollie I wouldn't until Sadie—"

Anger flared inside him. "Then why'd you tell Billy you were?"

"Because we will be, soon." She shook her head. "I didn't want him to get his hopes up about going to school here."

"So you'd rather he broke his leg instead?"

"No! I—"

"He doesn't want to leave, so was going to hide out in the bell tower. The others were going to bring him food."

"What?"

"You heard me." They were still whispering, which was hard when he wanted to shout.

"Who told you that?"

"He did, and so did the other boys. There was no reason to tell him you were leaving until it was time to go." Getting madder by the second, he added, "There's no reason to keep hanging around here, either, giving others hope that you might stay."

She twisted hard enough he had to break his hold or physically hurt her.

Taking a step back, she asked, "What are you talking about? Giving who hope?"

"Oh, pretending you don't know again?" On a roll, releasing the rage that was tearing at him, he continued, "Why do you think every bachelor for a hundred miles around is eating at the hotel three times a day? They want a wife, and besides you, Bella's the only eligible woman left in town. No man wants to marry a woman twice as big and mean as they are."

If he'd seen anger before, he now saw outrage almost as strong as what lived inside him.

"You are the most rude, ignorant man on earth. How dare you speak about Bella like that. How dare you—"

Cutting her off, he hissed, "Oh, that coming from a woman married to an outlaw. How dare you let those men think you're available when you're still married?"

"Get. Out. Of. Here."

Giving her a sneer as glaring as the one she was giving him, he said, "I can't. I need to carry Billy up to his room."

"I'll ask Mr. Blackwell to do that," she snapped. "Or one of the other men who aren't as downright nasty and mean as you." Lifting her chin, she marched around him and into Billy's room.

"Fine, do that," he muttered, knowing she couldn't hear. He didn't care, either. Not one ounce.

He wasn't even out the door before admitting he was lying, and being an ass.

Brett was on the front porch. "Wagon's here. I'll get those boys out of there."

Tom nodded, and followed a few steps back into the room where he grabbed a blanket off the sofa.

"That's what I was coming for," Sylvia Graham said. "I'll take it out while you get Billy."

Tom was about to protest when he heard Billy.

"Where's Tom? Why can't he carry me?"

"Right here," he said while crossing from the outer room. Once in the examination room, he didn't look at Clara. Couldn't. He hadn't meant to be so mean, to say such hateful things, and was ashamed by his behavior. "It'll take both Brett and me. We have to keep that leg straight and steady."

Fiona ushered the other boys out of the room and Clara held the doors open, and kept the path to the wagon clear. Once Billy was settled in the back, Wally set the horse moving forward at a slow and steady pace. Tom walked on one side, Clara on the other, and though she spoke often to Billy, she never looked his way once.

He couldn't blame her.

At the hotel, Brett once again helped him carry Billy inside and up the stairs. Clara ran ahead to open the door to their room. Walking backward, Tom had to keep glancing over his shoulder, and each time he saw her face, the blood in his veins ran colder. She no longer looked mad, more like heartbroken. And that pained him like nothing ever had.

Billy was quickly settled, and people cleared out of the room with well wishes and promises to visit soon. Tom stayed put.

"You can leave, too," Clara said.

"I'll help you get his clothes off." Nelson had cut the pant leg open just like she'd done his to see to his wound. "Don't want him jostled too much."

She stood at the door. Holding it open. "I can manage."

"Clara—"

"Don't you think you've already said enough? I do."

Billy was looking at both of them curiously, and Tom, knowing she was right, patted the boy's hand. "I'll stop by to see you tomorrow."

"All right," Billy said, still glancing between him and Clara. "'Bye, Tom."

"'Bye, buddy."

As he walked out the door, she hissed, "Don't bother stopping by."

The click of the door felt like a slam.

Holding the doorknob, Clara couldn't move. She was numb, inside and out. The anger that had run hot enough to blister her earlier was gone and the pain left behind was too much to bear, so she pretended it wasn't there. Just like she had so many other pains, so many other things.

"Ma?"

She turned around, and though she should, she couldn't even muster up a fake smile.

"You're really mad at me, aren't you?"

Leaning against the door, giving herself time, she said, "I'm not happy about what happened, and I'm very sad that you were hurt, but I'm not mad."

"Why not?"

"Because I'm too sad." Pushing off the door, she walked to the side of the bed and sat in the chair. Sad wasn't the only thing she felt. Guilt completely filled her. "You could have been hurt worse than a broken leg." Hoping Tom had been wrong, she asked, "What possessed you to climb the bell tower?"

He bowed his head. "I don't want to leave. I like it here. I was going to hide in the bell tower until you left."

Taking a hold of one of his hands, she asked, "Do you think I would have left without you?"

He shrugged and wiped at his eyes. "No, but I didn't know what else to do."

She didn't know what else to do, either. "Well, climbing the bell tower was not a good idea."

"That's what Tom said." Billy sighed. "I didn't mean to make you sad, Ma." Looking up at her, he said, "I didn't mean to get hurt, but leaving here makes me sad."

"I know, and I didn't mean to make you sad, either. And I certainly didn't want you to get hurt." But he had gotten hurt, and it was her fault. She was pretty sure Tom hadn't meant to hurt her, either, but he had. And that was her fault, too. She shouldn't have told Billy, and she shouldn't still be here. The one thing she hadn't wanted to happen was for someone else to get hurt, yet that was exactly what had happened.

A knock sounded on the door, and she considered not opening it. Was still contemplating if she should or not when it cracked open and Sadie poked her head around the door. "I brought up some warm milk. Figured it would help him sleep."

"Thank you," Clara said.

Sadie set the tray on the dresser and then wrapped her arms around Clara. "It's hard seeing those we love hurt, in pain."

Clara didn't trust herself to speak.

"All we can do is love them more," Sadie whispered. "Just love them more."

Clara nodded and stepped out of the hug before the tears pressing hard to be released won the battle and broke loose.

"I'll help you get his clothes off," Sadie said.

Clara didn't decline the help, was indeed thankful for the assistance. Sadie didn't leave until Billy was settled beneath the covers and had emptied the glass of milk. In no time at all, Billy was asleep, and Clara, sitting in the chair, let the tears fall.

They fell until she felt completely empty and sore, and then she laid her head on the table as a few more tears fell. When those tears dried up, she sat up and looked at her son. No matter what she tried to do, it turned out wrong. So wrong.

Knowing sitting here wouldn't help anyone, not her, not Billy, not Tom, she rose. Dr. Graham had said Billy would sleep for most of the day, and ultimately, needing even more funds now in order to pay the doctor, she washed her face and went downstairs to help with the evening meal.

Sadie, Rollie and Bella all tried to send her back upstairs, but she insisted there wasn't anything she could do. Sitting by the bed wouldn't make Billy heal any faster, and she'd left the door open to hear if he called.

They finally gave in and let her get to work, first peeling potatoes and then frying pan after pan of chicken.

Hours later, there were only a few pieces left, meaning any late eaters would have to settle for something else, when Sadie tapped her shoulder. "Altina's been fed and sound asleep. I'll take over."

Clara started to say no, but concern for Billy filled her.

Sadie must have sensed that because she said, "Billy's sleeping. I checked on him, too. You are the one who needs to rest now."

Clara was exhausted, but sleep wasn't going to help. Her body wasn't tired. It was her mind, and heart. With a nod, she walked over to hang up her apron.

"On your way through the dining room, stop at table four," Bella said. "They want to compliment the cook."

A sickening sensation rippled her stomach. She'd never made the connection of the men eating at the hotel like Tom had, and really didn't want, in any way, to encourage any of them to think she might possibly be interested in getting married again. She wasn't and never would be.

She peeked out the door, and a smile touched her lips as her eyes settled on table number four. Angus waved. She crossed the room and stopped at his table. Of all the people in Oak Grove, she would miss him the most. Well, second most.

"Compliment the cook?" she asked.

His eyes sparkled as brightly as his silver hair. "I just checked on the lad. He's sound asleep." Reaching over, he pulled out a chair. "And you know I don't like eating alone." With a grin, he pointed to the extra plate at his table. "You never know which meal might be my last."

"Angus O'Leary," she said. "You're too sly for even your Maker."

He chuckled. "Wouldn't that be dandy? Eat up, lass, while it's still hot. That's some of the best fried chicken that ever crossed my lips."

"Thank you, but I can't. Billy has to be hungry by now."

"Well, then, I must admit, I had Bella give me a helping for the lad, and sat with him while he ate it."

"You did?"

"I did."

"Fried chicken is his favorite."

"He said that." Angus shook his head. "I dare say, when it comes to wee ones, lads that is, there is very little left to the imagination. Why, if me own dear sweet ma knew about all the things I did as a lad, all the things I climbed, I may not be here to tell you about it."

"I can believe you were a handful." Sitting down, she added, "And that you had her as wrapped around your finger as you do most of the women in town."

"Aw, you're a smart one, on to me already."

The wink of his aging eye made her giggle. "As are you."

His expression grew thoughtful. "You know what I've learned, lass? That there are some people who are just plain mean and nasty for no real reason, and then there are those who are kind and sincere, but when something happens and they're hurting, or they believe someone they care about is hurting, they can say things that they wouldn't otherwise say. Do things, too."

"If you're referring to—"

"I'm not referring to anyone, other than meself."

Certain he'd been talking about Tom, she asked, "You?"

"Yes." Nodding and frowning, he said, "Me."

"What did you do?"

He leaned back in his chair and cast a sorrowful gaze her way. "I may have started a rumor."

"A rumor? You?"

"Yes."

Having not heard anything out of the ordinary or any spiteful gossip, she asked, "What sort of rumor?"

"Well, lass, I've gotten quite attached to you and your

lad, and after learning from our own mayor that you will be receiving a reward, well, I got to worry that you might be considering leaving our quaint little town." Letting out a heavy sigh, he said, "So, I may have made mention that you might be looking for a new husband."

"You didn't."

"I may have."

"May or did?"

"A man who's never been in love before does funny things, because he's not thinking straight. It's that way for women, too. Kind of like a dog that's eating something it shouldn't and someone reaches down to grab it away. They're gonna get bit. Folks say you can't blame the dog. That you gotta blame the person. Yet the person didn't know any better, either, 'cause they were just as focused on what the dog was eating as the dog was. So, my question is, what was that dog chewing on anyway?"

Clara shook her head, trying to grasp what he had said, and the meaning behind it. Then it hit. The *dog* he referred to was chewing on things she'd said. Tom was hurting because of what she said. Billy was hurt because of what she said. Things that had hurt them. She of all people knew inner wounds could hurt worse and take longer to heal than outside wounds. She owed them both more than an apology. She owed them the truth.

Angus grinned and sighed. "The truth will set you free."

Chapter Seventeen

Tom sat at his desk, twirling his badge between his thumb and finger. He'd blamed Clara for Billy's accident, and that was as wrong as everything else he'd done. In fact, he hadn't done a whole lot right lately.

Stopping the badge from spinning, he held it by one point, staring at the bullet lodged in the center. The new one he'd ordered had arrived, but he hadn't pinned it on yet. This old badge may have saved his life, but it was also the reason that bullet had been fired at him.

He flipped the badge around a couple of times. It wasn't very big, but he'd been hiding behind this tiny hunk of metal for years. Julia's death was the reason he'd first pinned a badge on, because he'd wanted to catch her killer. And he'd kept one pinned on ever since because he'd never wanted to feel that sort of pain ever again. Behind that badge, he didn't need to feel. Behind that badge, everything was justifiable.

Over the years, he'd let this little chunk of metal grow until it fully encircled him. Consumed him. Made him believe the law, being a sheriff, gave him everything he needed, wanted. It had worked because there was something about a badge, about a lawman, that kept people at a distance. Even here, in Oak Grove. He was respected, even liked, but even here, everyone identified him as Sheriff Baniff, not Tom Baniff. He never minded that. It kept things neat and simple, and it gave him protection.

Until he met Clara. That little piece of metal may have stopped a bullet, but it hadn't been capable of stopping him from falling in love with her. It couldn't stop him from loving her, either.

Or from being jealous. Even before she'd woken up from her injury, he'd been jealous of Hugh Wilson. He hadn't realized it, nor would he have admitted it, but it was the truth. And he was jealous of all the men eating at the restaurant. Which was unjustified because they'd always eaten there.

The last two weeks of staying clear of her had been hell. He kept telling himself that was how it had to be. What she wanted. What he wanted. But it wasn't what he wanted. Not at all.

The walls of his office had become like a prison. He'd even come to hate this badge, blame it, but what he failed to realize was it wasn't the badge's fault. It was his.

A man was his own man no matter what his occupation. He'd told Clara she was strong enough to do whatever she wanted. Well, it was time he gave himself that same advice.

Tossing the badge onto his desk, he stood and walked

to the door. On the boardwalk, he nodded to those who looked his way, but kept his focus on the hotel up the road. The dinner rush had to be over by now. If not, he'd wait.

He was half a block away when Josiah walked out of the hotel, with Bella Armentrout on his arm. Tom's ears burned remembering the rude things he'd said about her. He hadn't meant them. He'd never stooped so low and never would again.

"Evening, Sheriff," Josiah said.

"Sheriff," Bella added.

"Evening."

"If you're hoping for some fried chicken, I'm afraid it's all gone," Bella said.

"I'm not hungry," Tom replied.

"Stop by my office tomorrow, will you?" Josiah asked. "That reward money should have already arrived for Mrs. Wilson. You need to check into that. With that kind of money, several men might be interested in marrying her."

Refusing to acknowledge another flare of jealousy at the idea of Clara marrying someone else, Tom said, "She refused the reward."

"What? Why?" Josiah asked.

"It was her choice." He had a choice, too. Tom stepped around them and entered the hotel.

"Oh, hello, Sheriff," Rollie said. "I'm sorry, but we're out of fried chicken. There is—"

"Where's Clara?"

Rollie's eyes grew wide as he pointed toward the stairs. Tom's heels didn't hit a step as he bounded up them. A moment of sensibility came to him as he arrived at her door. Billy was most likely sleeping, so he only knocked once, softly.

The door opened. Afraid Clara would close it again, he grasped her arm. "We need to talk."

"Excuse me, Sheriff."

Tom twisted. Angus hadn't been there a moment ago. How the old man could appear out of nowhere was almost as wearisome as his riddles. Just last week, he'd spouted one off about the way to a man's heart being through his stomach. Tom had caught on to that one quick enough, knowing Angus referred to Clara cooking for all the bachelors in town.

"The lad's sleeping, so why don't you and the lass use my room?" Angus had stepped around him and was already pushing the door open wider and shoving Clara out. "I'll sit with the lad."

The door to Angus's room was open, so Tom pulled Clara that way.

"Hold up," Angus said. "The lass dropped these."

Tom grabbed the envelopes in his free hand and ushered Clara into Angus's room with the other, then kicked the door shut.

"Still mad, I see."

His stomach fell. He tossed the envelopes on the table and let her loose. "I'm not mad. I'm—"

"Mad."

"Fine, I'm mad. But not at you. I'm mad at myself for the way I've acted. I apologize for what I said earlier." He took off his hat and ran a hand through his hair. What man in his right mind asked for this? Asked to fall in love? He sure hadn't, but he had. He'd fallen. Head over heels, *damned if I do, damned if I don't*, in love with her. Tossing his hat on the table, he said, "I didn't mean any of it, and shouldn't have treated you the way I did. I'm sorry. Very sorry."

She walked around the table, stopping on the opposite side from him. Then, without a word, she took the glass globe off the top of the lamp. He hoped that lighting the lamp was a signal she was willing to talk, because it wasn't that dark outside yet.

Once the flame was going, she replaced the globe and looked at him. "I'm sorry, too, Tom."

"For what?" He'd been the one in the wrong, not her. "You didn't—"

"Yes, I did. I said things I shouldn't have. They caused Billy to get hurt—"

"That was an accident." She had to understand that. "I should never have said that was your fault because it wasn't. Little boys get hurt. People get hurt. You can't be blaming yourself for that. No one can."

"I can, because it's true. And that's what scares me."

"There's nothing to be afraid of, Clara."

"There is for me." She turned and walked to the window. "Since the moment I met Hugh I've been afraid. With reason. He approached our wagon in a small town in Nebraska, told my father that for a fee he'd protect us from the Indians. When my father declined, he said, *'I warned you.'* Ever since then, he kept warning me. And those warnings kept coming true. My parents. Uncle Walter."

The fury Tom had hosted toward Hugh returned,

tenfold. Along with compassion for Clara. "He'll never hurt you again, Clara, I swear to you."

"He even had the dog killed because he'd warned me that anyone, anything, that tried to protect me would die."

She turned around. Tears rolled down her cheeks, and Tom wanted to kick himself for all the time he'd spent hiding behind his badge rather than letting her know what had been happening, how he'd been protecting her.

"That's what I'm afraid of, Tom, and why I said I had to get as far away from you as possible. I don't want you to die while protecting me."

"Hugh's in Leavenworth, with no hope of parole." He started to walk around the table, but she held up a hand.

"I know he is, but his warnings aren't." Walking to the table, she picked up one of the two envelopes and handed it to him. "I'd like you to read this."

He didn't want to read anything, but the pleading in her eyes made his spine tingle as he took the envelope. Opening it, he pulled out several folded pages. The first thing he did was flip to the last page to see whom it was from. There could be more going on in Wyoming than he was privy to.

The letter was from Karen Ryan. He glanced up at Clara.

"It arrived this afternoon," she said, "but I just read it a few minutes ago."

Tom read swiftly, past the niceties and assurances that the cows and chickens were fine. Then he slowed in order to catch each word about the men who'd stopped at the Ryans', looking for Clara and Billy, and about how Sheriff Puddicombe had been out to their place, too. Ultimately, Puddicombe had captured the men. The letter ended with Karen stating that as soon as they received the reward money for helping Puddicombe capture the men, they would like to buy Clara's ranch, if she was interested in selling it.

Tom had no sooner finished reading the last line when Clara said, "Hugh had warned me they'd come, and they did. And I'm sure there will be others."

"No, there won't be," Tom said. He'd already known most of what he'd just read, but hadn't told her because a lawman couldn't share information about an ongoing investigation. Which was nothing more than an excuse. One he was now ashamed of.

He laid the letter down on the table. "While in Hendersonville, I asked Puddicombe to be on the alert, and to inform the Montana authorities about the Double Bar-S. He did, and besides those men Karen Ryan wrote about, several others have been arrested. The Double Bar-S ranch foreman had been cycling stolen money, making it almost impossible to track. He's in jail, and if they haven't already been arrested, posses are on the trails of any gang he'd been working with."

She stared at the envelope for a few moments before looking up at him. "Why didn't you tell me any of this?"

"Because you'd already been through enough." As soon as he said the words, he knew it wasn't enough. Not for her or him. It was time he stopped hiding the truth. "And because I love you, Clara." He started to walk around the table. "I'm not sure how it happened, or when, but it did. I fell in love with you. And with my love comes my protection. Anyone who ever had anything to do with Hugh will never come near you again."

She covered her mouth with both hands as he rounded the table.

"I should have told you, but I didn't want to worry you, didn't want you to know until the last one has been caught." Stopping in front of her, he admitted, "Because I thought once that happened, once I knew for certain that you'd be safe, I could stop loving you. But I was wrong. That will never happen. I'll never stop loving you."

Clara kept both hands pressed against her mouth, afraid if she said a word, a single word, Tom might disappear. That this all was merely a dream. Taking a breath, she determined there was only one way to find out. Sliding her hands off her mouth, she said, "I'll never stop loving you, either, Tom." The smile that flashed across his face reminded her of the first time she'd seen him. The moment it had all begun. "Do you remember the morning I woke up, when you and Billy gave me breakfast in bed?"

He took both of her hands. "Yes."

"That was when I fell in love with you. You and he were eating breakfast in the other room and you were telling him the important things a man needed to know. You entered my heart right then and there, and haven't left since." Squeezing his hands tightly, she added, "That was also the moment I started fearing for your life."

She wasn't certain if he moved first or if she did, but

either way, they were in each other's arms. Holding on to one another as tightly as they could.

Tom kissed the top of her head, the side of her face, and then her lips. She hadn't realized how strong, how encompassing, her love for him was until that moment, when every ounce of her being became consumed by kissing him in return.

She was breathless and still wanted more when Tom ended the kiss and grasped her face with both hands.

"As soon as I got to Hendersonville, I sent a horse and wagon back for you, but you'd already left. Why?"

She wrapped her hands around his wrists. "Because not knowing wasn't enough," she admitted. "I had to know that you'd made it to Oak Grove safely. I hadn't even found those stolen items yet, didn't go looking for them until…"

"Until what?"

"Until I'd already decided to come to Oak Grove." She released his wrists to wrap her arms around his waist again. "It was just like you described. The town. The people."

He kissed the top of her head. "The choice is yours. We can stay here, or go back to Wyoming."

Leaning back, she asked, "Why would I want to go back to Wyoming?"

"Because you said it was home. If that's where you want to be, then that's where you should be." He shrugged. "It'll take a while to build up a herd of cattle, but I have money saved. We'll get by."

He was amazing. So wonderful and kind and caring, and unselfish. "I don't want to go back to Wyoming," she said. "I'll gladly sell my land to the Ryans. I fell in love with you because of who you are, and you are as much a part of this town as—" She glanced around the room. "Angus O'Leary. I would never expect you to give that up for me."

"There's nothing I wouldn't give up for you, Clara, nothing at all."

He was an honest man, and she didn't doubt his words in the least. Leaning against his chest again, she asked, "Oh, Tom, why have the past weeks been so awful? Why didn't we just admit we loved each other?"

"Because we were trying to protect each other," he said softly. "And ourselves. I thought I had everything I could ever want, until I met you and realized I didn't have a single thing I wanted. That scared me."

His admission had her hugging him tighter, even though she couldn't imagine him being afraid of anything.

"So I used my badge as protection."

Not understanding his meaning, she leaned back and looked up at him.

"As a sheriff I had reason to talk to you, offer my protection, correspond with Puddicombe, converse with Alfords. I couldn't do any of that as a regular man."

The seriousness in his tone and his eyes had her taking a step back. "Why not?"

He let out a heavy sigh and then nodded. "Because you're a married woman, Clara."

Relief washed over her so fast she wanted to giggle, but couldn't because he was being very serious and she could see his point of view. A lawman and a married woman taking up company could cause a scandal. Even in Oak Grove. A seriousness overtook her, too. There was something she sincerely wanted him to know. "I never wanted to marry Hugh. I begged Uncle Walter not to force us to get married, but I was pregnant with Billy, and no matter how he came to be, I'll never regret having him."

Tom pulled her into another comforting hug. "I know," he whispered. "I know." He kissed her then, too. A kiss that made her forget about the past and think about the future. She stopped the kiss in order to grab the other envelope off the table.

"I have something else I want you to read," she said, already pulling out the top sheet of paper.

"Another letter?"

The disappointment in his tone, which said he'd rather be kissing her, made her laugh. "Yes." She held up the paper for him to read.

Her heart flipped at how his eyes lit up and he grabbed the paper.

"Divorce decree?"

Biting her bottom lip, she nodded. "Yes."

"When did you do this?"

"That's what I needed to see Judge Alfords about the night Sadie had her baby."

"Why didn't you tell me?"

She crossed her arms and tried her hardest not to smile.

He tossed the paper on the table and laughed. "Come

here." Grabbing her by the elbows, he pulled her close. "From now on, we'll just tell each other everything."

She giggled. "I can agree to that."

Leaning close, with his nose almost touching hers, he asked, "So, now that you're not married, do you have any interest in getting married again?"

Happiness exploded inside her. Remembering how they'd teased each other back at Uncle Walter's, she shrugged. "Well, that would depend on who's asking."

"Hmm," he said with a nod. "Well, he's tall, not so awful-looking, but could use a haircut. He likes horses and kids and dogs—"

Laughing inside, she asked, "But not cabbage?"

"No, definitely not cabbage, but he has a bank account and will build you a new house and till up a garden where you can grow as many cabbages as you want."

The desire to kiss him again, be kissed by him, was growing so hard and fast she could hardly hold still. "I don't like cabbage, either."

"Good to know."

She placed her hands on his shoulders. Those broad, wide shoulders that she'd admired too many times to count, and that touching right now had her blood heating up. "There's only one man I'd ever consider marrying," she whispered. "He's an amazing sheriff of a quaint little town in the middle of Kansas."

"If I know such a man, when would you consider marrying him?"

"Yesterday. Last week. Last month." Rubbing the tip of her nose against his, she admitted, "I've thought about marrying him since I met him."

"What about tomorrow?"

All sorts of desires were springing forth inside her. "I'd marry him right now." Unable to stand more, she planted her lips against his.

The kiss lasted an extended length of time, and left her entire body swirling with anticipation and desire for more when Tom stepped back.

"Hold that thought," he said. "I'll be right back."

She grabbed his hand with both of hers as he spun around. "Where are you going?"

"To get Reverend Flaherty."

She pulled his arm around her waist while stepping closer. Happiness so pure she might burst filled her, yet she said, "We can't do that. Seriously, we can't."

He placed a quick kiss on her lips while running his hand up and down her sides. "Well, I can't wait too long, I'll tell you that."

"Me, either," she declared. "Me, either."

"You really don't mind?" Clara asked, her heart leaping with joy.

"Not at all," Julia said. "Jules and I would be honored to share our wedding with you."

"I have the perfect dress for you to wear," Martha said. "I just finished it last night. Angus suggested I start sewing it last week. Amazing—every time he suggests that, a wedding happens."

Clara, too happy to care if someone thought she was crazy, asked, "Is he a leprechaun or not?"

The hotel dining room, full of women who had gathered shortly after breakfast to plan the food for Julia's wedding this afternoon, burst into laughter. When she'd walked in the room earlier, they'd all already known Tom had asked her to marry him last night. A few hours ago, besides her and Tom, the only other person to know that had been Angus.

As the other women started talking about the dual wedding this afternoon, happiness like she'd never known filled her. She wanted to be married as soon as possible—now that she knew what love was, she didn't want to waste a moment—yet she said, "I'll need to ask Tom."

"Now's your chance." Rebecca Swift, the banker's wife, pointed toward the door.

Tom was in the doorway, with one hand braced against the frame. He was so handsome. So perfect. And above all, hers.

Never taking her eyes off him, Clara stood and crossed the room. The excitement dancing inside her grew with each step. She couldn't wait to be his wife. Couldn't wait to spend the rest of her life with him.

Stopping in front of him, she asked, "What are you doing here?"

He pulled her into his arms. "I missed you."

"I missed you, too."

She loved his smile. Loved how his eyes sparkled. Loved him. Everything about him.

After a quick kiss, he said, "I heard from Puddicombe this morning."

Fear should fill her, but it didn't. With Tom at her side, nothing scared her. "And?"

He grinned. "The last one's been caught."

The sigh she let out cleansed her entirely, right down to her soul. "So it's over."

"Yes, it's over." Tom then glanced at the women behind her. "What's happening here?"

Running a finger around the star badge on his vest, she asked, "What do you think about getting married this afternoon?"

Excitement danced in his eyes as he pulled her tighter yet. "I think that sounds like the best idea ever."

Amazed, she shook her head. "I can't believe this. It's—it's like—"

She stopped because out of nowhere, Angus appeared next to them.

"A wee bit of magic, lass?" Angus said with a wink and nod before walking out the door.

Not caring who was looking, Clara laughed and kissed Tom soundly. "Oh, I love you," she said. "I love this town. I love my life."

His hands, roaming up and down her back, had her insides igniting with delight.

His voice was husky as he whispered, "You're going to love it more, tonight."

"I know." She stretched on her toes so her lips could brush against his. "Our wedding night."

The effect of that kiss, so deep and powerful it left her floating on air, lasted all day.

Their dual wedding with Julia Styles and Jules Carmichael that afternoon was perfect. Even more perfect than Clara had ever dreamed about. All of it. Including the huge community picnic that followed the ceremony. There was music and food and laughter.

Even Bear, Wayne Stevens's huge dog, gave out a joyous bark when Billy, who was lying on a bed in the middle of the meadow next to the church, announced, "If I'd known all I had to do was break a leg for Tom to become my pa, I would have done it weeks ago."

Clara looked up into the laughing, handsome face of her husband. The man who'd already made so many of her dreams come true. "I would have, too," she said. "I would have, too."

* * * * *

*If you enjoyed this story,
you won't want to miss these other
great Western reads by Lauri Robinson!*

*UNWRAPPING THE RANCHER'S SECRET
THE COWBOY'S ORPHAN BRIDE
WINNING THE MAIL-ORDER BRIDE
MARRIED TO CLAIM THE RANCHER'S HEIR*

HOME on the RANCH

HRCBPA18

Get 2 Free Books,

HARLEQUIN

SPECIAL EDITION

Plus 2 Free Gifts—

just for trying the

Reader Service!

Get 2 Free Books,
Plus 2 Free Gifts—
just for trying the Reader Service!

HARLEQUIN *Presents*